"Why isn't your father here?"

"He's sailed for Canada. He left a letter explaining why he'd taken the remainder of our funds and sailed for Halifax."

"Good God, he left you with *nothing*?" Dev exclaimed, appalled.

Lady Theodora's resolute expression returned and she straightened her slender shoulders.

"He left me my name and my pride, Sir Develin, and the hope of his eventual return. Be that as it may, I didn't come here to discuss my father's recent actions. I have a business proposition."

A business proposition? That was as unexpected as her arrival.

"A goodly portion of the sum you won from my father was intended to be my dowry," she went on briskly, giving him no chance to interrupt with either comments or a question. "I propose that, since you've got my dowry, you now take the bride."

Dev had had the wind knocked out of him once before. He felt exactly the same way now. "*What* did you say?"

Author Note

I'm often asked where I get my ideas. In the case of *A Marriage of Rogues*, another question might be, How long have you had this idea?

The answer is years. Literally, years.

In fact it's been so long I don't remember *when* I first got the notion of a heroine confronting a hero and saying—basically—'You won my dowry...now you get the bride.'

Why did it take so long for this idea to grow into a book? I did write one version—an unsuccessful novella. I put it away and wrote other stories. However, the idea just would not go away, and I was delighted to get the chance to try again—this time with a full book in mind.

Then 'life' happened—in the form of not one but two major medical crises in the family. Two starts went out of the window, and I thought the story was doomed never to see the light of day. However, thanks to very understanding editors, I was given time to weather the crises and begin again. In the end I think the story is all the better for the time and effort required to bring it to fruition.

I hope you enjoy Dev and Thea's romance. They've waited a long time to have their happy ending!

A MARRIAGE OF ROGUES

Margaret Moore

First published in Great Britain 2017
By Mills & Boon, an imprint of HarperCollins*Publishers*
1 London Bridge Street, London, SE1 9GF

Large Print edition 2017

© 2017 Margaret Wilkins

ISBN: 978-0-263-06772-9

Printed and bound in Great Britain
by CPI Antony Rowe, Chippenham, Wiltshire

Award-winning author **Margaret Moore** has written over fifty romance novels and novellas for Mills & Boon, Avon Books and HarperCollins Children's Books. Her stories have been set in the Dark Ages and medieval Britain, Restoration, Regency and Victorian England, and pre-Civil War Massachusetts. Margaret lives in Ontario, Canada, with her husband and two cats. She can be found online at margaretmoore.com, margaretmoore.blogspot.com and @MargMooreAuthor on Twitter.

Books by Margaret Moore

Mills & Boon Historical Romance

The Knights' Prizes

Castle of the Wolf
Bride for a Knight
Scoundrel of Dunborough

Stand-Alone Novels

The Overlord's Bride
Bride of Lochbarr
The Duke's Desire
The Notorious Knight
Knave's Honour
Highland Rogue, London Miss
Highland Heiress
In the King's Service
A Marriage of Rogues

Mills & Boon Historical *Undone!* eBook

The Welsh Lord's Mistress

Visit the Author Profile page
at millsandboon.co.uk for more titles.

Dedicated to the newest members
of our family. They're already enriching
our lives in so many ways.

Chapter One

Cumbria, Northern England, 1814

Muttering an oath, Sir Develin Dundrake rose abruptly from the desk in the study of his country house. Crossing the oak-paneled room to the French doors leading to the terrace, he watched in amazement as a lone female marched along the pebble path toward Dundrake Hall. Judging by her ugly ensemble and determined air, the woman had to be some local busybody bent on asking for a charitable contribution. Why else would such a creature venture forth on this cool, misty autumn morning? And did she not know better than to approach the manor house from the garden?

Whoever she was and whatever she wanted, he was in no mood to be harassed by an overbearing female, however noble her cause. He already gave a considerable sum to several charities of his own choosing and he hadn't had a decent night's sleep in days.

He looked out again to see where she was—and nearly jumped out of his skin. She stood just outside the French doors looking into the study like Banquo's ghost.

A surprisingly young, not terribly homely ghost, in spite of that ghastly pelisse the color of dung and droopy straw bonnet.

He strode to the doors and wrenched them open. "Who are you and what do you want?" he demanded.

With a little gasp of surprise, the young woman took a step back, giving him the upper hand, or so he thought until an expression of determined resolve came to her not-quite-homely features. Her arched brown eyebrows lowered over storm-gray eyes, the nostrils of her slender nose flared and her full lips thinned before she replied in an unexpectedly husky voice, "Good morning, Sir Develin. You *are* Sir Develin Dundrake, I assume."

"Visitors should call at the front entrance," he replied without any attempt at courtesy or directly answering her query.

"Have I the *honor* of addressing Sir Develin Dundrake?"

Was that sarcasm in her voice? "Yes, I'm Sir Develin," he said shortly, and with slightly better grace. If she was here on a charitable mission, he was wrong to be rude, even if she didn't observe the rules of etiquette.

"I beg your pardon for not calling at the main entrance," the young woman answered, her tone conveying neither remorse nor regret. "I intended to walk around to the front until I saw you. Given that my business with you is of a very personal nature, I decided it wouldn't be amiss to speak to you directly and in private."

No doubt she'd *decided*. She seemed nothing if not decided, and unfortunately for her, that was not a point in her favor. His father had been decisive, too. As for any business of a personal nature, he'd never seen her before in his life, of that he was certain. He would remember those large eyes and full lips, if nothing else.

Nevertheless, there *was* something about her that seemed familiar...

"May I come inside?" she asked. "Or if you would rather remain where you are, I have no objection. However, I must and shall speak with you today, Sir Develin, whether in your garden or your house."

No matter how resolute this woman was, he could easily have her removed from the premises and charged with trespassing, too.

Yet he did not. What he did next surprised him then and ever afterward. He opened the door wider and stepped aside to let her enter.

The young woman walked into his study and stopped in front of the marble hearth. A portrait of his father hung over it and she regarded it as if fascinated. Sir Randolf Dundrake had been painted seated at the desk that still dominated the room, one hand curled in a fist, the other on a book, even though he hadn't read a book since he'd left school some thirty years before the portrait was painted. The only background was a dark curtain, making his pale, hard face stand out like a mask. His black hair was thick, like his son's, and brushed back from a high forehead. He had the same brown eyes and strong jaw as his son, too, but thank God Dev hadn't inherited his father's thin lips and wide nose.

The young woman turned toward him. "That isn't you."

"No, it is not," he confirmed, wondering if he should ring for the butler. Perhaps it would be wise to have another person in the room.

He started toward the bell pull.

"I am Lady Theodora Markham."

God help me. Trying to calm his suddenly racing heart, Dev took a deep breath and slowly swiveled on his heel to face her. "I beg your pardon?" he said.

He'd heard her as clearly as if she'd been standing right beside him, but he needed time to think.

"I am Sir John Markham's daughter. I'm sure you recall the name. My father lost a great deal of money gambling with you in London a fortnight ago."

Recall the name? He couldn't forget it or Sir John Markham. More than once Dev had suggested ending their game, but Sir John had insisted they continue playing even after he began losing, going so far as to call Dev a poor loser and a coward for wanting to quit. They had played on until the man had lost all the money he'd had with him and written Dev several promissory notes.

The game had finally ended when Dev realized the man would never willingly quit. Ignoring Sir John's increasing scornful remarks, he'd finally walked away from the table.

Since that night, he'd been half expecting Sir John to appear on his doorstep to plead for time to pay his debt. That would have been bad enough, but to send a female relative to plead in his stead, even one as apparently self-possessed as this, was the act of a blackguard.

However, the question now was, how was he to deal with this forthright relative?

Before he could come to any conclusion, she spoke again, her tone just as forceful. "In fact, Sir Develin, he lost *all* his remaining funds except for a very small sum that was in my keeping at the time."

Although that was unwelcome and distressing news, Dev fought to keep any expression of guilt from his features. After all, it wasn't his fault the man had kept gambling, or so he'd told himself a hundred times. "It was his choice to play."

"I'm not sure 'choice' is precisely the right term to use," Lady Theodora countered. "I realize you are likely unaware that he had sold the family estate some time ago, as well as all the plate and horses and carriages, to pay his gambling debts. All we had left were some clothes and the money he played with the night he lost to you. That was the last of his fortune, except, as I said, for a small sum in my care."

"Have you come here to ask me to release him from his debts?" Dev asked, deciding that would be the easiest way to deal with her, and his own remorse. "Or perhaps to ask for another loan?"

Her expression as stern as Sir Randolf's, she shook her head. "I am not a beggar, Sir Develin."

His eyebrows lowered with confusion. "Then why *have* you come? If it's to chastise and berate me, you may spare yourself the trouble. I gave your father every opportunity to leave the game."

Finally she blushed, yet she still kept her steadfast gaze on his face. "However it came about, you were the beneficiary of my father's final wagers."

A dreadful thought came to him. Men had killed themselves over smaller debts. "Why isn't your father here?"

"He's sailed for Canada."

Relief washed over him, and yet— "Without you?"

Her blush deepened. "He was too ashamed to tell me of his plans. He left a letter explaining why he'd taken the remainder of our funds and sailed for Halifax."

"Good God, he left you with *nothing*?" Dev exclaimed, appalled.

Lady Theodora's resolute expression returned and she straightened her slender shoulders. "He left me my name and my pride, Sir Develin, and the hope of his eventual return. Be that as it may, I didn't come here to discuss my father's recent actions. I have a business proposition."

A business proposition? That was as unexpected as her arrival.

"A goodly portion of the sum you won from my father was intended to be my dowry," she went on briskly, giving him no chance to interrupt with either comments or a question. "I propose that since you've got my dowry, you now take the bride."

Dev had gotten the wind knocked out of him once before. He felt exactly the same way now. "What did you say?"

"I said, since you've got the dowry, you should also take the bride."

He still couldn't believe he understood her correctly. "What exactly do you mean?"

She continued to regard him steadily with those grave gray eyes and spoke with that same stern resolve. "I mean, Sir Develin, that you should marry me."

"Marry?"

"Yes," she confirmed. "I need a home and you need a wife. You are nearly thirty, Sir Develin, as well as rich, titled and handsome. Since you haven't yet taken a bride, I gather you enjoy the freedom to do what you will, when you will, with whomever you want.

"However, because you are rich, titled and handsome, you are also the target of every marriage-minded young lady and her mama in England. If you marry me, in return for the comfort and security being your wife will afford me, you will have a wife who will run your household and maintain a position in society. My family may have become poor, but it was not always so. I've been properly educated and know what's expected of a baronet's wife. I will also give you the freedom to do as you will within the bounds of the law. I will not question where you go or what you do or with whom you do it. In short, I will have a comfortable life free from worry and you may have the carefree life of a bachelor without guilt or harassment from your wife or other marriage-minded females."

Dev could only stare in amazement. This brazen, yet undoubtedly serious, dowdily dressed young woman standing before him had just made the most outrageous proposition he had ever heard—and he had heard a few outrageous ones in his time. To be sure, there was a certain logic to her suggestion...but her proposal was still outrageous and out of the question. "You must be joking," he said at last.

"I am quite in earnest, I assure you," she replied with that same calm determination. "Being a woman and without funds, I have limited opportunities. I could become a governess or teacher or a lady's companion, but I thought first I would see if you would accept a measure of responsibility for what you've done in a way that will also relieve you of some difficulties."

As she spoke, he managed to regain his composure. "I didn't bring your father to that gaming hell, or force him to play cards, and I am not the one who left you without resources, so my conscience is quite clean in that regard," he replied, even if it wasn't...quite.

But although he had some regret for what had happened that night, he had no intention of binding himself for life to this bizarre woman.

Or so he told himself until he remembered the last ball he'd attended and the women who had watched him like a cat stalking a mouse. His objections diminished further when he recalled the trap the daughter of the Duke of Scane might have set.

Lady Theodora was right about certain elements of his current existence. And what other lady of his acquaintance would let him do as he liked and without complaint once he was wed?

None came to mind.

Regardless of whatever appeal her proposition held, there was something else she'd apparently failed to consider. "Suppose I were to accept this outrageous proposal, what about children, Lady Theodora? Have you considered that in your planning? I shall want an heir and a spare at least."

If he thought he'd found the chink in her armor, the way she raised her head and thrust out her chin proved him wrong. "I am not an ignorant school-girl, Sir Develin. I shall do what is required."

"Required? Hardly an enticement," he noted dryly.

She raised an eyebrow. "It's my understanding you need very little enticement."

He would not be embarrassed or ashamed of his natural appetites. "I enjoy the pleasures of the bedroom and make no apologies for that."

"None are necessary," she replied. "As I said, I shall do what is required of your wife and expect you to do what is required of a husband. What else you do will be your own affair."

He strolled closer. "Provided I agree to this astonishing proposal."

She nodded. "Yes, provided you agree."

"I just might," he murmured before he pulled her into his arms and kissed her full on the lips.

Surprised and stunned, Thea's immediate instinct was to pull away and slap Sir Develin's face—except that this was no harsh, demanding, punishing kiss. It was tentative, tender and tempting. And she had come here to ask this man to marry her.

Moreover, the man kissing her was Sir Develin Dundrake. He was the most handsome man she'd ever seen, with those dark eyes, fine nose and strong jaw. She also knew a kind heart resided in that manly form, in spite of what had happened with her father.

Leaning against his body, she parted her lips and let his tongue slid into her mouth, not even moving back when his hand slid up her side and beneath her pelisse to cup her breast. Instead she held him closer still, gliding her hands over his back, feeling the play of his muscles through his broadcloth jacket. This was what she'd dreamed of since she first saw him months ago.

Nevertheless, reality was far more overwhelming, just as he was even more good-looking up close. She'd only seen him from a distance before. Here, in his impressive house, wearing those fine, well-fitting trousers, shirt, jacket and expertly tied cravat, his thick, dark wavy hair slightly disheveled as if he'd recently awakened, he was the perfect example of the perfect man.

He broke the kiss and drew back, a strange expression on his remarkably handsome face.

What was it? Surprise? Confusion?

Then he smiled, a roguish grin that was both merry and seductive. "I begin to appreciate the merits of your proposal, my lady."

She was beginning to appreciate that, in spite of her vivid imagination, she had not been prepared for that kiss, or the desire it created.

"If I were to agree," he went on, "when and where shall we marry? I assume you've thought that out, as well."

It took her a moment to realize he both looked and sounded as if he might be seriously considering her proposal—something she had scarcely dared to hope. Trying to regain her precious self-control, she said, "You should meet me at the village inn early tomorrow morning. From there, we can go to Gretna Green and be married at once."

"I see. What explanation do you suggest I give for my sudden elopement with a woman I've never met before?"

She had an answer for that, too. "I was raised in Ireland before my father lost his money. I understand you've traveled there in the past, so you can say we met in Dublin. And my family is in DeBrett's, should anyone care to look."

Sir Develin immediately went to a shelf beside

the portrait of the stern, cruel-looking man. He pulled out a book and leafed through it before running his finger down a particular page. "Ah yes, there you are, or at least your family."

He closed the book and returned it to the shelf. "I confess myself surprised you're willing to marry a man you've never met before."

"Naturally I made inquiries before coming here," she truthfully replied. "No matter how desperate my circumstances, I have no wish to tie myself to an inveterate gambler or a sot or a lecher. You gamble rarely, you don't drink to excess and while you've had several liaisons with a variety of women, you aren't a seducer of innocents. Nor are you a dandy."

And when you stroll down the street, you move like a warrior prince, she thought, but didn't say.

"You *have* made inquiries. But perhaps I have no wish to marry a woman I've only just met."

"You had only just met my father the night you won all his money."

"Marriage is hardly a game of chance."

"Is it not?" she returned. "How well do you think most men of your rank know the women they wed—*really* know them? Don't they more often marry based on family lineage and the limited acquaintance of shared social gatherings?"

He studied her for a long moment, then glanced at the portrait before looking back at her. "You seem to have thought of everything."

She, too, had believed she had, until she was actually in Sir Develin's presence and shared a kiss. Now her nerves were strained nearly to the breaking point. If this conversation lasted much longer, they might get the better of her, so she decided to get directly to the heart of the matter. "Are we to wed or not, Sir Develin?"

He smiled slowly, as if he had all the time in the world to answer. "Surely I may be allowed to think it over. After all, it isn't every day I get a proposal of marriage. In fact, this is the first."

His manner, both amused and condescending, roused her pride and her ire, too.

"This situation may be vastly amusing to you, Sir Develin," she retorted, "but I assure you, it's very serious to me. If you cannot give me your answer today, I shall consider that a refusal."

"No need to be so hasty or so angry," he said, his visage turning as grimly serious as that of the man in the portrait. "You must admit I have a right to take some time to contemplate your offer."

She readied herself for his refusal and for what she would say when he did.

"I agree."

Her lips parted and her eyes widened with astonishment. "You do?"

He nodded, and to her even greater amazement, a look of what could be amusement twinkled in his brown eyes. "I do," he said with an affirming nod. "I shall meet you tomorrow morning at the Maiden's Arms in the village of Dundrake as you suggest. Rather appropriate under the circumstances, don't you think? Now I suppose you ought to stay to dinner."

Torn between confusion, delight and relief, afraid he might change his mind if she stayed any longer, Thea rapidly shook her head. "No, thank you. I have to pack my things," she replied, moving quickly to the French doors.

"Let me call a carriage for you. It's a terrible day for walking."

Her hand already on the latch, she half turned to answer. "No, thank you. I don't mind. I enjoy walking. It's not far and I'll be halfway to the inn by the time the carriage is ready."

Before he could say another word, Thea was out the door and walking across the terrace as fast as her dignity would allow until she reached the steps leading to the garden. Then her dignity gave way to excited relief and she broke into a most unladylike run.

Once out of the formal garden with its trimmed hedges and into the wilder wood bordering Sir Develin's estate, she stopped to catch her breath, leaning against an ancient oak where she couldn't be seen from the manor house. The very large manor house with its stone carving and that paneled room that seemed to embody the ancient and noble family that resided within.

But it was not of the garden, or the house, or the furnishings or the wood that Thea was thinking.

"He agreed!" she whispered, not quite able to believe what had just happened. "He agreed!"

She was going to be married to a rich and titled man. She would never live a life of poverty and want, cold and hunger, ever again. Even better, she didn't have to resort to the plan she'd prepared if Sir Develin had refused.

And he'd done more than simply agree. Her fingers went to her lips that he had kissed with such passion. It was as if he actually found her desirable, and when she thought about their wedding night...

It would be wise not to think about that too much, she told herself as she pushed off from the tree and walked rapidly toward the village.

He could, after all, change his mind.

By the time Dev reached the French doors, Lady Theodora had disappeared into the morning mist like some kind of sprite or other supernatural being.

Maybe she was, he thought as he turned away. A vision conjured up by his guilt and remorse. Or perhaps he was feeling this combination of confusion and excitement because he'd never before met a more bold and determined woman, or one who kissed with such unbridled, unstudied passion.

He crossed to the table bearing the brandy bottle and glasses and poured himself a drink. Now that Sir John's daughter was no longer there, with her big gray eyes and distracting, tempting lips, he could surely think more rationally.

She was right about his feeling of being on display in a shop. It had reached the state where he dreaded going to balls and parties. Her other arguments in favor of the marriage she proposed were well taken, too. And how many men were offered the chance to be married and yet still live the life of a bachelor?

Her unexpected, undeniable passion was a point in her favor as well. She had responded not with the practiced ease of his former lovers, but with a guileless desire that increased his own.

Yet what would his friends and the rest of the ton say if he appeared with a bride nobody knew and who many wouldn't consider beautiful? They wouldn't necessarily notice her shining, shrewd eyes, lithe and shapely body or soft, full lips.

His solicitor would surely think he'd lost his head and a doctor should be summoned.

He glanced again at the portrait of his father over the mantelpiece. That judgmental gentleman would have had Lady Theodora cast out of the house and the dogs set on her the moment she revealed who she was. He would have been completely unmoved by the look of desperate yearning that had crept into Lady Theodora's large, luminous eyes as she waited for his answer to his proposal, a look that not only appealed to his honor, but touched his lonely heart.

Dev downed another drink, then wandered toward the French doors, looking out at the sodden garden again. At this time of year, no flowers bloomed, so the only greenery came from the neatly trimmed hedges and cedar border, and the wood beyond. It seemed like his life—merely existing while waiting for the warmth of spring and summer.

Putting aside such fanciful thoughts, he contemplated what he ought to do. Marrying Lady Theodora would assuage the guilt he'd been carrying ever since he let his pride, his need to win at all costs, keep him at the gaming table in spite of Sir John's growing panic and despair.

But did he have to pay for that mistake by binding himself to a woman he didn't love or even know?

Let Lady Theodora fend for herself. She certainly seemed capable enough.

After all, as he had said, her father could have left the gaming table. She wasn't *his* responsibility and never had been and need never be.

Except...

He had agreed.

And the die had been cast, although not that morning when Lady Thea appeared and made that unexpected proposal. He had cast it himself the night he gambled with Sir John Markham.

And cheated.

Chapter Two

"Can I get you anything, miss? Some bread and butter? A cup of tea, perhaps?" the servant girl asked Thea the next morning as she sat by the window in the main room of the inn overlooking the yard.

It was a large chamber and comfortable, with wide chairs and a fire blazing in the hearth—comfortable, provided you weren't waiting to discover what your future would be. Or if you were not the object of curious stares and whispers, as Thea had been since she arrived on the coach from London two days before, alone and with only a small valise. It would surely cause more talk when—if—Sir Develin arrived and she left with him.

"No, thank you," Thea replied to the plump young woman. The maidservant's hair was mess-ily tied in a loose bun. Her dress and apron were clean and neat, though.

Thea was glad she had so much experience keeping her expression placid. The ability had stood her in good stead with angry merchants and landlords for many a year and had proven rather impressive at curtailing gossip, or the persistent inquiries of curious people.

The young woman nodded at the hearth. "Maybe you'd rather wait by the fire."

Thea shook her head. "No, thank you." She preferred to stay where she was, watching the yard for any arriving carriages.

"We're not expecting any coaches for some time yet," the servant girl noted. "You *are* waiting for a coach, aren't you? To go back to Liverpool? Or London maybe?"

Thea wasn't about to tell her where she was bound. After all, she wasn't really sure herself. In spite of what Sir Develin had said the day before, he might not keep his word.

When Thea didn't reply, the maid frowned, then shrugged and mercifully went away, leaving Thea to watch the activity in the yard. Although the day was getting off to a cool and misty start, the yard was already a-bustle with grooms, stable boys and servants mucking out the stable or washing down the cobbles, filling the trough and bringing wood to the kitchen. Steam issued from the door of an outbuilding Thea assumed was the laundry—judging by the huge baskets of linen being carried there by strong-armed maidservants—any time it was opened. A cart full of large milk cans arrived and unloaded at the dairy, where a glimpse inside showed at least one young woman churning. A fishmonger came next, with baskets of freshwater fish and eels. The cook, wiping his hands on his apron, came out to appraise his offerings.

Then, when she was beginning to believe Sir Develin must have changed his mind, a shiny, black barouche-landau pulled by four beautifully matched white horses rolled into the yard. A coachman in dark green livery expertly brought the vehicle to a halt. When the coachman got down from his seat and opened the door, Thea's heart leaped with relief. Sir Develin Dundrake, resplendent and handsome in a tall black hat, three-caped greatcoat and shining boots, stepped out.

Thea wasted no time. She grabbed the worn

handle of her small valise and hurried outside, walking as fast as her pride and dignity would allow before coming to a halt a few feet from the barouche and Sir Develin. She also did her best to ignore the inquisitive stares of the coachman and other servants in the yard.

"Good morning, Sir Develin," she said, managing to sound much calmer than she felt.

"Good day to you, Lady Theodora," he replied, running his gaze over her from the crown of her bonnet to the hem of her pelisse.

She was aware her garments were not pretty and his intense scrutiny only made that fact more painful. Undaunted, however, she returned his perusal, noticing that in spite of the energy with which he'd disembarked from his coach, he was clearly exhausted. There were dark circles under his eyes, as if he hadn't slept all night.

Perhaps he had had second thoughts and had come to tell her—

"We'd best be on our way if we're to reach our destination before the day is out," he said, giving her a smile and holding out his arm.

He hadn't changed his mind! He was going to marry her!

As exhilarated as she was at that moment, though, a sense of dread haunted her, too. But it was follow through with her plan, or live in poverty and insecurity the rest of her life.

She put her hand lightly on Sir Develin's forearm, aware at once of the muscle beneath the fine clothes.

"We're going north," he said to the coachman. "To Gretna Green."

Ignoring the shocked look on the face of the coachman, Thea straightened her shoulders, lifted her chin and climbed into the carriage.

As the barouche rocked and bumped its way north toward Gretna Green, Dev surreptitiously watched the woman seated across from him. She'd squeezed herself into the opposite corner, as far away from him as it was possible to get within the small confines. What did she think he was going to do? Attempt to seduce her right there in his barouche?

Even if he was tempted to do so—and he was, a little—he was too exhausted to make the effort. He hadn't slept well for the past fortnight, and last night was even worse. He'd paced the floor for hours, trying to decide if marrying her was the right thing to do, for either of them. In the end, the arguments she'd presented in favor of the marriage had outweighed his objections.

At least for now.

Until the ceremony was concluded, he could still change his mind. And so could she.

"How long do you think it will take us to reach Gretna Green?" she suddenly demanded, one shapely eyebrow arched in query.

"By midday, I should think, if the roads are dry," he answered.

"Your coachman looked quite surprised when you said we were going to Gretna Green. Did you not tell your household where you were going and why?"

How could he, when he wasn't even sure she'd be waiting for him at the inn despite her boldness the day before? "I said I was meeting a lady."

"That's *all* you told them?"

"That was all they needed to know." He crossed his arms and regarded her with a serenity he didn't feel. "After all, you might have changed your mind."

"Not I," she swiftly and firmly replied before she went back to looking out the window.

She was certainly determined. That made her an interesting female, but was that really a quality he wanted in a wife? On the other hand, she had kissed with a boldness that had been quite exhilarating. No squeamish missishness from her!

As for the wedding night…

He wouldn't think about that. Instead he took the opportunity to study this woman he had pledged to marry.

She wasn't beautiful, but she was pretty. Her movements were graceful, her fingers long, and her body slim and shapely beneath that horrible pelisse. Her straw bonnet was equally unattractive and cheap. It looked like the sort of thing a farmer's wife would wear. A very poor farmer's wife.

She abruptly turned and fixed him with her powerful gaze. "Has no one ever told you that it's impolite to stare, Sir Develin?"

Like a green lad, he felt a flush steal over his face and damned himself for it. "Those are the ugliest garments I've ever seen," he said, his embarrassment making him sound more harsh than he intended. "Surely that wasn't the only color of fabric available. It looks like snuff. *Used* snuff."

She did not blush. Instead she regarded him with what could only be called a glare. "It was the best fabric I could afford. The color made it less expensive. I daresay the cost of clothing is something a privileged scion of a noble house never has to consider."

He didn't bother to defend himself, in part because she was right. Although he wasn't extravagant, he rarely paid attention to the cost of his clothes. "After we're married, you'll need better garments as soon as possible."

"I quite agree," she said. "Will you expect to oversee the selection?"

"I can think of nothing more boring."

She nodded, then went back to looking out the window.

He slumped against the squabs and closed his eyes. If she didn't wish to speak to him, so be it. Indeed he should welcome the silence broken only by the rhythmic thudding of the horses' hooves as they galloped along the road.

And he should use the time to once again try to

decide if he was doing the right thing, he thought drowsily. It wasn't too late to change his mind.

Perhaps he should, perhaps he should, perhaps...

Thea awoke from a restless doze and rotated her stiff neck. She had no idea how long she'd been asleep in the carriage. She'd nodded off some time after Sir Develin had. A quick glance showed he was still sleeping on the seat across from her.

She studied the face of the man she was going to marry. Sir Develin was almost thirty, but he looked much younger when he was asleep, especially with that lock of dark hair hanging over his brow.

As for the rest of him, he was broad-shouldered, narrow-hipped, tall and as well dressed as she was not. No wonder he was so popular with the ladies.

She looked down at her pelisse. He was right, of course. It was terribly ugly and she hated wearing it, but what else could she do when her choice was buy cheap and homely fabric or go without food? She would welcome a new wardrobe more than he could ever know, and she was doubly glad to think he would let her choose it.

She was wondering how much she would have

to spend when the carriage rattled to a halt and the coachman called out, "Gretna Green!"

The baronet awoke with a start and looked confused for a moment before he brushed the lock of hair off his forehead and said, "There already?"

"You've been asleep."

"Oh," he said with a yawn as the coachman opened the door, revealing a cobbled and busy inn yard. Beyond, the large main building of the inn, half-timbered and covered with ivy, looked comfortable and prosperous.

Sir Develin jumped out with the same alacrity as before, then reached up to help her disembark. He was regarding her so gravely she feared he was going to tell her he was going back to Dundrake Hall and leaving her there.

She hadn't come that far, hadn't made that presumptuous proposal, to be thwarted now.

Her lips pressed together with determination, she put her hand in his and, ignoring the sudden rush of heat that action prompted, stepped down. As soon as her feet touched the ground, she immediately left Sir Develin and approached the nearest servant, a stable boy carrying a basket of oats, and asked, "Where is the smithy?"

She hadn't only learned all she could about Sir Develin before going to Dundrake Hall; she'd made sure she understood how and where marriages were conducted in Gretna Green.

The lad grinned, revealing a gap where one of his front teeth should be. "Out the gate, turn right, can't miss it."

"Thank you," she said. She looked back over her shoulder at Sir Develin, who had stayed near the carriage. "Shall we?"

He didn't immediately reply and she held her breath, waiting with anxious anticipation for him to either speak or move.

"Yes, we shall," he said at last.

In later years, Thea remembered very little of the actual marriage ceremony, in part because there was very little *to* remember. A few words spoken over an anvil by a large, potbellied man who, she suspected, did no actual smithing, with a witness who seemed half in his cups. Afterward they returned to the inn, where she was shown to what would be their nuptial chamber.

It was an unexpectedly large room, with white-washed walls, a sloped ceiling and casement windows. A large, four-poster bed with clean-looking blankets and woolen bed curtains dominated the room, which also contained a washstand with an unexpectedly pretty porcelain basin and ewer, as well as plenty of fresh linen. There was a high-backed wooden chair in the corner opposite the door, a worn carpet on the floor and a folding screen in the corner. A fire had been kindled in the small hearth, making the room pleasantly warm. She also noted two valises by the bed, a large and very fine one that must be Sir Develin's and her own small and shabby one.

The slender, gray-haired landlady suggested a bath, and Thea eagerly agreed. It was a bit awkward when the landlady inquired about her maid; fortunately Thea had a ready answer for that, too. "I don't have one traveling with me today. I can manage on my own for one night."

"Especially on your wedding night, eh?" the woman said with a grin before she left the room.

Thea barely had time to catch her breath—or so it seemed—when a brisk rap sounded on the door heralding the arrival of two servants. A red-haired lad in homespun breeches and jacket and white linen shirt carried a tin bath, and a slender young woman in a simple calico dress and clean white apron held two large pitchers of steaming water. She also had more fresh linen over her arm. The boy set the bath down with a bang near the hearth and moved the screen to shield it from the door and drafts before he departed with a tug of his forelock. Meanwhile, the serving girl began to fill the tub with water from the pitchers.

"There's soap over there," she said, nodding at the washstand on the far side of the room, opposite the bed that Thea was determined to ignore for as long as she could. "I'll bring a pitcher of cold," she added.

"Thank you," Thea murmured.

"Which one is yours?" the girl asked with a friendly smile as she picked up the pitchers. "The skinny fella?"

"My husband, you mean?"

"Aye, which one's yours, if you don't mind me askin'?"

If he had been "the skinny fella," Thea might have minded. As it was, she felt a sudden rush of proud triumph before she said, "The handsome one."

Her delight lasted only another moment, for the

girl frowned, ran a doubting gaze over Thea, then shrugged and headed out the door.

Thea went to the mirror hanging over the washstand. Was it really so incredible that a man like Sir Develin…?

She drew up her hair and turned her head from side to side. No, she was no aristocratic beauty and never would be. Her eyes were too large, her lips too full and her chin too pointed. At least her nose was good, but a man like Sir Develin would surely have preferred a woman with more to recommend her than a shapely nose and not too plump a figure.

Nothing could be done about her features, she thought with a sigh as she began to take off her clothes.

She caught a glimpse of herself in the mirror, wearing only her thin cambric chemise and petticoat. The next time she was so attired and only so attired, she would be with a man. Sir Develin. Her husband. And shortly after that…

She quickly doffed her undergarments and stepped gingerly into the tub. It was hot, but bearable, and she began to splash water over her face. Another knock sounded on the door—the serving girl with the cold water, no doubt. Her eyes still closed, she called out for her to enter.

"I don't need any cold water, thank you," she said, reaching for a square of linen with which to wipe her eyes.

"Good, because I didn't bring any," Sir Develin said.

With a little shriek, Thea dropped the small square of linen and reached out to grab a larger one to cover herself, nearly upsetting the tub in her haste. "What are you doing here?"

"The innkeeper's good wife has made it clear that she expects me to share the tub with my bride," he replied, sounding as if he was completely at ease.

"After I've finished!" Thea declared, for once unable to hide her perturbation as she tried to stand and wrap the towel around herself at the same time.

"There's no need for you to cut your bath short. I can wait."

"I'm finished." She suddenly realized all her clothes were on the other side of the screen, where *he* was.

"I suppose two won't fit even if I was welcome."

"No. Now please leave the room."

"Don't you think that would look a bit odd? We *are* newlyweds, after all."

He was, unfortunately, right. "Then please get my underclothes and dress. Hang them over the top of the screen," she added, lest he come around it.

"I didn't expect you to be so bashful."

What *had* he expected? That she would throw herself, naked, into his arms? "Will you please do as I ask?"

Much to her relief, he did.

"Not quite where I'd envisioned spending my wedding night," he mused aloud while she hurried into her clothes.

She swallowed hard and felt the heat of a blush color her face, and other warmth spreading through her body. She'd been too afraid he wouldn't agree to her proposal to imagine the wedding night, at least until she'd returned to the inn in Dundrake. Last night she'd scarcely been able to avoid thinking about it. Now, when it was imminent, she was torn between curiosity, dismay and a longing that she could hardly describe; in other words, she was the opposite of calm and composed, while her husband apparently didn't find this situation at all out of the ordinary.

"I always thought it would be Dundrake Hall or my town house in London."

She was immediately glad they were here rather than his ancestral home or town house staffed by his servants. It was humbling enough knowing he had more experience between the sheets. If they were in one of his homes tonight, she would feel completely out of her depth in more ways than she already was.

There was another knock at the door. That must be the maidservant with cold water, Thea thought as she peered around the screen. Sir Develin's greatcoat and jacket were on the bed, and so was his cravat. His shirt, still tucked into his trousers, was open at the collar, exposing a portion of his chest.

Regardless of his state of undress, Sir Develin opened the door, to reveal the waiting maidservant holding another pitcher.

The girl's eyes widened in surprise, and then her expression turned admiring and even flirtatious. That was surely the usual female reaction to Sir Develin Dundrake, and Thea ordered herself not to take offense.

"I've brought some cold water, sir," she said.

"Thank you, but it's not necessary," he replied. "Nor will it be necessary to disturb us again. We'll come down when we're ready to dine."

"Yes, sir," the maidservant said, bobbing a curtsey and smiling even wider when Sir Develin handed her a coin.

Thea came out from behind the screen. She was about to suggest she go below when the man who was now her husband closed the door and turned toward her. As his gaze held hers, he began to unbutton his trousers.

Chapter Three

With a gulp Thea immediately started for the door. "I'll leave you to enjoy your ablutions in peace."

"Stay."

Hesitating, she glanced over her shoulder. He hadn't completely undone his trousers, but he'd taken off his shirt. She quickly looked away. "You're half-naked!"

The only other men she'd seen so undressed had been laborers in the fields or on the docks, large, beefy men who reminded her of a lumbering bear she'd once seen at a fair. Compared to them, Sir Develin was like a lean and muscular stag.

"Since we're married, we'll have to get used to seeing each other less than fully clothed," he said, running a measuring gaze over her that made her feel as if *she* might as well be naked. "I never kissed you at the wedding."

She took a step backward and hit the door. "It wasn't necessary."

"It would have been the proper thing to do."

Proper? The word was like a dash of cold water, but it helped settle her rattled nerves. "Yes, I daresay it would have. But no matter. Now if you'll excuse me, I'm going downstairs. I'm rather hungry."

"Need I remind you that we're supposed to be newly married? We should go together, or it might cause unwanted speculation."

He did have a point. There was going to be enough gossip among the ton when word got out about their marriage. She should avoid causing more.

"Very well," she replied, doing her best to keep her voice steady and her features expressionless in spite of the tumultuous feelings that made her feel like she was on a runaway horse. The desire to be with him as a wife should be and the hope that he would like her tangled with the fear of looking foolish, of doing something wrong, of seeming ignorant or silly.

"Good. Now I'm going to have a bath," he said, walking around the screen.

Thea perched on the edge of the chair and tried to ignore the sound of Sir Develin removing the rest of his clothes: the dull thud of his boots landing on the floor, the softer sound of his stockings and trousers following.

No doubt he was used to having his valet pick up his discarded clothing.

She was not his valet and she was not about to go around that screen, not for anything.

And yet, when she heard the water sloshing in the tub, she couldn't resist the urge to peek through the nearest opening where the screen folded. His muscular back was to her and she watched as he washed his broad shoulders, dampening the dark hair curling at the nape of his neck.

And then he stood up.

Blushing like a thief caught red-handed, she averted her gaze while also wondering—fearing—he had looked through the same opening at her. Which way had she been facing?

"Will you be so kind as to fetch my valise?" he asked serenely, as if he bathed in the company of women all the time.

Perhaps he did. After all, this wouldn't be his first night with a woman. He'd probably been seen naked by several, and more than once.

Although she was a virgin, he might not be pleased if she acted like a skittish horse, and she did want him to want her.

She walked over to the bed, picked up his valise and went behind the screen.

Sir Develin stood beside the tub with a towel wrapped around his narrow waist, riding low on his hips. With his dark hair brushing his shoulders, he looked like a wild young god, or Alexander the Great come to life.

Her heart racing, forgetting that she wanted to appear worldly-wise, she handed him the valise and hurried back to the chair, where she did her best to regain her composure. She would not look through that gap again, in spite of how tempted she was.

At last he came around the screen, fully dressed and looking as polished as he had seemed primitive and uncivilized before.

While she suddenly felt like a beggar made a guest at a feast.

Nevertheless, she rose, straightened her slender shoulders and said, "I would like to dine now."

With a regal nod, her husband held out his arm and together they made their way to the taproom.

"Here you are, my lady and gentleman," the inn-keeper exclaimed, hurrying toward Dev and his bride and grinning like a benevolent uncle.

He led them past several other couples to a table close to the brightly flickering fire in the hearth. A majority of customers were young, some looked very young and one or two were clearly past middle age.

Obviously Dev and Thea were not the only people who'd come to Gretna Green to be married that day, although Dev was fairly certain theirs was the only marriage where the bride had proposed to the groom.

He suspected more than one of the young couples had come to Gretna Green to marry over their families' objections, too. One or two—like the middle-aged couple near the door—seemed oblivious of anything except each other.

He, too, was very aware of his wife, but for a different reason. Her conduct in the bedroom had not been at all what he'd expected. Based on the kiss they'd shared, he'd believed she felt some degree of desire for him, and when they were alone, he'd done everything he could short of taking her into his arms to encourage her to make the first move toward intimacy. Instead she'd acted as if he were some kind of barbarian who'd abducted a virtuous maiden with the sole intent of ravishing her.

"The wife's outdone herself for you!" the boisterous innkeeper, who was as bald as an egg, continued. "A fine savory beef stew, we have, and the best bread to be found between Liverpool and Glasgow, if I do say so! And cake, o' course. We've got some cake. Wouldn't be a proper wedding dinner without cake!"

Dev nodded his appreciation as he waited for Lady Theodora to take her seat, her expression as calm and unreadable as ever.

Perhaps the passion and desire in Lady Theodora's kiss had been feigned, intended only to get him in the marital noose. Once she'd succeeded, she would do only what was necessary in the bedroom, with as much joy and delight as shoveling out a stable.

He had seen firsthand what happened when desire died, and he had no wish to repeat his mother's sad existence.

And could a marriage based on the groom's winning some games of chance, his subsequent guilt and remorse, his pity and lust for the bride, really stand a chance of succeeding?

He should suggest they end this charade of a marriage right now, before it was time to retire. If they didn't make love, his solicitor could seek an annulment and likely get it.

He would forgive her father's debts and she would be free to go her own way. He would be free, too, as he'd been before. Alone and lonely, but free.

The innkeeper and his wife appeared bearing two steaming bowls of stew, a basket of warm bread and a tray with a bottle of wine and two glasses. For the next little while and although he didn't have much of an appetite, he tried to eat while ignoring everyone else in the taproom.

Lady Theodora, on the other hand, ate like one who had been starving, albeit with good table manners.

Perhaps she hadn't had much to eat in the past

several days, thanks to her father's gambling losses. Pity, however, was no better a basis for marriage than lust or guilt.

"And now the cake!"

They both turned to see the grinning innkeeper carrying a platter toward them, followed by an equally plump and jolly older woman who must be his wife.

"Can't be a proper wedding dinner without the cake!" the innkeeper repeated as he set down the platter bearing two slices of what appeared to be fruitcake. Petrified, dried fruitcake.

Dev struggled to keep his expression placid. "Alas, I'm unable to contemplate another morsel after that excellent dinner."

"Oh, surely you can manage a bite!" the innkeeper's wife insisted. "Just a wee one."

Feeling like a minor martyr, Dev picked up the cake and took a bite. Sawdust would have tasted better. He managed to swallow, then immediately reached for his wine.

"Good, eh?" the innkeeper suggested.

"Never tasted anything quite like it," he replied honestly.

"Now you, my lady," the innkeeper's wife prompted.

He must not have been as subtle as he thought, for his bride quickly and emphatically shook her head. "I'm sorry. I fear I really couldn't eat another bite."

When both the innkeeper and his wife looked about to insist, Dev rose. "It's time my wife and I retired," he said in a way that would brook no protest. "Please call us first thing in the morning. We want to be on our way as soon as possible."

The innkeeper and his wife looked disappointed, until the wife said, "I'll wrap a piece up for you to take with you. For your first baby's christening."

At the mention of children, Dev glanced at Lady Theodora. Her cheeks had turned a light shade of pink and—somewhat surprisingly—her smile appeared genuine when she said, "Thank you."

"We'll call you just after dawn, sir."

"Good," Dev said, holding out his hand to his wife.

Theodora ignored the gesture, instead leading the way up the stairs.

Just as well. Her touch had a most disturbing effect upon him and should he require wit-

nesses for an annulment, they could honestly say
there was a distinct lack of affection between Sir
Develin Dundrake and his bride.

When they reached the bedroom now lit by
candles on the washstand and bedside table, Dev
faced Theodora and said, "If you'd rather not share
my bed tonight, you need not. I can find accommodation elsewhere."

Her eyes widened and her hand went to her
cheek as if he'd hit her. "You don't want to make
love with me?" she asked in a soft, sad whisper.

He thought she'd be relieved by his offer, yet
she was undeniably upset. And surprisingly vulnerable.

Where had that brazen, resolute and bold Lady
Theodora gone?

However she looked at him, he had to resist both
her appeal and his baser urges. He had to think,
not feel, if he was to be master of the situation.

Yet despite his own resolve, Dev simply couldn't
tell her that he'd reconsidered their arrangement
and was thinking of annulling the marriage. "I
thought you might be too tired. It's been a long

day and we have another journey tomorrow," he said instead.

"I slept in the carriage and so did you," she noted, splaying her hands on his chest, her eyes full of longing.

This was the reaction he'd expected before. What had changed? Why was she so different now?

Until you know, it would be better to resist the urges of your body, his mind declared.

Yet she cannot be insincere in her desire, his heart replied. *Her eyes aren't lying. And you know what it is to long for affection. For love.*

"I thought you enjoyed the pleasures of the bedroom," she whispered, winding her arms about his neck. She raised herself on her toes so her lips were less than an inch from his. "Or so I've heard."

"Where did you hear such things?"

"London. You are quite well-known, you know."

"Gossip. Rumors," he replied, his breathing quickening, his yearning increasing even as he fought to restrain it.

"Were they lies? Do you not enjoy the pleasures of the bedroom?"

He lost the battle to resist. "I did. I do. I will," he murmured before he embraced her and captured her mouth in a fiery kiss.

As Sir Develin held her close and kissed her, Thea's doubt and dread ebbed away. He wanted her as much as she wanted him. She could sense it, feel it, was certain of it. It was like a thick, soft rope between them, drawing them closer and binding them. She'd been afraid her bashfulness had caused him to reconsider and regretted acting like a naive girl. But he was proving her fears groundless. However he had behaved during the meal, he wasn't sorry he had married her. She was Sir Develin Dundrake's bride, and this was their wedding night.

Tonight she would have no fear, no shame, no embarrassment, no restraint. She would be his wife in every way, as he would be her husband.

Still kissing him passionately, she slipped her hands beneath his jacket to feel the muscles of his powerful chest. She remembered the sight of his naked back. The taut flesh. The narrow valley of his spine.

Her need growing, she pulled away. Keeping

her gaze on his flushed face and questioning eyes, she reached back to untie the laces of her gown, then wiggled out of her dress that was as ugly as her pelisse until it puddled around her ankles and she stood before him clad only in her chemise and petticoat, stockings and boots. As he continued to watch, she pulled the pins from her hair until it fell loose about her shoulders.

Still he hadn't moved, so after she set the pins on the washstand, she blew out the candle there and returned to him. Without speaking, she began to remove his clothes, starting with his jacket. He made no effort to help or hinder her while she continued with his shirt, undoing the buttons as far as they went. That wasn't so easy, because her fingers were trembling, but in the end, she succeeded and pulled it over his head.

Regarding her steadily, he reached for the buttons of his trousers.

She was not, she discovered, quite as prepared for what was to come as she thought.

She hurried to the bed, tugged off her boots and stockings and got beneath the thick coverings before blowing out the candle on the bedside table and plunging the room into darkness.

"Do you still want me to stay?" he asked, his voice low and deep and seductive.

"Yes," she replied, although she pulled the covers up to her chin.

The bed creaked and the feather bed dipped as he got in beside her.

She waited, breathless and excited, until his lips found hers for a tender, seeking kiss, exactly what a bridegroom's kiss should be.

She put her arms about him, letting him deepen the kiss and slide his tongue between her lips. His hand grazed her breasts, his thumb flicking ever so gently over the nipple that had grown stiff. The warmth flooding her body increased.

She put her hands on his shoulders and slid them down his arms, feeling the strength of him as she moved to caress his back, moving lower until she felt the rise of his buttocks.

That was as far as she dared while he untied the drawstring of her chemise and slipped his hand inside to stroke her naked breasts.

She moaned and arched and he inched closer, cradling her against him, before he broke the kiss and put his lips over her nipple, licking it gently with his tongue. It was like nothing she had ever known. Thrilling. Exciting. Arousing.

She closed her eyes and arched again, panting, while he continued to pleasure her with his lips and tongue. His hand moved beneath her petticoat and crept up her thigh to touch her intimately.

"What are you doing?" she gasped.

"Trying to ensure that you're ready for me," he answered in that deep, soft voice.

"By touching me *there*?"

"Yes," he whispered. He shifted lower and kissed her shin, then moved his lips steadily upward.

"Oh!" she gasped when he reached the inside of her thigh.

Surprise quickly melted into desire. Her knuckles whitened as she held tight to the sheet and let his tongue go where it would, do what it would. She felt no more shock or shame, only a delicious building tension.

Rising, he put his hands on either side of her and hoisted his body between her legs. His mouth returned to hers, taking it not so tenderly this time, but with a fiery, heated passion that kindled a similar blazing desire in her. She ran her hands over his shoulders, his back, his ribs, his chest, thrilling to the feel of his hot flesh and taut muscles, the welcome weight of him as he shifted his hips.

Again he pleasured her breasts, and now she arched to meet his licking, teasing tongue. Panting, she groaned as he stroked her below. And then his finger slid inside.

Her eyes flew open and he raised his head, his breathing swift and ragged. "I think you're ready. Are you *sure* you want this?"

She was ready for anything her husband might do. "Yes!"

He reached down and placed himself where his finger had been. Then, slowly, he eased himself inside.

It didn't hurt.

She smiled with joy and relief until he leaned down to take her mouth with his. Instinctively she wrapped her legs around him and encircled his neck with her arms. Breathing became gasps and small groans. She closed her eyes, the delicious tension building more and more, as well as a growing sense that something was about to happen, like the uneasy calm before a storm.

He moved faster. She, too, began to move, rising to meet his thrusts. Gripping him harder, tighter. No longer kissing, their gasping breaths joined until, in a shattering moment, the tension broke, sending wave after throbbing wave through her body. At the same time, he groaned like a man about to expire, his body bucking.

He stopped and, panting, lay with his head in the crook of her neck while she slowly, slowly returned to a place where she could think. And speak. "Is that…all?" she asked in a breathless whisper.

He pulled away and moved to lie beside her. "It's enough for tonight. And now that we're so intimately acquainted, you should call me Dev."

"And you should call me Thea."

"Good night, Thea," he replied, rolling onto his side, away from her.

"Good night, Dev," she said, also turning onto her side.

But she couldn't sleep. After a while, she got up and washed, then crept back to bed, trying not to disturb him as she lay wide-awake. He needed his rest, for he must surely be exhausted.

But Dev was not asleep then, or for a long time afterward. He was trying to decide what, if anything, he should do.

Although he'd agreed to marry Thea Markham

out of guilt, remorse and his distaste for the marriage mart, she also intrigued him. Her passionate responses had thrilled him, too, perhaps because she was so serene and practical and resolute at other times. But when it appeared she may have feigned her desire, he'd begun to question all the reasons for his decision and been prepared to seek an annulment—until she'd looked at him with apparently sincere longing. Then, and despite whatever reservations he still harbored, he'd been unable to resist his lustful urges, just as his father always said.

What should he do now? Stay married and trust that her desire was as genuine as it seemed and that their marriage could succeed despite its unusual origin, or give up the hope that any union based on such a foundation could be happy and seek an annulment?

In the end, he decided only one thing: until he was sure of his course of action, he should not touch his wife again.

No matter how much he wanted to.

Chapter Four

Seated in the barouche the next morning, Thea kept her gaze on the passing countryside while they continued their journey back to Dundrake. The rugged beauty of the lakes and mountains, and the play of the light and shadow caused by the sun disappearing behind clouds, were a wonderful change from the squalid areas of London where she'd been living. Sometimes she would catch a glimpse of a waterfall or wild river, the water rushing over rocks. Occasionally they would pass a farmstead, the yard alive with chickens and geese, and sometimes a dog or a child quietly watching the fancy coach pass. Or they passed through a small village dominated by a little stone church, a smithy and a few shops around a green where some farmers and their wives were buying and selling.

Yet Thea couldn't completely enjoy the scenery. She was too distracted by the grimly silent presence of the man sitting opposite her.

After finally falling asleep last night, she had awakened to find that Develin was already up, washed and dressed in expensive, well-made traveling clothes. He bade her a good morning and said little else. Unsure what to do or say to her husband, she quickly washed and dressed. She was relieved that, in spite of the intimacy they'd shared, he'd kept his gaze averted. It was different being alone with him in the brighter light of morning than it had been in the candlelit room last night.

At breakfast, he'd been polite but still nearly silent.

Perhaps he was simply tired, exhausted from the events of the day before and especially the night that followed. After all, she was weary, too. She'd lain awake most of the night wondering if she'd pleased him as much as he had pleased her and trying not to contemplate the other women with whom he'd been intimate.

"We're nearly at Dundrake Hall," her companion abruptly announced, his tone matter-of-fact. "The next curve should see us at the gates."

Thea's heartbeat quickened. What would his servants think of her? And his friends? Although she was educated and knew how to behave in polite society, she was a stranger and no beauty. She fervently hoped she could hold her own with the ton, or at least not be an embarrassment to her husband.

Despite her self-assurances, her pulse increased again when the coach rounded the curve and she had her first glimpse of the imposing iron gates of Sir Develin Dundrake's estate. They looked like they belonged to a prison.

Perhaps one of the horses would throw a shoe or an axle break and delay their arrival. All she needed was a little more time to prepare herself.

Unfortunately no disaster impeded their progress.

When they reached the gate, the door to what had to be the gatekeeper's lodge opened. An old man, gray-haired and bent-backed, hurried toward the gates from the wattle-and-daub cottage.

"Ah, it's Sir Develin back, eh?" he called out in a thin, reedy voice as he peered inside the barouche. "And not alone, neither. I wish you joy, Sir Develin."

"How the devil—?" her husband began, echoing her own surprise before a frown darkened his features.

The cat was clearly out of the bag, the news arriving via a visiting relative, peddler or tradesman perhaps. However their marriage was discovered, curiosity and speculation were no doubt going to be the reaction that greeted her introduction as Lady Dundrake, and likely not just among the servants.

She had had worse receptions. She suspected Develin had not, though, as his subsequent actions proved.

He leaned out the window and rather forcefully asked, "Is there a difficulty, Simpkins?"

"No, sir, no!" the gatekeeper replied, his gaze now fastened on Thea, who wished she had a better bonnet.

"Then open the gates," her husband snapped before he returned to his seat, where he frowned and crossed his arms.

Since she was Lady Dundrake, it was time to

begin to act like it, she told herself, so she gave the gatekeeper her best smile as they drove by.

Her smile disappeared when she saw the house. The Georgian structure with its grim gray stone and several gleaming windows had seemed vast and imposing when she approached it from the garden. It seemed vaster and more impressive from the front, with a wide stone portico and stairs and ornamental plinths and cornices. Dundrake Hall must have cost a fortune and taken years to build.

"My father did have a few good qualities," her husband noted as the coach rolled along the gravel drive. "He had excellent taste and knew how to get what he wanted from a builder."

"The house was your father's design?"

"Yes, all of it, inside and out."

"Did not your mother…?" She fell silent when she saw the warning look that flashed across Develin's face. Clearly his mother was a subject to be avoided, at least for now.

So she stayed silent as the coach reached the house, where the servants were lined up like a firing squad in maids' uniforms of dark dresses and white aprons and caps, or fine green livery for the footmen.

She took a deep breath and managed to sound composed when she asked, "How many servants are there?"

"Twenty-five or thirty, depending on the season. Mrs. Wessex can tell you how many are currently employed. She and Jackson, the butler, have been with the family since before I was born," her husband replied.

Mrs. Wessex must be the housekeeper, and it was no comfort to Thea to find out she had been at Dundrake Hall for so many years. Servants of such long standing might very well look askance at a wife who had apparently appeared out of nowhere. "I daresay they're surprised that you're returning with a bride."

He shrugged a shoulder. "They're used to my impulsive decisions."

"That is not quite the same as bringing home a wife they know nothing about."

"I'm sure they'll manage." His brow furrowed. "You did say you knew how to run a household."

Although there were some things her husband should never know, it was probably better to be honest about this. "Yes. I've just never actually done it before."

* * *

She'd never run a household?

He really shouldn't be surprised, Dev supposed. After all, there was much he didn't know about her and little that he did. And of course, if her family had their income drastically reduced in recent years, she wouldn't have had the opportunity to learn the intricacies of running a manor.

Yet she seemed so supremely competent, he still found her admission unexpected.

He also began to wonder what else the woman who was now fully, completely his wife had been less than forthcoming about. What other things might he learn that would make him even sorrier he'd agreed to her proposal and made love with her last night?

He should have ignored her shining, longing eyes, the temptation of her body, the sultry sound of her husky voice and stayed away. He should have used his head.

One of the liveried footmen stepped forward to open the door. Dev disembarked and took a better survey of the gathered servants. No doubt they all wanted to see the new Lady Dundrake, who was still wearing that horrible pelisse and bonnet. Gad, even the scullery maid was there.

He shouldn't have been in such haste to leave Gretna Green. He should have insisted she get new clothes made before they returned—another mistake it was too late to correct. All he could do now was pretend not to notice.

He slid a glance at Thea and caught her furtively straightening her bonnet and adjusting the collar of her pelisse. Perhaps she wasn't as completely impervious to the call of vanity as she had seemed and seeing the servants arranged like soldiers on parade might be intimidating even to a woman not easily intimidated.

A memory suddenly arose, strong and vivid, of the day he'd been waiting outside the vicarage while his father criticized the rector's last sermon. Some of the boys from the village had been taking turns jumping over a mud puddle. When he'd wandered closer, the oldest studied him a moment, then shrugged and let him join the game.

He'd slipped and fallen headlong into the puddle. When his father had seen him, dripping and muddy, the knee of his trousers torn, he flew flown into a temper, charging him with acting like a little ruffian and looking like one, too.

He'd made Dev wear those torn, muddy clothes for a week.

He had thought he'd never forget that humiliation, but he had, until today.

He opened his mouth to say something encouraging. Before he could, though, Thea's expression altered. It was like seeing her transform from vulnerable young bride to impervious Amazon.

Obviously his wife didn't need any reassurance from him, he thought as he got out of the barouche and reached up to help her from the carriage.

Thea disembarked with the poise and expression of a visiting empress, and as if she were attired in the finest Paris fashion.

The pride he could understand, but her haughty demeanor was unexpected and unnerving, and not the way to impress the servants.

He led her toward the tall, distinguished-looking older man at the head of the line of servants. Jackson's expression was as stoic as usual, his manner betraying neither surprise nor curiosity. "Jackson, this is my bride. My lady, the butler."

"Jackson," she repeated with a slight—very slight—inclination of her head.

"My lady," Jackson intoned, bowing.

Dev pressed his lips together and continued toward the housekeeper. As always, Mrs. Wessex was impeccably neat, in a dark dress with not a single spot of lint, her ample waist encircled by a leather belt holding a large ring of keys. A pristine white cap sat atop her equally white hair.

"Mrs. Wessex, my bride," he announced. "My lady, this is the housekeeper.

"My wife has no maid," he added as Mrs. Wessex dipped a curtsy. "We shall have to hire one immediately. I'll leave that in your capable hands, Mrs. Wessex."

Thea's grip tightened on his arm and this time, it did not lead to a passionate response. It was painful.

"I trust I am to be consulted on the selection," she said with cool authority, a tone not likely to endear her to the servants any more than her behavior.

This was not the time or place for criticism, however, so he merely nodded and said, "If you wish."

"I do."

Annoyed, Dev decided it would be better to postpone the rest of the introductions. "It's been a tiring journey, so the rest of the introductions can wait until later," he said to no one in particular.

"Since the servants are all assembled here, I see no reason to postpone," Thea replied. "If you'd like to rest, I'm sure Jackson and Mrs. Wessex can tell me who everyone is."

She made it sound as if he were old and feeble and easily fatigued. Gad, what sort of woman *had* he married? "Of course if you'd prefer to meet the servants now, you may. Mrs. Wessex, please do the honors, then show my wife to my lady's bed-chamber. I have business to attend to."

That wasn't strictly a lie. As the owner of a large estate as well as a town house in London, he always had some business to attend to, of one kind or another.

He strode into the house and, without bothering to remove his hat and greatcoat, continued to his study. After throwing his hat and coat onto the nearest chair, he poured himself a stiff drink from the decanter of brandy on the side table, glanced up at the portrait of his father and muttered, "Yes, Father, this time you're right. I was too impetuous."

He downed the brandy in a gulp, then slumped into one of the worn wing chairs.

He'd married with the notion that he was making amends, but that act could well prove the old adage that two wrongs don't make a right.

With a scowl, he rose from the chair and went to his desk. He was no helpless victim. He was Sir Develin Dundrake, baronet, heir to an estate and the toast of the ton. There was no need for him to continue this unfortunate liaison. After all, he had the best solicitor in London and he would write to Roger at once.

After the introductions had been completed and the servants dismissed, Thea was given a brief tour of the main floor of the house. There were two wings leading in opposite directions from the entrance hall. One wing was composed of the formal drawing room done in shades of Wedgwood blue and white, a large dining room with mahogany furniture brightly polished, a slightly less formal sitting room and the morning room, a very pretty chamber papered with depictions of songbirds. Like the room in which she'd first met her husband, this, too, opened onto the terrace. The other wing held the library, study, a large ballroom with mirrored walls and immense chandeliers, an anteroom for refreshments and the billiard's room. Mrs. Wessex didn't say the house was set up as if to separate the female members of the family from the male, but it certainly seemed that way. Nor did Thea give any sign that she'd been in the study before.

Not surprisingly she was not shown the lower level, where the kitchen, pantry, buttery, servants' hall, laundry and wine cellar were located. Nor would she be shown the topmost level, where the servants slept, no doubt with the maids on one side and the male servants on the other.

After returning to the hall, she followed Mrs. Wessex up the ornately carved staircase to the family and guest bedrooms and dressing rooms.

"The guest rooms are to the left," Mrs. Wessex explained, nodding at the wing over the masculine side of the house.

She gestured at the first door in the right corridor, on the side that would overlook the garden. "This is the master's bedroom, with his dressing room just beyond." She continued to the third door. "And this is your room. I do wish we'd had more notice about the wedding. All Sir Develin said before he left the other day was 'Make up my mother's room. It will be needed when I return.' Well, you could have knocked me down with a feather. This room hasn't been used in years."

Thea smiled in response, trying to make up for the way she'd acted when she first got out of the barouche. She was unfortunately sure she had made a terrible first impression. She had been too tense, too anxious, too stiff and unyielding. But she'd also been too aware of the strange nature of their marriage as well as her lack of beauty and fine clothes to be more herself.

Develin's attitude hadn't been helpful, either. He'd been cold and formal, then deserted her.

Yet she couldn't lay the blame for her unfortunate first impression at his door. It was her fault, so it was up to her to try to undo any damage her manner had caused.

"It must be even more shocking that he came home with a wife," she offered, speaking in her usual tone.

The housekeeper blushed. "Unexpected, to be sure, but he's always been an impulsive fellow. His father used to chide him for his heedless ways."

Thea remembered the portrait of that stern man in the study and wondered what it would have been like to be chided by him—surely far from pleasant.

"I can be rather impulsive, too," she said, "although I more often take time to consider."

"Do you, now?" Mrs. Wessex murmured as she opened the door to the lady's bedroom and moved back to let Thea enter first.

She stepped into the bedroom of her dreams.

Tall windows provided ample light and a canopied bed dressed with light green silk coverlet stood against one wall papered with twining leaves. Across from the bed was a fireplace with a marble front, carved with vines and plump little cherubs. A looking glass rested in one corner, and a delicate dressing table boasting another mirror was against the other wall. Silver candleholders rested on the two bedside tables.

"Oh, it's lovely!" she cried, clasping her hands as if offering a prayer of thanks, which wasn't far from the truth.

"I'll leave you to rest, my lady, and I'll send Ella to help you dress for dinner," Mrs. Wessex said.

"I can manage for myself," Thea said, wanting

more than anything to be alone. So much had happened today and in the few days before that… and then she saw the furrowed brow of the house-keeper. "Until Ella arrives," she hastily added.

Mrs. Wessex gave her a very small smile, nod-ded and left her.

Alone at last, Thea wandered around the lovely chamber. This was also what she'd dreamed of when she decided to ask Develin Dundrake to marry her—a beautiful home, evidence of a new and prosperous future. She need no longer dread that she would be all alone in the world, poor, cold and starving, with no home and no family, no husband, no children.

But what of love, Thea? a little voice inside her queried. *Don't you want to be loved?*

Surely love would come, too, if not from her husband, at least from her children.

Thea didn't see Develin again until he joined her in the drawing room before dinner that evening.

She had ignored Ella's shocked expression when the maid discovered Thea had only three dresses to her name, and the one she wore now, of plain blue taffeta, was the finest. The youthful maid had hesitatingly offered the information that there was an excellent dressmaker in the village, as well as a milliner. Thea had thanked her and silently vowed she would visit them as soon as possible.

Upon entering the drawing room, whose glories she had only glimpsed earlier that day, she'd managed to avoid gawking like a stunned peasant. She had never seen so much gilt furniture richly upholstered in blue velvet, or so many delicate figurines as those on the mantle, not to mention the silver sconces and candelabra and the very fine pianoforte in an alcove.

She'd wondered if her husband would expect her to play. If so, he would be disappointed. She'd only begun her musical education when the family funds started to be depleted, and her music lessons had been one of the first economies.

Although she'd waited with growing impatience for her husband to appear, she hadn't chided him when he finally arrived to escort her in to dinner. Nor had she pestered him with questions or forced him to make conversation as the meal progressed. After all—and so she fervently hoped—he might not be annoyed with her. He might simply be a quiet man.

And what a meal it was! There was a lovely cream of mushroom soup, followed by breaded haddock, then roast beef and chicken with peas and carrots in a thick sauce. The dinner ended with three kinds of pie, a cake and other confectionaries arranged on a tiered plate. There was also ample wine, although she was very careful not to drink too much. She was unused to fine wine and wanted to keep her wits about her. She had made enough mistakes already today.

At last the meal ended, and she retired to the drawing room again, alone. She perched on a gilt chair near the ornate marble fireplace where a fire warmed the room. After a time, Mrs. Wessex arrived, as well as Ella bearing a tea tray. The silver service gleamed in the firelight, and more delicate cakes and sweets were on a pretty china plate beside it.

"Shall I pour, my lady?" the older woman deferentially inquired.

"No, thank you," Thea replied, determined to prove she wasn't completely ignorant about such things.

She didn't get the chance. The housekeeper simply nodded and she and Ella left the room.

With a heavy sigh, Thea poured a cup of tea and sipped it while she waited. And waited some more.

Just when she had decided Develin wasn't going to join her, he strolled into the room as if no time at all had passed since dinner. Or as if she was of no importance whatsoever.

"I was about to give you up for lost," she said, trying not to sound irate or frustrated, although she was both. "The tea is probably cold. Shall I ring for more?"

"No, I don't want any tea," her husband replied. He walked past her and leaned against the mantelpiece, his forearm casually draped across it and all the while regarding her with an enigmatic expression.

"That was a very sumptuous meal," she said at last.

Still no response.

"Do you usually have such meals? It seemed quite extravagant."

"I'm quite rich."

She would not continue this uphill struggle to have a conversation. If he was upset with her, she would rather find out. He did have some cause to be annoyed—but then, so did she.

She rose and faced him squarely. "I appreciate that I may not have acted as you might have wished when we arrived here today."

He lowered his arm and raised an eyebrow, but did no more than that.

Even if he was going to persist with his silence, she would admit the truth, at least about her feelings that day. "I was afraid."

"Afraid? *You* were afraid?" he repeated, as if that was hardly to be believed. "Of my servants?"

"Not precisely. But I…that is, this house…" Annoyed with herself for being so incoherent, she began again. "This house is so large and there are so many servants, I was afraid of making a mistake, or saying the wrong thing. Instead I may have appeared more haughty and arrogant than I intended."

Her husband's lips turned up a little at the corners in a manner that struck her as condescending, as if she were a naughty child. "I did wonder what had gotten into you," he said, his tone no less patronizing.

Her pride piqued, she rather tartly replied, "If

you'd talked to me more in the carriage, I might not have been so anxious."

Develin frowned. "I suppose it didn't occur to you that *I* might have some cause for concern about how we would be received when word of my marriage got out."

"Did you not take that into account when you accepted my proposal?"

"I didn't expect you to act like an arrogant—"

"I've explained that," she interrupted. "I suppose I shouldn't expect a man like you to understand. As for arrogant…" She ran a coolly measuring gaze over the man standing arrogantly before her. "I believe I've met my match in that."

"If I am arrogant, at least I have cause to be," he returned. "I am a baronet, you're the daughter of an impoverished gamester who abandoned you. Yet you acted like the Queen of Sheba—hardly a way to ensure good relations with the servants whose help and favorable opinion you're going to need if this house is to run smoothly."

"I may not be the Queen of Sheba," she replied frostily, "but I am the woman you married. I'm the woman you made your wife in *every* way.

Whatever you may be thinking, there's no undoing that now."

He didn't answer. He simply regarded her with cool, unnerving confidence.

Dread flooded through her. They were married, truly married. Surely nothing could change that.

Except that he was a rich and titled man. He would have powerful, influential friends and could afford the best attorneys, men capable of finding ways to overturn any contract or agreement.

"We had a bargain," she reminded him, her voice rising even as she fought to maintain her composure. She went closer to him, until she was a mere handbreadth away. "If you're an honorable man, you will keep it, as I shall keep *my* word. I shall run your household as required, and first thing tomorrow I will go to the village and order some new clothes from the dressmaker there. Ella has informed me she's quite excellent, and I'll visit the milliner, too. And tonight, should you wish to come to my bed, I will not refuse you."

She caught the sharp intake of his breath, saw the flash of desire in his dark eyes. Yet that look of bridled passion was followed quickly by another frown.

Not wanting to hear his response, Thea turned on her heel and marched out of the room.

Breathing hard, frustrated and aroused in spite of all his efforts not to be, Dev was tempted to slam the door behind her, but that would only alert the household that something was amiss between the baronet and his bride—although they'd probably find that out soon enough, just as he had come to realize he'd made a grave mistake.

He should have told her before dinner that their marriage was wrong. That he wanted to annul it and would find a way to do so.

But the words had stuck in his throat then and afterward. Even when she was so obviously angry and despite her haughty behavior, he hadn't been able to tell her he was sorry they had married.

It must have been his pride that kept him silent on the subject of an annulment. Now that he was aware of that weakness, he could surely find the right words to inform her of his decision. He would secure the annulment and provide her with a sufficient sum to live on for a few years, as well as foregoing any repayment of her father's promissory notes. If she still balked, he would offer his solicitor's assistance in securing lodgings in any city that she named, although preferably far from London. Surely then she would be willing to end what was clearly a misalliance, and he could be free of any guilty obligation.

Whatever happened in the future, however, one thing was clear: he would not be going to her bed tonight.

Chapter Five

After another restless night with little sleep during which her husband did *not* arrive, Thea wasted no time summoning the carriage to take her to the village of Dundrake. Whether her husband regretted their marriage or had simply tired of her already, she was his wife in every way and she would do whatever was necessary to remain so, beginning with a new wardrobe suitable for a baronet's wife.

Mrs. Wessex looked a little askance when Thea told her she was going to the village, but being a servant, she could ask no questions. The butler, who seemed more statue than human, helped her into the carriage and told the coachman where she wanted to go. The drive wasn't unpleasant, and she was curious to see more of the estate and surrounding area, or as much as she could from the road.

It was very pretty country, still wild enough to be ruggedly beautiful, but tame enough to have decent roads and prosperous farms. The village itself, named after the Dundrakes, was charming, with a large church built of weathered gray stone, an ample green and several shops in addition to the Maiden's Arms and at least one other tavern.

She wasted no time before calling upon the dressmaker, a petite Yorkshirewoman named Mrs. Lemmuel who wore a simple gown of dark blue wool that fit her hourglass shape perfectly. Her light brown hair was neatly parted in the middle and pulled back. More important, although she took in Thea's cheap and ugly garments in a single glance and probably estimated to the penny what they had cost, she gave Thea a welcoming smile.

"Good day," she said as Thea studied the display of Mrs. Lemmuel's work and the bolts of fabric on shelves nearby.

Thea returned her greeting, then voiced the purpose of her visit. "I've heard you're a most excellent dressmaker. I require some new dresses and two ball gowns. Also some undergarments."

Mrs. Lemmuel's brown eyebrows rose. No doubt she was wondering how a woman currently dressed in such cheap and flimsy garments could possibly afford so many new and costly items.

"I'm newly married and have been traveling, so my wardrobe is in a very sad state, as you can see," Thea offered, telling herself that little lie was forgivable. "My husband says I'm to purchase whatever I require. Cost is no consideration."

Mrs. Lemmuel's expression softened. "Most generous! Are you to live in the vicinity?"

"I understand my husband's family has lived here for quite some time."

Confusion came to the dressmaker's face.

The servants at Dundrake Hall had somehow learned of her marriage; word would soon spread beyond those confines to the village, so there was little point in prevaricating. "I recently married Sir Develin Dundrake."

"Sir Develin Dundrake!" Mrs. Lemmuel cried, her voice so shrill it was almost a squeak.

Then suddenly it was as if Thea had announced she was indeed the Queen of Sheba come to shop. The dressmaker's attitude became if not exactly fawning, certainly much more accommodating.

"You *must* look at this silk," she insisted, running her hand over a silver-colored bolt. "It will suit you admirably and bring out your eyes."

From that better beginning Thea spent the next part of the morning choosing a pattern for a ball gown to be made of that silk, as well as fabric and patterns for several day dresses and another ball gown, that one of deep sapphire blue trimmed with wide lace.

"That color makes your eyes more blue than gray," Mrs. Lemmuel said of the sapphire, her manner as satisfied as a cat after a bowl full of cream, or as if she were purchasing the costly gown for herself. "Is there anything else you require? Something for riding perhaps?"

"Not today," Thea answered in words, and "not ever" in her mind. Her father had sold all their horses before she'd learned to ride.

Develin could ride well, though.

As she'd waited for the carriage to be brought around to the portico, she had seen her husband mount a feisty, prancing black saddle horse as if it were as calm and quiet as a mule. He'd only touched his heels to the animal before it took off at a gallop down the long drive.

He apparently hadn't noticed her at all or, if he had, was determined to ignore her.

Just as he had last night, when she'd slept alone in that large, beautiful bedroom, and this morning when he didn't join her for breakfast.

The door to the shop burst open, pulling Thea from her unhappy recollections. A tall, slender young woman wearing spectacles, dressed in a fashionable ensemble of buttercup yellow, her pelisse caped and her bonnet brim wide, stumbled inside. She quickly righted herself, blinked in a manner reminiscent of an owl and smiled ruefully. She wasn't exactly pretty, but she was striking in an Amazonian sort of way and despite the spectacles.

"Dear me, so sorry," she said in a rich contralto voice and with a plumy accent. "Tripped on my hem. Must be more careful, of course. Thank heavens I'm good at recovery. Too much practice, Mater would say, but what can one do? I do hope I didn't startle you too much. Apologies if so."

"Good day, my lady," Mrs. Lemmuel said with a somewhat strained smile. "Unfortunately your gown is not yet ready. The lace from Brussels is late."

"Oh, is it? That's a difficulty. I wanted to wear it to church this Sunday. A bit showy for devotions, perhaps, but I've always found contemplating important things easier if I'm not wondering if I look a fright."

"The lace should arrive tomorrow. I can have the dress finished and sent round by Friday."

"Wonderful! Thank you. Much obliged, I'm sure." The stranger turned to Thea and gave her an apologetic smile, displaying excellent teeth. "I'm sorry! I didn't mean to interrupt. Mater's waiting in the carriage, though, so time is of the essence." She gave a little curtsey. "I'm Gladys, Lady Gladys Fitzwalter, I should say. My father's the Earl of Byford."

"I'm Lady Theodora Mark—Dundrake," Thea replied, giving a little curtsey, too.

"Delighted to make your acquaintance. Are you staying somewhere nearby?"

Thea gave her a friendly smile. "Dundrake Hall."

"She is *Lady* Dundrake," the dressmaker supplied.

Behind her spectacles Lady Gladys's hazel eyes widened. "Not really!"

"Yes, really," Thea replied genially. It was impossible to think Lady Gladys's reaction was anything but simple, guileless surprise.

"Oh dear, you must think me a terrible dunce," Lady Gladys said, blushing as red as the silk flowers on her bonnet, "but I thought you said your name was Markdundrake and I was rummaging in my mind for a reference."

"And *I'm* sorry," Thea said. "I've only recently married and I started to say my maiden name."

Lady Gladys laughed. It was a sound as deep and rich and pleasant at her voice, and full of good humor. "So you've got the prize, have you? I'm sure there'll be many a maiden sobbing into her pillow when the news gets about. And not just maidens, too. Mind you, *I've* never believed all the stories about Develin. He's handsome and a very charming fellow, but I don't see how it would be possible for a man to have as many lovers as... as..."

Lady Gladys suddenly looked as if she'd been caught stealing. "There I go again, putting my foot right into my mouth. It's a wonder I have any tonsils left. Don't mind me, my lady. Just silly rumors, that's all."

Thea was well aware of the reputation of Sir Develin Dundrake, and that it was not undeserved. She'd also learned his lovers—always married women known to have had paramours before— continued to speak of him with affection after the affairs had ended, something that *was* rare.

The shop door opened again and a young woman entered. She was dressed in the extreme of fashion, her bonnet brim almost too wide to fit through the door, trimmed with flowers and ribbons, in a Spencer jacket of green and a much-pin-tucked dress in a shade that approximated apricot or perhaps the wrinkled peel of an orange left out in the sun. Hurrying past them, she ignored both Thea and Lady Gladys and snatched the bolt of sapphire fabric from Mrs. Lemmuel's hands.

"Mama!" the rude young woman cried when an older woman, also dressed in the extreme of fashion in a puce gown that would have been juvenile on a juvenile, entered the shop and pushed her way past Thea. "This is the fabric I told you about. Is it not lovely and just the thing for my new ball gown?"

"It would do, I suppose," the vision in puce replied before fixing her stern gaze on the dress-maker. "How much does it cost?"

"I'm sorry, Your Grace." Mrs. Lemmuel sounded sincere, but her eyes suggested something else as she took the bolt from the young woman and placed it on the counter. "This fabric has just been purchased."

The vision in puce, who must be a duchess to be so addressed, finally acknowledged that there were other people in the shop. However, she barely glanced at Thea, instead turning her attention to Lady Gladys. "Good day, Lady Gladys."

"Good day, Your Grace," the young woman said, moving down the counter toward a display of ribbons that she immediately knocked over with her elbow, sending rolls of ribbon to the floor.

"Oh dear, I'm so sorry!" Lady Gladys cried as she bent down and started to pick them up. Thea hurried to help her while Mrs. Lemmuel gathered the last.

The duchess and her daughter did nothing until all the ribbons were on the counter.

Then the duchess coldly remarked, "Perhaps you should stay home, Lady Gladys, or have a servant always nearby to assist you in case of accident."

Thea didn't have to see the hurt in Lady Gladys's eyes to grow angry. "Perhaps *some* people should learn better manners," she said just as coldly.

Lady Gladys regarded her with outright astonishment, the dressmaker began to back away as if expecting an explosion and the duchess's daughter frowned while the duchess glared at Thea like an indignant ostrich. "How dare you speak to me in that insolent way?" she demanded, the wattles of her neck shaking.

"I dare because I'm right."

The duchess turned her withering gaze onto Lady Gladys. "Who *is* this creature? If she's in your employ—"

"I'm Lady Theodora Dundrake," Thea interrupted with proud disdain, secretly thrilled she could say so.

"Are you claiming to be related to Sir Develin?" the duchess demanded, running a skeptical and scornful gaze over Thea.

"I am his wife."

"His...*what*?" the duchess's daughter cried. "That's...that's impossible!"

"That is not in the least bit amusing, you brazen hussy," the duchess declared after shooting her daughter a look that was as good as a command to keep quiet. "Who are you really—and don't lie! My husband, the Duke of Scane, can have the magistrate arrest you at a moment's notice."

"I assure you, it's quite true," Thea replied. "Sir Develin Dundrake is my husband and I am his wife."

Lady Gladys recovered the power of speech. "Your Grace, allow me to introduce you to Lady Theodora Dundrake. Lady Theodora, this is the Duchess of Scane and her daughter, Lady Caroline."

"If this astonishing state of affairs is true, why haven't I heard about it?" the duchess demanded.

"You're hearing about it now," Thea replied.

"Well, I certainly never expected this!"

Thea glanced at the duchess's silent daughter. It looked like Lady Caroline didn't know whether to scream with rage or cry with despair. Perhaps Lady Caroline had harbored matrimonial hopes now thwarted. If that was so, Thea could find it in her heart to pity the young woman, especially with such a mother.

However, her purchase concluded, her identity revealed, she decided it would be best not to linger. "If you'll excuse me, Your Grace, I am off to the milliner's. Thank you, Mrs. Lemmuel. Good day, Your Grace, and you, too, Lady Caroline. Lady Gladys, I hope we'll meet again soon."

"I'm leaving, too," Lady Gladys said swiftly, starting for the door.

Neither the duchess nor her daughter responded as Lady Gladys followed Thea out of the shop. Thea could see a carriage in the lane and suspected it belonged to Lady Gladys's family.

"Oh dear me, that was wonderful!" Thea's companion exclaimed. "I don't know how you could be so calm. The duchess quite terrifies me. I always seem to find myself even more awkward and foolish when I'm with her and wish I could hide." She grew more serious. "Grateful as I am for your assistance, I fear you've made an enemy. The duchess has a lot of influence and powerful connections. If she cuts you, so will the rest of the gentry hereabouts."

"I wouldn't want that woman for a friend," Thea

replied firmly even as misgiving began to creep in. It wasn't difficult to believe her husband would be displeased by what had just transpired.

"Surely Sir Develin is popular enough that any faults of mine will be overlooked for his sake," she continued, hoping that would prove to be true.

Lady Gladys's smile brought some relief. "You're quite right. Everyone likes him, including the duchess."

And the duchess's daughter? How did she feel about Sir Develin? How did he feel about her?

Did it matter? She had promised him freedom from the rigid rules of society, and if he choose to break them with Lady Caroline, she could neither prevent that nor condemn him.

"You must come and meet Mater," Lady Gladys continued. "She'll be delighted, I'm sure, especially when she hears what you had to say to the duchess. She hates the duchess with a passion, although she never shows it."

"Another time, if you don't mind," Thea replied. "I'm really not fit to be seen in these traveling clothes and I wouldn't want to make a bad first impression."

Again.

Lady Gladys seemed to notice her clothes for the first time and looked rather taken aback before she said sincerely, "Mater won't care, truly. She only pays attention to *my* clothes."

As Thea hesitated, a gloved hand appeared at the window of the coach and slapped the side.

"Oh dear, she's getting impatient. Best delay the introduction perhaps. Good day, my lady!" Gladys cried as she hurried away and climbed into the coach.

Thea didn't wait. She swiftly made her way to the milliner's before the duchess and her daughter came out of the dressmaker's. She had had quite enough of those two for one day. If she was fortunate, it would be weeks before she had anything more to do with the Duchess of Scane and her daughter.

And that Develin would understand why she'd spoken to that horrible woman as she had.

There was nothing like a morning ride in the countryside to make Dev feel rejuvenated. He loved the high hills and deep lakes of Cumbria, the wind and the rain and the woods that scented the air, the sharp tang of smoke from the cottages and the pleasant greetings of his tenants as he rode past. How different from the fog and coal smoke of London, and the noise of the streets—carriages and heavy wagons rattling over the cobblestones, street sellers hawking their wares, maids beating rugs and gossiping and the occasional cry of alarm when the picking of a pocket was discovered.

So often in his youth and childhood he'd sought solace in the woods and fields, where the only thing to disturb the silence was the call of birds or chittering of squirrels, and the occasional lowing from a herd of cows or the bleating of sheep. No one criticized or chastised him there, and he was free to dream, or ride as fast as he liked if he craved the wind in his hair. Spring, summer, autumn or winter, the seasons made little difference. There was always something to look at and admire, accompanied by that sense of freedom.

This morning was more than half over when he returned to his manor house and found the butler waiting for him in the yard—a sight so unusual he feared something terrible had happened.

"What is it? What's wrong?" he demanded as

he dismounted from the champion gelding he'd bought the year before.

"There is no cause for alarm, Sir Develin," Jackson replied in his deep bass voice, "and I regret giving you any reason to think so. The Duke of Scane is awaiting you in the drawing room."

That was a relief, but although Dev had always liked the good-hearted, slightly dim duke, he would prefer not to have any visitors until the matter of his marriage had been settled.

He was about to concoct an excuse when Jackson frowned and said, "The duke suggested rather forcefully that I inform you of his presence *immediately.*"

That would explain why Jackson was in the yard.

Perhaps it was news about the duke's son, Dev's best friend from school.

Dev quickly handed his crop, hat and gloves to the butler and hurried to the drawing room.

Thankfully Thea wasn't at home. Before he'd ridden out that morning, the groom told him she had called for the carriage to go to the village, just as she had said she would. There was no sign of it, or Thea, in the yard, so hopefully he'd be spared having to explain her presence. If he was careful and given the duke's rather singular preoccupation with his own interests, he might be able to avoid mentioning his marriage altogether.

"Ah, here you are, m'boy!" the stocky duke cried when Dev entered the room that hadn't been redecorated since his mother died fifteen years before. "Just found out you'd come back from London. You're to and fro like a mast in a stiff breeze. Would have come sooner, but my gout was playing up. I've come at last, though, and with an invitation, too. Dinner party a week today, if you'll still be here."

The important matter was only a dinner party?

He supposed that, to the duke, it was.

He didn't want to disappoint the kindhearted fellow, but who could say where he would be in a week, especially if Roger was able to get him out of his present difficulty? Even if he was still here and still married to Thea, the duke's wife was not someone she ought to meet, so a dinner party was something to be avoided. "I'm not sure I'll be able to attend, Your Grace. I may have to go to London again to meet with my solicitor."

"Ah, the clever Mr. Bessborough. Spot of legal trouble, eh?"

"Perhaps, although I hope to avoid any serious legal entanglement."

The duke leaned closer, bringing with him the scent of horse and dog. For all his bulk, the duke was a keen and excellent horseman, and he loved his hounds dearly. "Entanglements, eh? Lord love you young rascals! Not that I blame you young bucks for sowing your wild oats while you can. I'm sure plenty of gels are chasing after *the young Apollo!*"

The duke always pronounced his son's name as if making a proclamation, and as always, Dev managed not to wince. Paul, as his son preferred to be called, hated his legal name, as he'd made clear the day Dev met him at Harrow.

When the other boys heard Paul addressed as Apollo, they'd begun to mock the skinny, pimpled lad. Paul had raised his fists and offered to take them all on. He'd been obviously afraid, but resolute—rather like Thea—and Dev had been impressed enough to stand by his side. The bullies had decamped and he and Paul had been fast friends ever since.

"Not that *the young Apollo!* is running wild," the duke continued proudly. "Indeed no! He's a model of gentlemanly behavior, I'm sure."

"I'm sure, too," Dev agreed, for if ever anybody could be described as "shy," it was Paul, who was also blessedly more intelligent than his father.

Even more to the point, Paul had always been naturally virtuous, and Dev doubted even having free rein in Europe with no parental supervision or lack of funds could turn him into a Casanova.

"The duchess thinks it's high time he settled down, though," the duke noted. "She said the whole country's going downhill with fellows like…"

He cleared his throat and flushed a little. "That is, with so many young men running wild and not marrying. I don't know how you young fellows manage to avoid it. I'd been married years by the time I was your age."

Dev considered the duke's marriage the equivalent of a prison sentence. The genial duke, however—and miraculously to Dev—didn't seem to mind.

"As I was telling the duchess the other day," he continued, rocking back on his heels, "I realize it will be difficult for *the young Apollo!* to settle on a choice. And you, too, eh? Not that I blame you. You have to be careful when you're as rich as Croesus."

As if on cue, the door to the drawing room opened and Thea walked into the room. She came to an awkward halt when she saw that Dev was not alone.

It was not her most graceful moment, and she was wearing that horrible pelisse and bonnet, too.

"I'm sorry. I didn't mean to intrude," she said, looking from Dev to the duke and back again.

At least she sounded genuinely apologetic.

"Well, now, who's this?" the duke said. Then his eyes widened as if scandalized. "Oh! I never thought…that is, in your own house!"

Dev had no choice now but to reveal that he was married, or the duke would surely tell all and sundry that Sir Develin Dundrake had brought his mistress to Dundrake Hall. "Your Grace, allow me to introduce my wife, Theodora."

The duke was even more shocked. "Your *wife*?" he cried. "You're *married*?"

"Yes, Your Grace."

"Wed before *the young Apollo!*" the duke exclaimed, as if that was the most remarkable thing of all, before feeling for a chair and sitting heavily.

A moment later, though, and before Dev could say another word, he shot to his feet and grasped Dev's hand, giving it a hearty shake. "Forgive me, m'boy! Best wishes and heartiest congratulations!"

He smiled at Thea, who smiled in return—a genuine, pleasant smile that highlighted her shining, luminous eyes.

She was even prettier when she smiled, and he was pleased to see that she was regarding the duke as if he was a gentleman to be respected. Most members of the ton treated Scane like a court jester, but Dev preferred the genial duke's open manner to that of most aristocrats and for that reason, easily forgave him his pride in his son.

The duke learned forward and waggled a finger at both of them. "Sly, you two, very sly! Not that I blame you. Weddings are such a fuss. Mind you, I'll have to write *the young Apollo!* at once." He ran his hand over his broad chin. "Where is he now?" he mused aloud. "Amsterdam, I think. Bruges?"

Thea's brow furrowed and the duke took the opportunity to brag. "I refer to my son and heir. He's a fine chap, as I'm sure your husband will agree, and so will you when you meet him."

"I look forward to it," Thea said. She gave them both another smile. "If you'll both excuse me, I'm rather tired. It's been a busy day."

"Of course, of course!" the duke cried.

Dev wouldn't have been surprised if he'd slapped her on the back.

Thea nodded at the two men, then left the room with her more usual grace.

She'd barely closed the door when the duke rounded on Dev and gave *him* an enthusiastic slap on the back. "You dog, keeping such a secret! Where did you find her?"

"She's the daughter of Sir John Markham of Ireland."

"Ireland, you say? No wonder we haven't met her. The duchess takes a dim view…" He cleared his throat again, like a dog growling. "Yes, well, Ireland's a lovely country and does produce some beauties, eh?"

"I think so. Others may not."

The duke laughed heartily. "Good God, m'boy, as if you'd marry a woman who wasn't! Such grace! Such a figure!" He nudged Dev hard in the ribs. "And that voice—a man could fall in love with that alone, eh?"

Never had Dev considered the duke a perceptive man. Obviously he'd been wrong. The duke had seen beyond Thea's clothes better than he had at their first meeting, and he flushed with shame.

"Look at you, blushin' like a schoolboy!" the duke exclaimed, grinning.

However, in the next few moments, he grew serious. "This news is going to astound my wife. Caroline, too. I'd best go home and break it to them at once.

"It's going to cost me at least a new gown or two for Caroline, too," he continued as they walked to the hall. "She'll say she'll need them or she'll look like a peasant next to Sir Develin Drake's wife. She and my wife will want to visit right away, no doubt. Likely first thing tomorrow, if I know the duchess."

Dev sincerely hoped the duchess would be indisposed or otherwise unable to leave her overfurnished manor for several days. Perhaps weeks.

The duke frowned as Jackson helped him into his coat and hat and, for the first time in Dev's experience, revealed that he might not be as blind to his wife's faults as he seemed. "Best prepare your wife, Dev."

"I will," he assured the nobleman even as he wondered if anybody could ever be fully prepared to meet the Duchess of Scane.

Chapter Six

After Dev waved farewell to the duke, he strolled toward his study, remembering what had happened at the last ball he attended. Caroline had followed him into the moonlit garden and done her best to coerce him into kissing her. He'd easily ignored those attempts and then her uncle had suddenly appeared, perhaps with the intent of forcing a marriage. While Dev had never believed the duke knew of any such scheme, he wasn't so sure about Caroline.

As for her mother…

When he opened the door to his study, he was surprised to find Thea waiting there, her shoulders tense, her back straight and a slight wrinkle of concern between her eyebrows.

She'd taken off that bonnet and pelisse, at least.

"I went to the village and ordered some dresses,

two ball gowns and several undergarments from the dressmaker," she announced. "I also purchased three new bonnets at the milliner's and some slippers at the shoemaker's, as well as a few other items." She nodded at the desk. "You'll find the cost there."

"Good," he said, meaning it. Even if the marriage didn't last, she should at least have better clothes.

He went to the desk and quickly examined the bills. The cost was much less than he expected, although enough that, along with the list of fabrics, he could tell she wasn't frugal to the point of unnecessary austerity. "You aren't extravagant, I see."

"Another reason you should be glad I'm your wife."

His jaw clenched.

Thea looked him directly in the eye and spoke as if issuing a declaration of war. "I also met the Earl of Byford's daughter."

That wasn't good news. "Did you introduce yourself?"

"I had to tell the dressmaker who would be paying for my new clothes. Mrs. Lemmuel told

Lady Gladys who I was. Lady Gladys was very nice to me."

"She's nice to everybody," he replied. That was quite true. The earl's family were all kind and generous, although the earl spent a great deal of time and money improving his stable, and the countess could be as acerbic and overbearing at the Duchess of Scane. Fortunately Gladys, their only child, had inherited the best qualities of both her parents, and if she was clumsy and not very pretty, she was an accomplished rider and played the piano unexpectedly well.

Also, unlike many other young ladies, she didn't seem on a constant hunt for a husband.

Unfortunately, Gladys liked to talk and her mother carried on a vast correspondence. Soon all the ton would know of his marriage. And when their marriage ended, everyone would hear about that, too.

Thea straightened her shoulders, took a deep breath and said, "Lady Gladys wasn't the only person who came into the dressmaker's shop. The Duchess of Scane and her daughter were there, too. Lady Gladys introduced me to them."

That was even worse.

"I may have been rather curt," Thea added as if that was merely an afterthought instead of a disaster.

"You were *curt*? To the Duchess of Scane?"

"The duchess was cruel to Lady Gladys," Thea replied defensively.

No doubt she was, and with that realization, his anger drained away, replaced by sudden concern. He could well believe the duchess had been unkind to Thea, too. "I suppose she had several unflattering things to say to you, as well."

"I've dealt with her sort before, so her words had little effect on me."

Although he was sorry to have his suspicions confirmed, he was heartened by his wife's unwavering response. He was also glad Thea had been there to come to Gladys's defense.

Thea knotted her fingers, but otherwise her expression didn't change. "Lady Caroline seemed quite upset when she learned that you were married."

Although there was no need to tell Thea about the possible entrapment, especially when he wasn't sure if Caroline was involved in the planning or not, he saw no point in dissembling. "Her mother wanted us to wed. I was not so inclined. Nor do I think Caroline has any significant feelings for me. If she was dismayed, it was more likely due to the dread of having to bear her mother's disappointment."

To add to his dismay, he realized it was quite possible that however angry the duchess might be about his marriage, she still might come to call. Indeed she might be even more inclined to do so if she could find evidence she could use to denounce him and his bride. It would undoubtedly be best if they gave her as little ammunition as possible. "Unfortunately the duchess rules local society, so it might be best to avoid her as much as possible. Should she come to call, tell Jackson to say you're not at home."

He hadn't anticipated the spark of fiery resolve that leaped into Thea's gray eyes or her firm response to the suggestion aimed at sparing them both. "Many people have scorned and mocked my father and me, so I am well prepared to deal with any slings and arrows aimed my way. And if the duchess does rule local society, we can't allow her to intimidate us or I'll never be accepted as your wife."

The spark dimmed a little. "However, I shall also be more aware that we have a position to maintain and temper my remarks accordingly."

She might not have to do that for very long.

He pushed away any regret about that. Nor did he mention the dinner party. Surely the mean-spirited Duchess of Scane would rescind the invitation.

Instead of comforting him, that realization made him angry. He didn't care if the woman snubbed him, but he would be hard-pressed to forgive the insult to Thea, who might still be his wife by the day of the dinner party.

He opened his mouth to say something comforting about the duchess's behavior, then hesitated. If Thea felt ostracized by society here, it might make the ending of their marriage less upsetting for her.

And him, too, he told himself.

"Mrs. Wessex has just informed me she has three candidates for a lady's maid waiting in the morning room for me to speak to," Thea said after another moment, breaking the silence. "Until later, then."

"Until later," he replied.

After Thea had left the room, Dev glanced up at the portrait of his father and smiled grimly. "It's too bad you aren't here, Father," he said aloud. "I'd like to hear what she'd have to say to *you*."

Seated in the morning room, Mrs. Wessex clasped her hands in her broad lap and regarded Thea expectantly. "So, my lady, which one did you like best?" she asked, referring to the three women of various ages who had just been interviewed for the position of lady's maid.

"They all had merit," Thea cautiously replied.

Being a lady's maid was a post of some importance and intimacy, so Thea knew she had to take great care in the selection. Unfortunately she'd been too preoccupied after leaving Develin to pay as close attention to the applicants as she should have.

Her husband's behavior baffled her. After a wonderful wedding night, he had seemed to regret their marriage, yet hadn't begrudged her the money she'd spent on new clothes. Nor had he been angry about her encounter with the duchess, at least not at her. Indeed at one point she thought he even looked pleased that she hadn't been cowed by the older woman. And it was good to discover that he liked Lady Gladys.

"Daphne Morris has the best references," Mrs. Wessex noted, calling Thea back to the business at hand. "She's visited here with Lady Chelmsford. Miss Morris is a nice, quiet young woman who knows her place."

Thea desperately tried to remember which one was Daphne Morris. The small, dark-haired, mousy one, she thought. There had been something furtive in her manner, though, the way her gaze darted around the room as if cataloging everything in it, that Thea didn't like. It reminded her of people she'd met in pawnshops, not always, Thea was sure, pawning goods they had come by via honest means. "She didn't say why she had left Lady Chelmsford's employ."

"No, no, she didn't," Mrs. Wessex agreed. She set Miss Morris's letter aside and picked up another. "What about Marianne Abbots? She was with Lady MacTundle."

Mrs. Wessex smiled. "I don't think there's any mystery as to why she left that household. The manor's at the far north of Scotland, and Lady

MacTundle never leaves it. Miss Abbots probably wants to be somewhere warmer."

While she could appreciate that yearning, Miss Abbots had been too dour. Having her for a maid would be like living under a perpetual rain cloud.

"What was the name of the older one, the one in the dark green dress?" she asked.

That woman had met Thea's gaze equally steadily and her hands, ungloved, bore the unmistakable signs of hard work.

"Alice Cartwright," Mrs. Wessex replied, her brow furrowing. "I don't think she'll do at all." She touched Alice Cartwright's letter of reference but didn't pick it up. "Maid to a manufacturer's wife who's gone to America with her husband. Born in a workhouse, orphaned and sent to a charity school at eight.

"No, she won't do at all," the housekeeper finished firmly.

"You don't approve of charity schools?" Thea asked.

Mrs. Wessex shifted uncomfortably. "Some are better than others," she offered. "The ones Sir Develin supports are no doubt excellent examples of their sort, but good ones are rare."

That her husband contributed to charity schools

was a pleasant surprise. In all her seeking of information about Sir Develin Dundrake, she hadn't heard anything about any charitable endeavors. His apparent desire to offer aid without seeking acknowledgment or praise met with her approval, too.

"But this school," Mrs. Wessex said, tapping Alice Cartwright's letter again, "I've never heard of it. Who can say what sort of education she received?"

Mrs. Wessex would no doubt blanch as white as a bleached sheet if she knew the sort of "education" Thea had received in addition to reading, writing and etiquette. "I think her wish to rise in life speaks very well of her. I'm going to give her a chance. If she proves unsatisfactory, we can advertise again. I shall write to her at once offering her the position."

"As you will, my lady," Mrs. Wessex said with obvious reluctance.

"Yes, as I will," Thea firmly replied.

When Dev entered Dundrake Hall by the entrance nearest the stables the next morning, he was surprised to find Jackson waiting there again. His first thought was that the duchess had

come to pay a gossip-gathering call and the butler wanted to warn him. "What is it, Jackson?"

"Mr. Bessborough has arrived and wishes to
see you at once, sir."

He'd been expecting a letter from his solicitor
in response to his own, not a personal visit.

He handed his hat and gloves to the butler.
"Where is he? The study?"

"Yes, Sir Develin."

"Has he been fed?"

"Yes, Sir Develin."

"Good." He started for the study, then paused
and looked back. "Where is Lady Dundrake?"

"I believe she's still in her bedroom, sir."

"Ah." It would be better, perhaps, if Roger and
Thea didn't meet, at least not yet.

"Mr. Bessborough and I aren't to be disturbed,
Jackson, *by anyone*," he added with emphasis.

When Dev entered his study a few moments
later, the broad-shouldered solicitor who was five
years his senior rose from a chair by the fireplace.
Dark eyebrows lowered, chiseled features grim,
Roger looked as stern as the late baronet when
he faced Dev. There was one distinct difference,

though—the solicitor's eyes were a startling shade of bright blue.

Roger was also impeccably turned out, his black, waving hair brushed back from his high brow, his face closely shaven, his shirt white as new-fallen snow, his cravat dark as his jacket and trousers and tied with skill. He wasn't exactly a handsome man, but his imposing build and lean, angular features, like he'd been carved out of granite, made him a man one looked at twice. Or, if he regarded you as he was looking at Dev, feel as if you'd been caught committing a heinous crime.

"How was the journey from London?" Dev inquired. He tried not to sound anxious, but he was as tense as he'd ever been facing his irate father.

"Uneventful," Roger replied, ignoring Dev's gesture suggesting he resume his seat. "I came as soon as I could after receiving your letter." His frown deepened. "You should have told me you were thinking of getting married."

"There wasn't time."

"Did you *have* to marry the young woman?"

Dev realized what he was getting at. "She's not with child."

"Then why the need for such haste?"

He was sweating like a horse after a long race and blushing like a lad. "Need? There wasn't exactly a need." Not on his part, anyway. "I was weary of being chased by a pack of marriage-minded young ladies and their mamas at every ball, party or fete."

"Yes, I can appreciate that burden," Roger said with what might have been a hint of sarcasm. "And you should have an heir."

Dev ignored the possible sarcasm. "Exactly."

"Since you've never mentioned your bride's name before, I assume she's of recent acquaintance."

"Very recent."

"How did you meet her?"

"I played cards with her father."

Roger's eyes narrowed ever so slightly. "Played—or gambled?"

"Gambled," Dev confessed.

"And he introduced you?"

Dev's cravat suddenly felt a bit too tight. "I met her after her father left the country."

"Who introduced you?"

"She introduced herself."

Although Dev would have thought it impossible, Roger looked shocked. "She introduced *her-self*? Where?"

"Here."

"In the village, you mean?"

Dev cleared his throat. "No, here at the hall."

"She was with friends of yours? Mutual acquaintances?"

"No." Gad, he hadn't expected an interrogation. "We married very soon after we met." No need, surely, to say it was the day after. "What do the exact circumstances matter?"

"Perhaps they don't," Roger replied. "I assume some of your friends know her or her family."

"I doubt it. She grew up in Ireland. Her father's in DeBrett's, though. I looked."

"And who told you that?"

"She did," Dev replied, his frustration growing along with his defensiveness. After all, he wanted to ask Roger about the possibility of getting the marriage annulled, not—

"Are you quite sure this woman is who she claims to be?"

Dev regarded Roger with stunned amazement. "I beg your pardon?"

"Since you met the young lady through no mutual acquaintance, how can you be certain she's Lady Theodora Markham?" Roger replied. "Or that a Lady Theodora even exists? I, too, checked DeBrett's and while there was a Sir John and his wife, I saw no mention of children. I also took the liberty of asking a few acquaintances in legal circles and only one had heard of a Sir John Markham. That Sir John had been threatened with debtor's prison over the matter of several pounds owing for lodgings."

Dev felt sick to his stomach. "It didn't occur to me that she could be anyone else," he admitted. "But why would she claim to be Sir John Markham's daughter if she wasn't? She would have nothing to gain by it. The man was a gambler and impoverished."

"She got you, didn't she?"

Dev felt for the arm of the nearest chair and sat heavily. "Good Lord."

"I'm sorry to upset you," Roger said with more sympathy than any of his fellow attorneys would ever guess he possessed, "but you're a very rich man with a generous heart and I know—none better—what sort of loveless life you've had. But if she's not Sir John Markham's daughter, who is

she? *What* is she? She could be anyone, any*thing*.
Who knows what unsavory history may be discovered in time? You have your name, your rank
and your future to consider."

"What do you suggest we do?"

"If she's not who she's claimed to be and we
can prove it, an annulment shouldn't be difficult."

Just what he had been thinking. Although...
"And if she *is* Sir John Markham's daughter?"

Roger's dark eyebrows lowered over his aquiline nose. "What do you mean?"

"I may still want an annulment."

His solicitor's expression changed to one of
slight confusion.

"I'm beginning to think I did marry too hastily," he admitted.

"And now you've changed your mind?"

Dev nodded and flushed under Roger's censori-
ous gaze. He knew from whence that condemna-
tion came, and it wasn't from Roger's experience
as a lawyer. "You needn't fear she'll suffer. I'll
ensure that she's never poor and she's a very intelligent, resourceful young woman. She'll surely
find another..."

The word *husband* stuck in his throat and the

thought of another man sharing Thea's bed filled him a pang of jealousy so sharp it was like a knife to the heart.

"Means to survive," he finished, managing to sound as if his mind wasn't tormenting him with images of Thea making love to another man.

"Are there other grounds for annulment?" Roger inquired.

"That's what I wanted to ask you," Dev replied, doing his best to focus on the legal nature of their discussion.

"Have you made love with her?"

More images, but of him with Thea this time, being in her arms, her body one with his, her soft cries of ecstasy echoing in the dark. "Yes."

Oh yes.

"Then unless she's an imposter, there's very little that can be done by way of an annulment," Roger said. He tilted his head ever so slightly as he regarded Dev. "You could seek a divorce."

Divorce? "On what grounds?"

"If you truly wanted one, I'm sure something could be arranged," Roger answered with a hint of disdain.

Dev had realized there would be a scandal when

he ended his impromptu marriage, but he'd never considered he might also lose Roger's respect. "I'd rather not drag my family's name through that sort of mud," he said by way of an excuse.

Roger's expression didn't change. He still regarded Dev as he might a man who preyed on weak and vulnerable women. "You must have had a reason for marrying her," he said coldly, "or couldn't you seduce her otherwise?"

"It wasn't like that," Dev protested vehemently. "I've *never* lied to get a woman into my bed, and I certainly wouldn't marry just for that."

"Then why, in God's name, did you wed this woman and in such haste?" his solicitor demanded.

There was no help for it. He'd have to tell Roger the truth.

He began with meeting Sir John in the gambling hell and how the man refused to give up the game no matter how high the stakes, even when he was losing. How he'd called Dev a dishonorable coward for suggesting they stop, how Dev had done everything he could think of to get the man to quit until he'd finally walked away.

He did not confess that he'd resorted to cheating, thinking Sir John would surely stop once he lost too much. He hadn't counted on the man's obsessive persistence.

Without mentioning his regret or remorse, he described Thea's arrival at Dundrake Hall and what she'd said about the consequences of that night of gambling, as well as the news that her father had absconded to Canada. He told Roger about the proposal *she* had made: that since he'd won her dowry, he should have the bride, explaining what a good bargain it would be for both of them.

Roger's bright blue eyes widened at that.

"That's how she put it to me," Dev confirmed. "I would have a wife to run my household and provide an heir and I would be free of the marital chase, as well as having other freedoms besides, while she would have comfort and security and children."

Roger rose and went to the fireplace, where he stared down at the empty grate for what seemed a very long time before he turned to Dev again. "Those are the only reasons for your decision?" he asked, his deep voice low and cautious.

"No, that's not all. I admired her resolve, her

determination to get what she felt she deserved," Dev replied truthfully.

"Was *that* all?" Roger asked, his tone the same.

"No. I found…find…her attractive. And she can be very passionate."

"That would explain the making love, then."

"Yes."

"I see."

Dev wondered if it was truly possible for a man like Roger—stoic, cold, practical in the extreme—to really see, to understand how he had felt, the emotions that had driven him. The desire. The need not just for passion, but affection, too.

But there was more to marriage than passion and mutual accommodation. "Unfortunately, however enjoyable that was, she really isn't suitable when it comes to other aspects of being a baronet's wife. She's already managed to make my social life more difficult."

"In a way that doesn't compensate for the benefits she suggested?"

"Yes."

"Have you told her you regret the marriage?"

Dev shifted his weight from one foot to the other. "I haven't said so, but she may suspect."

Frowning, Roger stared at the empty hearth again, then straightened, his expression as full of resolve as Thea's could be. "Here is the case as I see it, Dev. If she's the daughter of Sir John Markham as she claims, there are no grounds for an annulment. You made a contract with her, and she has fulfilled the terms, or as many as she's able to at this time. However, should we discover she is *not* the daughter of Sir John Markham— and we have, after all, only her word that she is— then it should be easy to dissolve the marriage.

"Until we have more information, you should neither do or say anything that might confirm any suspicions she may have that you wish to end the marriage. If she has defrauded you, we don't want to give her a chance to flee. If she's an imposter, there could be consequences for her under the law, should you choose to pursue the matter."

Dev didn't want to think about other consequences. Not yet. First, he had to find out if Thea really was Sir John Markham's daughter. "We'll deal with that if and when it becomes necessary. In the meantime, I should act as if all is well? *All?*" Dev repeated with emphasis, hoping Roger would guess what he meant.

Roger's lips thinned a little. "Well, not *all*. That would serve her cause, not yours." He frowned. "Provided you can restrain yourself."

"I can," Dev grimly assured him.

"It might be easier if you go to London for the next few weeks."

"If I leave, her curiosity will surely be provoked. I'll stay."

Roger nodded, then said, "Has she ever asked you for money?"

"No, not directly."

"Her father hasn't contacted you and demanded money?"

"How could he? He's on a ship to Canada."

"Again we have only her word for that. From what port was he allegedly sailing?"

Dev ran his hand through his dark hair. "I don't know. She said he was bound for Halifax."

"Liverpool probably, but I'll send agents to other ports as well. What part of Ireland did she say she was from?"

"Dublin, I think."

"Try to find out for certain. Ask her questions about her family and where she's been living and send the information to me. Any details she can supply that we can verify will help us determine if she is who she says she is or not. I shall also set my agents to finding out what they can about her."

Dev nodded his agreement and added, "You'll stay the night, I trust."

"I think it would be best if I left without meeting your wife. If she is an imposter, she's a clever one, and meeting her might cloud my judgment."

Again Dev nodded and didn't disagree. After all, she might have clouded his.

Chapter Seven

A few days later, Thea sat at her dressing table staring at her reflection in the mirror while Alice Cartwright arranged her hair. The petite young woman with auburn hair had arrived promptly in response to Mrs. Wessex's letter offering her the position of lady's maid. From the moment Alice Cartwright took charge of Thea's wardrobe, as well as the other responsibilities of her job, it became clear she intended to do her best, and her best would be exemplary. She had mended a few small tears in Thea's old garments with stitches so tiny they were nearly invisible. She proved adept at getting clothes clean, too, so much so, she impressed even Mrs. Wessex, who had asked her how she managed to get out an ink stain. Apparently she had used milk.

The only fault Thea could find with the maid—

and it could hardly be called a fault—was that Alice Cartwright's efficiency and skills meant Thea had more time to think about other things, like her husband and his changeable moods.

She was never quite sure how Dev was going to react to anything she said or did—whether he would be glum and silent as he had been the day after they married, or apparently pleased, as when she told him about meeting the duchess. Lately he'd been charming and friendly, telling her how he had befriended the duke's son at school and doing a genial impression of the duke saying "*the young Apollo!*" like he was making a public proclamation. He had asked about her childhood and she'd told him of her days in Ireland, while he described his friends and life in London. He listened with sympathetic interest when she talked about what it had been like to grow gradually poorer, or spoke of the death of her mother, yet he never once mentioned his parents.

But despite his genial attitude and her own amiability, he never came to her bedroom at night. Hoping he would, she'd waited and was always disappointed.

Nor did he ever meet her for breakfast. The

first morning he was absent, Jackson had stonily informed her that Sir Develin had gone for his morning ride, as he did every day and regardless of the weather.

"You've lovely thick hair, if you don't mind me saying so," her maid ventured, interrupting Thea's thoughts as she put the last pin into place. "Makes it easy to do."

Thea gave the young woman a smile. "Thank you. I've never seen hair like yours, either," she replied.

Although Alice brushed her hair into a tight bun at the nape of her neck, it waved smoothly over her scalp like ripples in a pond.

"It's a nuisance, m'lady," the maid said with wry bitterness. "Like a rat's nest if I don't brush it a hundred times every day. Used to get me in trouble at school, that did, brushes not being easy to come by."

"It was difficult for you at school?"

"Oh, it wasn't so very bad, m'lady," Alice replied. "At least we got to eat."

Thea could unfortunately imagine the sort of fare the students had been offered—watery gruel and stale bread, most likely. After such a childhood, the young woman's genial good humor was even more impressive.

A sound like the scratching of a mouse came from the vicinity of the door leading to the hall.

Only one person in the household announced himself like that, the youngest under-footman. Harry seemed to think a regular knock would shock them into apoplexy.

Alice went to the door and opened it. The bashful, blushing Harry gravely handed her a silver salver bearing a white calling card.

Harry was normally as serious and grim as an undertaker, so it wasn't his manner that caused Thea's sudden anxiety. Ever since she'd encountered the duchess and her daughter that fateful day in the village, she'd been worrying they would eventually come to call—not that her maid or any of the servants needed to know that, so Thea put on a serene expression as she took the card.

Which belonged to Lady Gladys.

Smiling with both pleasure and relief, she rose from the stool and addressed the waiting footman. "Harry, please tell Lady Gladys I'm most certainly at home to her and show her to the morning room."

"Yes, m'lady," the youth said, speaking as if he'd just been given a most serious and vital mission before he turned and left.

Smoothing down her dress, Thea glanced at her reflection in the tall looking glass. Some of her new dresses had arrived, including this one in a very pretty light blue with tucks around the hem and white ribbon about the neck. With her new dress and fashionably arranged hair, she felt the equal of anybody.

"Please go to the kitchen and have some tea sent to my morning room," she said to the maid who was already tidying the dressing table. "I'll probably be some time with Lady Gladys."

"Yes, m'lady," Alice returned before Thea departed and hurried down the stairs.

She looked for any sign of her husband's return, but saw none. Since it was a fine morning, with the sun doing its best to warm the autumn air, she suspected it would be some time yet before he finished his ride. Then he would appear as suddenly as a genie from a magic lantern, a genie in well-cut riding clothes and shining boots, his hair ruffled by the wind and speed of his horse. Sometimes he had a hound or two at his heels.

She wasn't used to dogs, but his were well trained and sat upon command. They never stirred again until told to, or given a wave of his hand. Otherwise they simply sat regarding their master with tongues hanging out, panting, their adoring eyes focused on his every move.

An attitude, she had realized, not unlike her own. Once that had occurred to her, she took pains to act less like a beholden servant and more like his partner in business, as apparently she was, although he hadn't quite adhered to all the provisions of their marriage bargain.

When she entered the morning room, the well-dressed Gladys rose swiftly from a chair near the French doors leading to the terrace. Her bonnet was covered in cream-colored silk that matched her pelisse, which was decorated with silk flowers in pink and light green. Its cream-colored trim also matched Gladys's cambric gown.

"Good morning!" Gladys exclaimed, hurrying toward Thea, her skirts brushing an ebony table and nearly knocking it over. Fortunately she caught it in time, then carried on as if that was nothing out of the ordinary for her, as Thea rather suspected was the case. "I do hope I'm not calling too early, but it was such a lovely morning—just perfect for a walk—and I thought I'd come for a visit."

Thea gave her with a warm smile and gestured for Gladys to sit on the nearby sofa. Like all the décor and furnishings of this room, the sofa was pretty and feminine, upholstered with green brocade. A few delicate figurines stood on the white marble mantelpiece and the top of the walnut secretary. On the walls were pictures of pleasant country scenes. However grave and grim Sir Randolf had been, he had an eye for decoration, or perhaps Dev had it wrong, and his mother had been given some say over the choices for her own rooms.

"I'm very glad to see you," Thea said as she joined Gladys on the sofa.

She'd been finding life rather lonely. Dealing with servants and planning menus was not the same as talking with a friend, and while her new maid was most agreeable, there was still the barrier of rank between them.

"I find fresh air invigorating," Gladys continued. "Indeed, I like nothing better than a brisk walk." She lowered her voice to a confidential whisper. "Unless it's a dip in the fishpond on a hot day."

Even Thea's vivid imagination couldn't quite conjure that. "Don't you worry that somebody will see you?" she asked. "Or that you'll catch cold?"

"The pond's quite secluded and I'm the picture of health," Gladys replied as Ella appeared with the tea tray and cakes.

As she set it down on the table in front of the sofa, Gladys continued as if they were quite alone. Unlike Thea, she was clearly used to the presence of servants and was able to ignore them.

"I've always been healthy," Gladys said, taking the cup of tea Thea poured for her after Ella had withdrawn. "Not like poor Papa. He's never recovered from that last voyage to America. We had considerable property there once. Gone now. Still, we're better off than many, for we have the estate here and the house in London and the cotton mills."

Gladys suddenly frowned and leaned toward her, squinting through her spectacles. "You'll forgive me for my impertinence, but I must say you're looking a little peaked."

"I'm rather tired, that's all," Thea replied. That

was not unexpected when you stayed awake for hours waiting for a husband who didn't arrive.

"Ah!" Gladys said with a smile whose significance Thea could easily guess.

"As far as I'm aware, I'm not with child."

Gladys flushed and set down her teacup. "I'm sorry! I'm always jumping to conclusions and saying things I shouldn't. Not that I'd be surprised if you were in that way, not with such a husband. I mean, I should think you'd want to…that is, it wouldn't be a hardship…"

"I quite agree," Thea said, coming to the red-cheeked Gladys's rescue and then changing the subject. "Did the lace for your gown arrive?"

"Indeed! Poor Papa nearly fell into a fit when he saw the cost, but Mater was a dear about it. She always is. I think she lives in hope that fine feathers will help me catch me a husband." Gladys grinned with frank good cheer. "Poor Mater! I'll never marry a man who cares more about my clothes and my fortune than my feelings."

Thea felt compelled to point out she was fortunate to have that choice. "Not all women are able to ignore the practicalities of a good match."

Gladys colored once again. "Oh dear, I didn't mean to offend."

Thea immediately regretted her words and hurried to reassure her. "I'm not offended. I applaud you for your willingness to put love above all else."

"Yes, well, it's the most important thing of all, isn't it?"

"It is," Thea agreed, even if not everyone was able to marry for love. But she was the one who'd made a bargain to wed without love, so she couldn't complain about a lack of it now.

Gladys sighed as she set down her teacup. "I suppose I shouldn't have said anything about a bad match in this house, not after what happened between Develin's parents. The late baronet might come and haunt me."

Her own disappointment momentarily forgotten, Thea said, "I know very little about my husband's parents. He never talks about them."

Gladys frowned and pushed her spectacles back into place. "Oh dear. Perhaps I shouldn't, either."

"I wish you would. It would help me to understand him and be a better wife," Thea said honestly.

If she couldn't have her husband's love, she

could at least aim for mutual comfort and consideration.

"Since you put it that way, I don't suppose it
would do much harm. After all, it's no secret,
not among the local gentry. His mother was the
only child of a very rich merchant. I heard her
dowry was nearly fifty thousand pounds, money
Sir Randolf—Develin's father—badly wanted.
Sir Randolf had a title, though, and that's what
her father wanted."

"Was she compelled to marry?" Thea asked,
having visions of a distraught young woman
beaten and locked in her room until she surren-
dered.

"Not at all. Mater says she was quite delighted at
the time, for Sir Randolf was very handsome, too.
Sadly their happiness was short-lived. He wasn't a
complete brute, but he was hardly sweetness and
light, especially when she didn't give him any
more children after Develin. His birth was quite
an ordeal, so Mater says, and the poor woman
nearly died, but that didn't seem to matter to the
baronet. Mater heard him say he wanted one son
to inherit the estate, one for the army and one for
the church, so he would have influence in every
sphere." Gladys lowered her voice again. "He

really was a most unpleasant fellow. I'm not surprised Develin stayed away from here for years. And I once heard him say he didn't care if he ever had children. I assume he meant beyond an heir."

Given his absence from her bedroom, Thea wondered if he even wanted an heir.

But he had made love to her on their wedding night, and he had been the first to mention children the day they made their bargain. "It's my understanding that he wouldn't be sorry to have more than one child," she ventured, hoping that was true.

"Is that why his solicitor was here the other day? Papa said he saw Mr. Bessborough in the village. He supposed Develin was making a will or revising a previous one because he'd gotten married. That would be a sensible thing to do."

Even though Dev's solicitor hadn't come to the hall or been introduced to her, that was no reason to suspect anything was wrong, Thea told herself. The earl was probably right. After all, a lawyer's visit was surely about a business matter, not a social call.

Gladys's eyes widened. "Oh, dear me, have I done it again? Did you not meet...? Papa could be wrong, you know. Perhaps his eyesight isn't what it was, although Mr. Bessborough is quite a striking personage and Papa can still hit a quail…but that was last hunting season. Maybe it's deteriorated in the interim. He's not getting any younger, after all."

Thea tried to put Lady Gladys, and herself, at ease. "Yes, perhaps he was mistaken, or if Mr. Bessborough wanted to speak to my husband about a legal issue, there was no need—"

"Good day, ladies. You're up and about bright and early, Lady Gladys."

At the sound of Develin's voice, the two women started as if they'd been caught raiding the larder and simultaneously turned to see him standing in the doorway. He still wore his riding clothes, and his casual attitude seemed to suggest he'd have been equally at home when noblemen were much less constrained by the rules of society, able to take what they wanted when they wanted it.

How long had he been standing there? Long enough to hear what they'd been talking about?

If he had been, he gave no sign as he tossed his crop on the nearest table and gave them both a charming smile, civilized once more.

The blushing Gladys rose in a rustle of fabric.

"If you'll excuse me, my lady, I think it's time I took myself off."

"There's no need to rush away," Thea protested as her husband strolled into the room.

"By all means, stay, Lady Gladys," her husband seconded. "We see very little of society."

Thea shot him a sidelong glance. What did he mean by that?

"Oh, but I must. Lots to do, you see," Gladys said. "I have to see Mrs. Lemmuel about another gown, for one thing. Mater's insisting that I have one for the duchess's dinner party."

Obviously they had not been invited, Thea realized with dismay. She glanced at her husband and discovered he didn't seem surprised or disturbed by the snub. Or else he hid it very well.

Whatever her husband was thinking and while she wasn't completely sorry she'd been rude to the duchess, she did regret not finding a less blunt way to make her point.

"No need to see me out. I know the way," Gladys continued, heading in the general direction of the door. She knocked over another little table and, bending to right it, hit a chair with her elbow and sent it crashing to the floor as well. "Oh dear! Pray forgive me!"

"There's no damage done," Thea assured her.

"Quite all right," Dev added, righting the chair.

"Yes, well, good morning!" the flustered young woman cried as she hurried out the door.

"I do believe the adage about a bull in a china shop might have been coined with Lady Gladys in mind," her husband noted dryly after she had gone.

"I think she's only clumsy when she's anxious," Thea said.

"Which is often, unfortunately," her husband unexpectedly agreed.

Thea had supposed a man would be impatient with Gladys's nervousness.

"There's not a bit of malice in her," he went on, coming to stand by the sofa. "She can ride as well as any man, too, and run like the wind. She's the only person who could ever beat Paul in a foot-race."

Dev's fulsome praise came as something of a shock—not his admiration for athletic prowess, but that the usually clumsy Gladys possessed any.

Yet when Thea considered Gladys's long legs and other physical attributes, she realized the young woman's speed and ability ought not to be so surprising.

However, it was not of Gladys she most wished to speak. "Are you upset we're not invited to the duchess's dinner party?"

As she waited for her husband to answer, Thea got the second surprise of the day, for he actually looked…sheepish?

"As a matter of fact," he said, eventually meeting her gaze, "we are. The duke invited us the day after we returned."

"Why didn't you tell me?" she cried before the answers came to her.

Because he doesn't want to go. Because he's ashamed of you. Because you were rude to the duchess.

"I thought the duchess would rescind the invitation after your…encounter…in the village," he replied, telling her she had guessed correctly.

"She has not?"

"No. Not yet, at any rate."

"Do you still expect her to?"

He ran his hand through his black hair already disheveled from his ride. "Perhaps."

"And if she doesn't?"

Now *he* looked surprised. "Since the duke himself invited us, we should go."

He made no reference to her previous insolence,

and for that she was grateful, and emboldened enough to broach something else troubling her. "I suppose we should expect to have more visitors soon," she ventured, trying not to sound as if she was seeking any specific information. "You will tell me when you invite anyone."

"Of course."

"Even if they're men of business, like your solicitor?"

His brow furrowed and his expression grew guarded. "If there's a reason for you to meet Mr. Bessborough, you'll meet him."

She regretted the change in his manner, yet she had to find out more or she would worry for hours. "I understand he's already been to Dundrake since we returned."

Cleary he wasn't pleased to hear that she knew of the solicitor's visit, yet he answered nonetheless. "I had informed him of our marriage and he came to discuss it with me. A change in one's marital status does have legal ramifications, after all."

"A new will might be in order," she agreed, "with provisions for children."

Dev's frown deepened.

"You did say you wanted children when we discussed our bargain," she said, coming to stand in front of him and trying not to think of the first kiss they'd shared.

"I do." His dark orbs seemed to pull her closer. "Very much."

Thrilled and even more encouraged, she softly noted, "We'll have to make love to get them."

"I'm aware of that. Very aware," he replied, and as he spoke, she saw a yearning in his eyes that matched her own.

She slid her hand up his arm. "Like we did on our wedding night. That was enjoyable, wasn't it?"

He nodded.

"I've been hoping to enjoy such…activity… again. I've been waiting for you every night."

He didn't reply, but neither did that look leave his eyes.

"Don't you want me, Develin? Don't you want to make love with me?"

He didn't answer with words.

Chapter Eight

Dev's arms went around Thea and he pulled her close to kiss. No tentative wedding night kiss this, but a passionate, heated embrace, almost primal in its intensity, as if the veneer of the civilized man was dropping away.

Or the last of his restraint cast off.

Yet for all his passion, it was Thea who deepened the kiss and insinuated her tongue between his lips, she who held him tight, leaning against him as if there was nothing more important in the world than being with him.

She didn't care where they were or what time of day it was. It seemed far too long since she'd been in his arms, kissing him and being kissed in return. Too many lonely days and anxious nights had passed during which she'd wondered if he still wanted her.

And now he was with her, holding her with what seemed desperate, growing need.

He drew her to a nearby chair and pulled her down onto his lap. Still kissing her, he pushed up her skirt and petticoat and eagerly caressed the soft skin of her thigh above her stocking. Her fingers went to his cravat, all but tearing it off in her haste. He slipped his hand into her bodice to stroke her breast while she undid the buttons of his shirt and thrust her hand through the opening to explore his chest. Shifting, she felt the evidence of his arousal through their clothing, a sensation that made her hot and moist, ready and anxious, to have him inside her.

She broke the kiss to undo his trousers, the hoarse sounds of his breath in her ear as he urgently kneaded and fondled her breasts. She freed him and swiftly straddled him before lowering herself. Gasping, he took hold of her hips, bringing her forward and not incidentally her breasts to his mouth.

As she rocked and ground her hips against his, glorying in the feeling of his erection deep within her, he laved and sucked her pebbled nipples until he threw back his head and growled with release.

In the next moment, she cried out for the same reason.

Panting, she laid her head on his shoulder while his rough breathing slowed.

A sharp rap sounded on the door.

With a shocked gasp, they both looked at the door as if it had suddenly become a window and people could see them.

"Who is it?" Dev loudly demanded while Thea hastily moved away.

She smoothed down her wrinkled dress and pushed a few errant locks back into place, fearing it would be obvious they'd been making passionate love on a chair in the morning room.

"I beg your pardon, Sir Develin," Jackson said from beyond the door. "The Duke of Scane has sent a messenger asking you to go to him at once. It's very important, the lad said."

Dev, who had returned his own clothes to a more normal state, although his cravat showed signs of hasty tying, darted a puzzled glance at Thea, then said, "I had best go at once."

Thea nodded. After all, there was no reason he should not.

So he did, leaving his wife to hope the long nights of anxious waiting were finally over.

As Develin galloped toward the duke's seat, his thoughts were less about the duke's summons than his wife. His pretty, passionate wife. His pretty, passionate, irresistible wife. Making love with her, whether in bed or elsewhere, was like nothing he'd experienced before. No other woman aroused him as she did. No other woman rendered him so eager to please her, or so satisfied when he realized he'd brought her to a climax.

But it wasn't only physical intimacy that he wanted with Thea. He wanted to simply spend time with her, to hear about her life and her experiences—and not just to report them back to Roger, either, although he had dutifully done so. She was an interesting, entertaining storyteller, and a woman of kindness and compassion, too, as her growing friendship with Gladys proved.

But what if she wasn't Theodora Markham? What if she had tricked him into marriage?

And what would Roger make of her talk of wills? It had certainly disconcerted him.

These thoughts and others, his joy and his suspicious dread, battled within Dev as he rode through the portal leading to the inner yard of the duke's manor. It was a huge edifice surrounding a cobbled yard and had once been an abbey. After dismounting and tossing his reins to one of the grooms, he went to the house where he was immediately shown to the duke's library.

The walls and shelves of that chamber were of age-darkened oak, the Aubusson carpet comfortably worn like the wing chairs and the scent of cheroots lingered in the air. Paul had once told him his father had bought all the books that lined the walls in one fell swoop and had yet to read any of them.

"Good day, young fella, good day!" the Duke of Scane cried, hoisting himself from his chair when he saw Dev. "Excellent day for a ride, eh? Thought of going out myself, but…well, I'll get to that later. In the meantime, I've been imagining what *the young Apollo!* will make of the news about your marriage when he gets my latest letter. Might even spur him to take a wife, eh? Not that he's lived like a monk, I'm sure. Such a handsome fellow's bound to have liaisons. But I don't have to tell you that, do I?"

Dev kept any hint that he didn't consider the thin, lanky, long-nosed Paul a handsome fellow from his features. "I'm sure he's very popular."

"Still, I'd rather he married an Englishwoman. I never could get the hang of any foreign lingo. Pity me if he comes home with a French viscountess or German baroness."

Dev decided he'd best get right to business before the duke started to discuss the possibility of grandchildren. "I was told you wanted to see me about a matter of some importance, Your Grace."

"Ah yes, I did. I do," the nobleman amended. He went to a table in an alcove and produced a large white, heavily embossed envelope. "This is for you and your charming wife." He grinned and before Dev could open it, said, "It's an invitation to the dinner I told you about. A formal invitation."

"I must confess I'm rather surprised," Dev said in a miracle of understatement. He'd been sure they would be excluded. He'd even been pleased and relieved about that until he'd seen the hurt and dismay in Thea's shining eyes.

Now he was relieved that they were being asked

to attend and in spite of whatever bad impression Thea had made on the duchess.

Or perhaps the invitation had come despite that bad impression. "Is this your doing, Your Grace?" Dev asked, hoping Thea hadn't inadvertently caused the duke any trouble.

"Mine? Lord love you, no! Wish I could say it was, but dinner parties and anything like that are my wife's bailiwick and I don't interfere."

"I asked because my wife told me she met the duchess in the village," Dev explained, "and I gather the introduction did not go well."

The duke's usually cheery visage darkened. "Yes, well, m'boy, there's no denying the duchess was in a bit of a state when she got back. She was shocked to find out you were married. But I told her I'd met your wife and found her a charming girl. Bit bold perhaps, but charming."

Yes, Thea was bold. And brazen and proud and exciting and altogether desirable.

"So was the duchess in her day," the duke continued, handing Dev the envelope. "Came right out and proposed…" The duke flushed. "Yes, well, she was bold. No doubt my wife's decided to let bygones be bygones, eh?"

Dev wondered if he should believe that.

The duke's smile broadened. "That must be it, considering what we plan to announce." His visage grew sheepish. "Wasn't supposed to say anything about that. But never mind. You'll keep the secret, I'm sure." He straightened and couldn't have looked more thrilled if he'd been named heir to the throne. "*The young Apollo!* is coming home at last!"

Dev tried to appear as pleased as his host, but he'd heard this sort of declaration before, and Paul had yet to return. "That's wonderful. When?"

"By All Saints' Day and maybe sooner."

Putting the invitation in his jacket pocket, Dev silently decided Christmas would be more likely, if at all that year. "I look forward to seeing him again. It's been a long time."

"Hasn't it? I'm sure his friends over there protest when he mentions coming home and so he stays to accommodate them."

"No doubt."

The duke pulled a cheroot from a carved wooden box on a nearby mahogany table and proceeded to light it with a straw put to the glowing embers of the fire in the hearth. "Have you heard about the new litter of puppies my best bitch has had?

Daisy's outdone herself this time—twelve pups and all healthy."

The man beamed as if he'd been given the keys to the kingdom.

Dev smiled in return, then said, "If you'll excuse me, Your Grace, I should go home at once and show my wife your invitation."

"Of course, of course! The ladies do get excited over a party, eh?" the duke said with a knowing wink as they walked toward the door. "And you won't let on I told you about the return of *the young Apollo*?"

"Not a word."

"Excellent!"

After Dev bade the duke farewell and headed toward the stables for his horse, he began to wonder if the duchess had a motive that was not kind or neighborly when she extended the invitation to her dinner party. He could more easily believe the mean-spirited, vindictive woman wanted to look for reasons to find fault with Thea, then spread word far and wide that Sir Develin Drake had married a terrible woman.

Perhaps it would be better—safer, less fraught—if they didn't go. Why risk more potential social disaster? Why take the chance?

Another reason not to attend came to him as he approached the groom holding the bridle of his horse that tossed its head and impatiently re-footed. If he intended to have his marriage an-nulled—and he did, didn't he?—he shouldn't want Thea to meet any more people in the vicinity. Doing so would only increase the gossip when the annulment occurred.

If he hadn't made that more difficult by loving her again.

"Sir? Are you quite all right, sir?"

The groom's anxious query pulled Dev from his thoughts. "Yes, I am," he replied, mounting his spirited horse and turning it toward the portal.

He made his decision. They would not go to the duchess's dinner party. He wouldn't even show Thea the invitation. He would wait a day or two, then send their regrets.

In spite of what had happened earlier that day, Dev didn't come to Thea's bedroom at night. Once again she waited, tossing and turning, wondering why not, although she no longer feared he didn't want her. That morning he had shown her that he did. No, something else was disturbing him, probably something to do with the duke or the duke's family, and unfortunately something that Dev obviously didn't want to tell her about.

After he'd gone to visit the duke, she didn't see him again until dinner. He'd said very little until she resorted to asking what the duke wished to see him about. Dev had replied that it was nothing of consequence after all, then lapsed into silence once more. She hadn't questioned him further, not wanting to risk ruining the intimacy they'd shared earlier that day.

Maybe all husbands were like that, she told herself, talkative and friendly one day, grimly silent the next. Passionate one moment, cool and aloof later. What, after all, did she really know about men and their desires?

She might simply have to accept things as they were, difficult though that might be.

At least she could take comfort in her opulent surroundings, fine clothes and good food, and enjoy the times her husband was friendly and attentive, or passionate and loving, whenever that might be.

Or so Thea reasoned before she finally fell into a fitful sleep.

* * *

The nightmare began as it always did. Clutching her father's hand, chased by men whose faces she couldn't quite see, Thea ran down a filthy, foggy alley. Other evil, twisted faces loomed out of the dark on either side and long-fingered, bloody hands reached for her.

Panting, terrified, she kept urging her father to run faster, faster! He kept trying to hold her back, crying "One more hand and I'll win! One more hand and they'll go away!"

Tonight, there was a new face among the monstrosities coming closer and closer. Her face twisted into a horrible, scornful grimace, her long fingers like talons, the Duchess of Scane grabbed Thea's shoulder. Thea screamed and tried to break free from the woman's awful grasp, but she couldn't. She was being dragged back into the darkness and there was no one to help her.

"Thea! Thea! Wake up!"

With a gasp, she did—and found herself in her husband's arms. Illuminated by a candle on the bedside table, Dev sat beside her on the bed and cradled her against his chest. "It's all right," he crooned in a low whisper, stroking her hair and brushing it back from her sweat-slicked face. "You're safe. You're safe."

Wrapping her arms around her husband's neck, she held him tight while her breathing slowed to normal. "I had a bad dream," she whispered.

"A terrible dream, by the sounds of it," he said softly.

"I've had it before. My father and I are being chased, but he slows down because he wants to keep gambling. This time, the duchess was there, too." She shivered as she recalled the woman's horrible grimace and talonlike fingers. "She grabbed my shoulder. I couldn't get away."

"I don't doubt the duchess is the stuff of night-mares," he said, his tone light and reassuring, too, "but she need not trouble you. We don't have to have anything to do with her."

Thea drew back and regarded him gravely. "That would be the easiest thing to do," she agreed, "but not the wisest. Gladys told me she rules society here, and if that's so, we mustn't ig-nore her or antagonize her more than I already have. We've been snubbed once because of my insolence. I can only hope that's the last reper-cussion we'll suffer."

He frowned. "We don't need the duchess's approval, or her dinner parties."

"Then we might as well go into exile."

"You exaggerate."

"You don't know what it's like to be shunned by society," she said quietly. "I do, and I don't want that to be the price you pay for marrying me." She thought of another reason he might not want to attend social functions, and her gaze faltered for the briefest of moments. "Unless you have another reason for not wanting to be seen with me?"

Perhaps she was too course, too ugly, too ungraceful or too bold. She had already embarrassed him by quarreling with the duchess and perhaps he feared a repetition of that grave social error.

"No, I don't, and if you're willing to put up with the duchess, you'll have every opportunity to do so. We're still invited to the dinner party Gladys mentioned. That's why the duke wanted to see me today—to give me the invitation."

"Why didn't you tell me?" she cried, relieved and yet still dreading she had cause for concern. "I'll try to control my temper and not do anything else that might embarrass you. Thankfully my new clothes will be ready, so you don't have to be worried about my attire."

He tilted his head to study her and a slow, seductive smile raised the corners of his lips. She was wearing one of her new nightgowns, a thin silken sheath that felt like gossamer against her skin.

"I like your new attire," he said, his voice low and seductive.

For the first time since she'd awakened from her nightmare, she noticed his clothes. His shirt was untucked and open at the neck, and his only other article of clothing were his trousers. He must have dressed in haste when he heard her cry out.

It would be easy for him to undress.

It was be easy for her, too.

Regarding her steadily, his eyes dark with desire, he grazed her right shoulder with his fingertips. "Is this where the duchess grabbed you in your dream?"

Her heartbeat quickening, her skin flushing with warmth, she nodded.

"Did she hurt you in your dream?"

"A little."

He bent his head to brush his lips where he had touched her. "You have beautiful shoulders."

She closed her eyes and shivered again, this time for a different reason.

Inching closer, he dragged his lips toward the curve of her neck. She leaned her head back and gripped his arms to steady herself.

"I should go," he suddenly announced, letting go of her, but not getting off the bed.

She didn't let go of *him* and didn't intend to. "Why? We're husband and wife. You do want me, don't you?"

He slowly nodded.

"Then have me, husband," she whispered.

For a moment Thea feared he was going to leave, until he tugged her into his arms and his mouth captured hers with fevered desire.

After a long and passionate embrace, Dev got off the bed, but only to remove his clothes. Eagerly Thea watched him strip off his shirt and trousers, reveling in the sight of his naked body. In the dim illumination of the candle, he did indeed look like a young god, his skin bronze in the flickering flame.

Even more exciting was the blatant look of need and longing in his dark eyes.

He quickly joined her in the bed and began to

caress her body through the thin silk of her nightgown. She had believed nothing could rival the sensation of his hands on her skin, only to discover the film of silk added to the thrill of his touch, sending more waves of pleasure coursing through her.

Nevertheless, she didn't regret it when he nuzzled the loose neckline of her garment lower and brought his mouth to her breasts. She arched to meet him and parted her legs in a silent invitation, one he didn't hesitate to accept.

He was inside her in an instant and began to thrust, the powerful motion increasing her arousal. She gasped and moaned and whispered words of encouragement, letting him know how much she wanted him. Needed him. Loved—

She had no more coherent thoughts before he reached the climax and so did she, the moment powerful and potent, a release and a delight. They were one, husband and wife, lovers, mates, joined by law and nature.

Panting, he lay down beside her, stroking her hair while she nestled against him and toyed with a lock of his dark, wavy hair. "Dev," she whispered, "do you want many children?"

He raised himself on his elbow to regard her quizzically. "I want as many as God may give us, as long as you're safe."

She felt as if the sun had suddenly come out. He wanted children and he must truly care for her if he was concerned about her safety in childbirth.

He lay down again. "Why do you ask?"

"Gladys told me you once said you didn't want children, perhaps because of your parents' unfortunate union and your less-than-blissful upbringing," she admitted. "I feared you meant it after I spoke of wills and you looked so upset."

"I wasn't upset."

Having seen his face when wills were mentioned, she didn't quite believe him. However, many people didn't enjoy discussing wills, so she decided not to pursue that course of conversation.

"What did Gladys tell you?" he asked, his voice sounding loud in the darkness.

"That your father was a cruel man, unkind to your mother, and that you stayed away from here for years."

To her dismay, he got out of bed and pulled his shirt over his head, then tugged on his trousers and began to button them. "No, I didn't have a particularly loving father," he grimly agreed. "As for my parents' marriage, it wasn't any worse than many marriages among their peers. My father got what he wanted and so did my mother, although she found out too late she had wanted the wrong thing. The wrong man."

She sat up. "I'm sorry, Dev."

"She's at peace now. I only regret I wasn't able to make her happier and protect her while she was alive, as you did with your father." He looked away when he added, "She died when I was at school."

She had never heard a man sound so lonely. She wanted to hold him, to put her arms around him to comfort him, so she got out of bed and hurried to stand between him and the door. "I'm sure you were a comfort to your mother, even if you weren't there when she died," she offered quietly.

His eyes widened, as if this had never once occurred to him.

She embraced him gently, her heart full of sympathy for the boy he'd been and the pain he had endured, in some ways like her own, but also different, too.

She touched his cheek and looked up into his handsome, stoic visage. "She should have left your father."

He shook his head. "She wasn't like you, Thea. She couldn't have managed on her own."

It was the best compliment she'd ever received.

"I wish you could have known my mother," he whispered.

"So do I. I think you must have her eyes. Is there not a portrait of her in the house?"

"No."

"Yet you keep your father's portrait in the study."

He stepped away. "To make certain I am never like him." He pointed to a red, mottled spot on the back of her arm usually hidden by her clothes. "How did you get that mark?"

She instinctively covered it. "I was burned by water from a kettle when I was a child."

"In Ireland?"

"Dublin. We were visiting the Reverend Mr. Pennyfeather and I pulled a kettle over."

"It must have been very painful."

"It wasn't so very bad a burn," she said, wondering what had prompted him to mention it.

"Good night, Thea," he said before he moved

past her, opened the door and, without another word, left her, quietly closing the door behind him.

Thea stared at the closed door. She wished she hadn't said a word to Dev about anything after making love, let alone his parents. She should have simply enjoyed the comfort of his presence, no matter how much she wanted to learn about the history of the man she'd married. Then he might have stayed.

But all was not to be regretted, her heart suggested. She had confirmed that he wanted children.

And next time they made love, she would say nothing afterward.

A few moments later, Dev slipped out of his bedroom and quietly made his way to the study. He got a sheet of fresh foolscap and began to write to the Duchess of Scane, telling her he and his wife would be delighted to attend her dinner party. That might yet prove to be a grievous error, especially if his marriage was annulled or Thea wasn't Sir John Markham's daughter, but he didn't want to see that dismay and disappointment in Thea's eyes again. Besides, he had endured rumors and nasty whispers before, as Thea had inadvertently reminded him. His parents' unhappy union had been fodder for gossip for years, and he had survived.

He also wrote another letter to Roger, telling him about the scar on Thea's arm. Now more than ever it seemed urgent that they find out if Thea was Sir John Markham's daughter or not.

He did not tell Roger he'd been unable to resist making love to her again and more than once. Yet when he remembered being in Thea's arms, the excitement, the passion, the craving she inspired and sated so well, losing the battle to resist the temptation to be with her didn't seem a mistake. Loving her seemed inevitable and right, as if they were meant to be together.

But it was wrong. He had married out of guilt and lust, not love. Surely any marriage so conceived was doom to fail, and the sooner it was ended, the better.

When he had finished his letter, Dev folded his arms on his desk and laid his weary head upon them.

This time, he wasn't pondering his conflicted

feelings for his wife, or wondering what he should do about his marriage.

He was thinking of his poor mother and how different things might have been if she'd been more like Thea.

Chapter Nine

There days later, Dev paced in the drawing room, waiting for his wife. The barouche was at the door and the coachman in his seat, ready to take them to the duke's manor for the dinner party. He wasn't used to waiting for a woman and couldn't imagine what was taking so long. Thea had had hours to—

His impatience disappeared when Thea appeared at the top of the stairs. She wore a gown of silver silk in the latest fashion, low in the bodice with little capped sleeves. The skirt fell in a glistening swath of glimmering fabric to reveal satin slippers with silver buckles. Around her shoulders she had a shawl of the finest cashmere. Her thick chestnut-brown hair was piled high on her head, with curls dangling at the back and smaller ones on her forehead above her brilliant gray eyes.

Little white flowers were woven into her hair as well, and her hands and arms were sheathed in long white gloves.

She was, simply, beautiful. As beautiful as any woman he'd ever seen or imagined.

And she was his wife.

Dev closed his parted lips and stepped forward to meet her as she came down the stairs with perfect poise, graceful and regal as a queen.

Yet something was missing and it took him only an instant to realize what. She should have a necklace around her slender neck, something as brilliant and shining as her eyes, if that were possible. He remembered a necklace of his mother's, one of blue sapphires set in silver she had particularly loved.

Thea must have it. Whatever happened between them in the future, she should have it.

He watched her maid put her evening cloak around her shoulders, then held out his arm to escort her to the carriage. Torches burned in sconces on the side of the vehicle to light the way, and thankfully the roads were dry.

Once inside with Thea seated across from him,

he knocked on the roof and the carriage lurched into motion.

The windows were covered against the evening chill, so he thought she might look at him. Instead she seemed preoccupied with the drawstring of her cloak.

He wondered what she would do if he joined her on that side of the carriage and kissed her. It was very tempting.

He was about to put thought into action when she suddenly looked at him with what could only be dread and said, "Do you suppose many people will be there?"

"Going by my experience of the duchess's dinner parties, probably twenty to thirty."

That was clearly not a comforting answer. "You look lovely," he said, smiling to ease her concern.

"I've never had such a fine gown," she said. "I hope I don't spill anything on it."

"I'm sure you won't, but if you do, your maid should be able to fix it."

"Yes, she will," Thea answered with more confidence, and her shoulders relaxed a little.

"How do you find her? I gather from a few comments Mrs. Wessex made before she arrived that she was afraid the girl wouldn't do."

The vibrant energy came back to Thea's eyes. "Only because Alice Cartwright was an orphan and went to a charity school. She's been most satisfactory."

"I thought she must be or Mrs. Wessex would have told me."

Thea folded her hands in her lap and fixed him with a steadfast gaze. "Mrs. Wessex said you support several charity schools."

"Yes, I do," he readily admitted. "I think education is a good thing, for anyone."

"I quite agree," she said, and how she smiled then! It was as if he'd never really seen her smile before—and perhaps he hadn't. Even better, she obviously approved of his charitable ventures and didn't begrudge the cost.

When the barouche turned and passed through the gate to the duke's estate, he reached out to cover Thea's clasped hands with his own. "No need to worry about the duchess. You're the equal of any woman there."

"I'm not afraid of the duchess," she said, so

calmly he believed her. "And Gladys will be there."

So would he, but apparently she didn't consider him much moral support.

Which was an unexpectedly distressing thought.

The barouche rolled to a stop and a tall, white-wigged footman opened the door. Dev disembarked and reached up to take Thea's hand. As she climbed out of the carriage, she looked up in wonder at the duke's manor. Every window of the enormous mansion was lit, and a whole line of servants could be seen waiting in the hall.

It was one thing to best the duchess in a shop, he supposed, and quite another to face her in her own manor house with the trappings of five centuries of wealth and privilege around her.

He squeezed Thea's hand and she glanced at him not with dread, but with grim determination, like a general before a battle.

Her pride and resolve were also clearly in command when they entered the vast and opulent drawing room, where it seemed a multitude awaited. Instead of blushing or looking anxious, his wife raised her chin and smiled at everyone.

"Good evening, Lady Dundrake!" the duke exclaimed from where he stood beside his wife and daughter. "You look a picture, my lady! Glad to see this young fella doesn't stint when it comes to his wife's clothes, eh?"

"My husband is very generous," she agreed, for the moment not acknowledging the duchess or Caroline beside her. "And please, I'd much rather my husband's good friend called me Thea. Lady Dundrake is so formal."

The duchess looked as if she'd like to call Thea something else. "I'm sure we wouldn't do anything so common," she declared acerbically.

Dev could have throttled the overdressed peahen of a woman on the spot.

Thea, however, smiled and ran a haughty gaze over the duchess in a way that would have done credit to the duchess herself. "I'm sorry, Your Grace. I didn't realize being familiar with one's friends was considered rude here. However, if that is so, you will have to call me Lady Dundrake. Long, of course, but shorter than Lady Theodora Esmerelda Persephone Grace Dundrake. The poor dean at St. Patrick's Cathedral in Dublin had such a terrible time with it at my baptism."

Dev had to choke back the urge to laugh out

loud when he saw the expression on the duchess's face, even as he made a mental note of all Thea's names and where she'd been baptized. He'd have to tell Roger about that. Surely she wouldn't make up something like that when there were baptismal records that could be checked.

"And of course I'm delighted to meet you again, Lady Caroline," his wife continued, moving past the duchess toward her daughter. "What a beautiful gown!"

Caroline was really quite lovely, but not when she was dressed in a scarlet gown with an elaborate, heavily embroidered overtunic and wearing a necklace of gold and rubies so heavy and cumbersome he was surprised she wasn't bowed down by the weight of it. Her mother must have chosen it for her, for the duchess's own gown was almost the same, albeit in a shade of chartreuse that did no favors to the woman's complexion. The duchess's diamond necklace drew more scrutiny to her wrinkled neck than impressed with its probable cost.

"I do hope you'll come to call on me soon," Thea was saying to Caroline, and with apparent sincerity. "Even with a wonderful husband, it's very lonely being in a new home, as I daresay you'll find out soon." Thea nodded toward a knot of young men, most of whom were understandably staring back at them. "I'm sure there are many vying for your favor."

And too many who might vie for Thea's, Dev thought with a sudden jolt of jealousy.

A few, like that rogue Leamington-Rudney, caught his eye and wisely looked away.

If he'd needed another excuse to stay home from this party, he would have found it if he'd known Lord Leamington-Rudney would be there.

"Oh, there must have been plenty of young bucks after you," the duke said to Thea. "Mind you, your husband should be glad *the young Apollo!* didn't meet you first, or he wouldn't have had a chance."

"Our son will have his pick of *suitable* young ladies when he returns," the duchess noted before she fixed her malevolent glare onto Dev and spoke as if Thea weren't there. "You must tell us how you met your wife. Nobody seems to have heard of her before."

"I was raised in Ireland, Your Grace," Thea answered before he could, "where the fields are so green in spring it almost hurts your eyes to look at them. As for how we met…" She gave Dev a secretive, seductive look that made him want to pick her up, carry her upstairs and make love to her in the first bedroom he came to. "That's between us. But I will admit it was love at first sight, at least for me, Your Grace."

"For me, too," Dev couldn't help adding as he took hold of her hand.

He had intended to merely silence the duchess, but as soon as he said those words and held Thea's hand, he felt a sense of confirmation. And when Thea looked at him and smiled, he felt that even more.

Caroline's eyes widened, while her mother's narrowed. "Indeed?" the duchess remarked skeptically.

"Indeed," Thea returned with conviction.

Lady Gladys appeared at the door to the drawing room, with an older couple behind her who were surely her parents. The man was slightly stout, but more muscular than fat, and with a thick mustache that matched his gray hair. He wore evening dress that was fashionable a decade or two ago and, judging by his satisfied air, was completely content. His wife, as tall as Gladys, with a back as straight as a poker, was fashionably attired in a black silk gown with beading on the bodice and a black lace shawl. Although the two women shared the same statuesque build, the countess didn't resemble her daughter in looks. Lady Byford's features were sharp and pointed, whereas Gladys's more pleasant expression softened any of the less attractive elements she'd inherited from her mother. She wore a flowing gown of pale pink satin trimmed with darker pink ribbons. It was youthful without being juvenile, and pretty without being overdone, like the duchess's daughter's unfortunate gown.

After the briefest of greetings to the duke, duchess and Lady Caroline, Gladys proceeded to introduce her parents to Thea.

The Earl of Byford said hello, smiled in a genial sort of way, then all but dragged Dev off to talk about his newest horse. As they moved away, more guests arrived to take the duchess and Caroline's attention, so Thea, Gladys and the countess moved farther into the room decorated in a fashionable Nile green. It felt rather like being under the sea.

"Well, you're a sweet little thing and no mistake," the countess announced, her voice sounding almost exactly like her daughter's as she ran a pleased gaze over Thea. "It's about time that young rascal settled down. He's a good lad, all in all, but needs a firm hand at the helm. You look like you can manage him."

"She's not herding sheep, Mater!" Gladys cried with an embarrassed laugh.

"*All* men need a firm hand," Lady Byford countered.

Thea smiled. "I don't think my husband will take well to guidance."

"Nonetheless, you'll manage your husband, I'm sure," the countess declared. "And so will Gladys once she gets married, if any of these silly fools will ever get some sense and see what a treasure she is."

Gladys blushed as red as Caroline's ball gown. "Mater, please!"

"Well, it's true. Not that Develin would have been right for her. I'm sure he's a delightful husband, but she would never have been happy with him."

"Mater!" Gladys pleaded.

Her mother shot her an unexpectedly sympathetic look. "Well, you don't love him, never did and never would."

Before Gladys could reply—if anyone could have replied to that—Lady Byford suddenly stiffened like a hound on the scent. "Come along, Gladys. We'd better get your father away from those young fools before he buys another horse from one of them! I'm positive Leamington-Rudney cheated him with that gelding."

With that, Lady Byford grabbed her daughter's arm and marched off toward the little knot of men around the earl.

Thea was going to go after them until Dev joined her.

"I see you've met the countess," he noted wryly.

"She's a very forthright woman."

"And very proud of her daughter. It's a pity Gladys—"

"So, this is the mystery woman!" a slightly drunken voice interrupted from behind them.

Dev and Thea half turned to find a good-looking young man with curling golden locks and tight-fitting breeches, extravagant cravat and elegant jacket, as well as dark circles beneath his eyes and a slightly red nose, soddenly smiling and swaying.

"Good evening, my lord," Dev said grimly. "May I introduce my wife? Theodora, this is Lord Leamington-Rudney."

Notorious cad and decadent dandy, he wanted to add.

Thea ran her cool, steadfast gaze over the viscount, whose features and voice betrayed that he had already imbibed freely of wine even though dinner had yet to be served.

"Good evening, my lord," she said, giving him the frostiest of smiles, suggesting she had the measure of the man without any help from her husband.

"Delighted to meet you, my lady," the viscount said, reaching for her hand.

Dev had never wanted to smack a hand away more than when Leamington-Rudney grasped his wife's and pressed his thick lips to the back of it. Thank God she was wearing gloves.

The duke's butler—six foot six and built like a brick tower—appeared in the doorway. "Dinner is served!" he announced, much to Dev's relief.

His relief didn't last long, though, for the duchess had him take Caroline into the dining room and Leamington-Rudney escort his wife.

Thea spotted Dev watching her out of the corner of her eye. He'd been doing so often during the dinner, although whether he was pleased with her behavior or making sure she didn't make a mistake or say the wrong thing, or was wondering how she was getting along with the ridiculous viscount beside her, she wasn't sure. Her husband was alongside the duchess, with Caroline to his left and the Earl of Byford across from him. The countess was on the earl's other side. The earl spoke loud and long about his last hunt while his wife seemed to be paying special attention to the place settings.

Thea was farther down the table and farther still from Gladys, who was mostly ignored by the two young men seated on either side of her. She'd met bakers' boys and blacksmith's apprentices with better manners, at least when it came to acknowledging others in their company.

Dev, however, was attentive and polite to all—a gentleman in every sense of the word. Unlike her, he clearly belonged there among the ton, and not only because of his wealth, his title, his bearing and his handsome features.

"So, where have you been hiding all this time?" the viscount asked Thea after taking another drink of wine.

He was already drunk and would likely be found passed out in an anteroom before the evening ended. The only difference between him and the men she'd encountered who frequented more lowly gaming establishments and pubs was his wealth, and she supposed the viscount might one day find himself sharing a fate similar to her father's if he didn't see the error of his ways.

That did not mean she was any more inclined to treat him gently when he put his hand on her knee and said, "If I had known you existed, I would have given Dundrake some competition."

She shoved his hand away and regarded him sternly. "Do that again, and you'll regret it."

The viscount made what she supposed he considered a contrite smile, although he really looked more like a grimacing monkey. "You're that sort, are you?"

"If you mean the sort that finds such actions annoying, yes, I am."

"I didn't mean to offend."

"You meant something else, I'm sure—something I would consider abhorrent. Now, unless you want me to stab you with my fork, I suggest you keep your distance."

"Oh, you don't mean..." he began with a lopsided grin before he got a good look into Thea's angry eyes.

After all, she was no gently reared innocent. She'd retrieved her father from some very dubious establishments where more than one patron had assumed she was a fallen dove looking for a customer and approached her accordingly, only to discover Thea was quite capable of defending herself with her sharp tongue, a slap or a blow from her reticule. Several had retreated with both bruised pride and a stinging cheek.

The viscount cleared his throat, then turned away to address the older woman on his other side, who seemed quite flattered by his attention.

"Pray tell us, Lady Dundrake," the duchess's daughter suddenly demanded, "how *did* you meet Sir Develin?"

Although Lady Caroline was regarding Thea as if she were some sort of bizarre, exotic species,

Thea gave her a serene smile. "We met in a garden. It was quite romantic, I assure you."

The duchess sniffed with disdain, while Caroline turned to look at Dev. "It sounds like something from a fairy tale. Was it truly that romantic, Sir Develin?"

Her husband smiled at Thea in a way that made her blood rush. "Yes, it was."

If only that were true.

"How charming," Lady Caroline coldly remarked before giving all her attention to the next course the footman set before her.

No one else said anything directly to Thea for the rest of the meal. In some ways, that was a relief; in another, she wondered if she should have been less forceful.

Just when she was beginning to wonder if the dinner was ever going to end, the duke tapped his wine glass and got to his feet. "My lords, ladies and gentlemen, a toast! To my son, *the young Apollo*! He is coming home at last!"

Thea raised her wine glass, and as she did, she glanced at Gladys. Her friend was sitting completely, uncharacteristically still, as if she'd been turned to marble. Only when everyone raised their glasses did she seem to wake up and reach for hers. Then, with great deliberation as if she were performing a very tricky medical maneuver, Gladys sipped her wine and put her glass down on the table, then folded her hands in her lap.

"I say, Your Grace," one of the impolite young men beside Gladys called down the table. "Did Paul—I mean, did Apollo say when he'd be arriving?"

"By All Saints' Day," the duke said, beaming, "if not sooner."

With a swish of silk, the duchess rose. "Shall we, ladies?" she said, signaling it was time for them to retire to the drawing room.

Thea dutifully complied, although she would rather have ventured into any gambling hell in London or Liverpool. At least there, she would have been prepared for overt curiosity and insolence rather than facing the more subtle gibes and inquisition of supposedly gently reared ladies.

The duchess pounced as soon as Thea entered the drawing room.

Standing beside a magnificent, brightly polished ebony pianoforte, her expression snide, the duchess called out to Thea, "Lady Dundrake, won't you favor us with some music? We have a lovely instrument."

Thea gave her a placid smile in return. "So I see. However, I'm sure my skills are very poor compared to others here. I daresay your daughter is a far superior pianist."

"Perhaps she could accompany you while you sing?"

"I cannot sing very well, either. Nor can I play the harp."

"If it's music you wish, I'll oblige," Gladys said with unexpected vim and determination. She sat down at the pianoforte before anyone could protest and immediately launched into a very loud and spirited rendition of a very complicated air, her mother smiling as if they were in a concert hall.

The duchess moved away in a huff and as soon as Gladys had finished her piece, Caroline took her place, playing an equally complicated ballad.

The countess loudly complimented her daughter, who smiled, then hurried to join Thea.

"You play very well," Thea said to Gladys when her friend reached her.

"Considering the amount my parents have spent

on good teachers, I should," Gladys admitted ruefully. She held out her hands and spread her long, slender fingers. "It's good to know large hands can be good for something, if not particularly attractive. Mind you, I do wish my mother wouldn't carry on as if I'm a prodigy."

"She's justly proud of you."

"I appreciate that, but it's embarrassing nonetheless," Gladys said. She nodded toward the piano. "Caroline has very pretty hands. That's why she prefers to play the harp in company. She's a rather competitive person. I keep wondering if she'll say anything to you about..."

"About my marriage to Develin?" Thea suggested after Gladys fell guiltily silent.

Gladys nodded vigorously, loosening a lock of thick brown hair that she hastily tucked behind her ears.

"Did Caroline have hopes of marrying Develin?"

"I suppose I really shouldn't say anything. I'm not a mind reader, after all, to know how anybody else really feels. I hardly know how *I* feel half the time."

Thea could sympathize with that sensation.

"So I can't expect to really understand how Caroline feels, and especially where love's concerned. It's not as if I have any experience in the matter."

Thea suspected that was not precisely true. Given Gladys's reaction to the duke's announcement, she might be as familiar with unrequited love as Thea had been. "Do you think Caroline had any reason to believe Develin wanted to marry her?"

Gladys frowned, obviously considering, before she said, "If you mean did your husband ever show any particular partiality toward Caroline, no. Not that I ever saw. He was polite, of course, and kind, as he is to everybody. But if Caroline didn't want him, her mother certainly wanted them to marry. Develin was the best catch in the county."

"I'm sure there are plenty of eligible young men who'd make a good husband for Caroline."

Gladys sighed. "Not that her mother approves of. She's always favored Caroline, probably to make up for the duke favoring Paul, so Mater says. And Carolyn might have got her hopes up because her brother and Develin were such good friends. He was here often and I suppose, if one is young and pretty, one could hope that a friendship with a brother might extend to a sister and turn into something else. And Develin does have much to recommend him, as you well know. Caroline wouldn't be the only young lady who would be disappointed when she found out he was married."

Thea wondered if she'd made a mistake about Gladys's feelings. "Did you...?"

"Oh, dear me, no! Not I!" Gladys cried, and she couldn't have looked more startled if Thea had pinched her. "I mean, Develin's a very nice man and good-looking, of course, but he's not my sort at all! I prefer a quiet life in the country, while he spends most of his time in London. I hate dancing, I'm a dunce at cards and, well, most dinner parties are an exercise in anxiety for me, while he likes balls and cards and dinner parties."

Develin had seemed content to be in the country, but then, they hadn't been there very long. Perhaps he was secretly yearning to return to Town. Maybe that explained some of his somber moods.

There was one other thing Lady Gladys had mentioned that caught Thea's attention. "Develin is good at cards?" she asked as if she didn't already know the answer.

"Oh yes. The best cardplayer at school, so I heard, and I gather he's won a few tidy sums in the city. Not that anybody talks about where he plays or with whom." She patted Thea's gloved hand. "He doesn't venture into the worst places, I'm sure. And there are other places he could go where there aren't any cards, if you follow me, but he never does, or so the other gentlemen claim when they think nobody's listening. Dear Papa is quite good at looking like he's half-asleep, but I assure you, he knows all the antics the young gentlemen get up to. That's why he's often said he's glad he had a daughter, not a son, even though I don't doubt he would have liked an heir."

"I'm sure you'll marry one day and then he can look forward to a grandson."

Her friend blushed and she looked down at the hem of her gown. "I doubt that. I do own a mirror and I can see perfectly well with my spectacles on. I'm not exactly a young man's dream."

"You have much to offer any man wise enough to see it," Thea said sincerely.

"That's easy to say when you have brains and beauty, too. Now, if you'll excuse me, I really ought to make sure Mater's not getting overheated," Gladys replied before she moved toward her mother, who was now seated near the hearth.

Thea bit her lip in consternation. She hadn't meant to upset Gladys. She truly believed many men would be fortunate to have such a kind-hearted woman for a wife. Perhaps the duke's son would—

"Proud of yourself, are you?" a voice hissed in her ear.

She turned to find Caroline behind her.

"What did you do to make him marry you?" the duchess's beautiful daughter demanded in a harsh whisper.

Despite her scornful tone, Thea saw something other than disdain in her eyes, something that made her sympathetic heart go out to the young woman.

"I didn't *make* him marry me," she replied with quiet compassion, but firmly, too. She could feel sorrow for Caroline, but she wasn't about to apologize for her marriage.

"You trapped him somehow and married him for his money!"

Some would say Caroline's charges were true, but they wouldn't know the whole truth. Not even

Develin knew all of the truth. "If my husband had wanted to marry you, he could have done so before he ever met me. He did not."

Caroline drew back as if she'd struck her. "He would have! One day he was going to see how I felt and realize…and see…he could have loved me. But *you* came along and tricked him. Or seduced him. Whatever you did, you don't deserve him and I hope you *die*!"

As Thea stared, dumbfound by her ferocity, Caroline covered her mouth with her hand and hurried away.

Dev realized something was wrong with Thea the moment he entered the drawing room. She was as pale as a new moon. He hurried to her and anxiously asked, "Are you ill?"

"No, no, I'm quite all right," she replied.

"You don't look all right."

To his relief, the color returned to her cheeks as well as the vitality to her eyes. "I have no intention of rushing away from this dinner party."

"Are you sure?"

"Quite!"

"Very well, then," he said. "We'll stay."

But he would find out who or what had upset her as soon as they were back at Dundrake Hall. Where they would not be interrupted.

Chapter Ten

Wearing one of her soft and pretty new night-gowns, Thea stood by the fireplace in her bed-room after returning from the duchess's dinner party. She and Dev had journeyed home in silence, although she'd been sure Dev had wanted to ask her questions. More than once she'd caught him regarding her with an inquisitive look, yet thankfully he never spoke.

Wrapping her arms about herself, Thea stared into the flickering flames, the only illumination in the room. The dinner party had been more exhausting than she'd expected and not only because of the late hour. It was wearying making polite conversation and fatiguing trying not to notice the curious stares and speculative whispers. At least Gladys had forgiven her for any dismay she'd caused talking about marriage. To Thea's relief, she'd rejoined her later and chatted quite genially about the food the duchess had served. Several of the dishes—squab and oysters and sumptuous pastries—were only a few of the excellent offerings. Clearly the duchess was keen on impressing her guests with the menu, and she'd certainly succeeded.

As for any other friendships that might have begun that evening, Thea feared the enmity of the duchess and her daughter rendered that unlikely. Fortunately she'd been right to think people wouldn't be willing to snub her husband, no matter what they thought of her.

But who wouldn't want to be his friend? He was charming to everyone, including Lady Caroline and her mother, so it was no surprise to learn that Caroline had wanted to marry him. Yet as she had said to that upset young woman, he had had his chance to marry someone else before he ever met her.

A soft knock sounded on the door leading to Develin's dressing room. "My lady? Thea? May I come in?"

It was Develin.

She glanced at the woolen bed robe over the nearby chair and left it there. "You may."

The door opened and her husband, still clad in his evening clothes save for his jacket and cravat, entered the room. She stayed where she was and he walked over to join her, his face bronzed by the firelight, his eyes deep in shadow.

"It was obvious something was amiss when the gentlemen rejoined the ladies tonight," he said, holding up his hand to stop her before she could deny it. "There's no point trying to tell me otherwise. Did the duchess say something to distress you?"

"Her venom is easy to dismiss," Thea replied with a shrug.

"Did Leamington-Rudney make lewd remarks? Or try to touch you?"

"There's nothing that vain puppy could say that I haven't heard before," she answered honestly. Indeed he was a rank amateur in lewdness compared to some of the men she'd encountered. "He did put his hand on my knee at dinner. He quickly removed it when I threatened to stab him with my fork."

"That...!" Develin rolled his shoulders as

if physically trying to subdue his emotions. "I wouldn't have blamed you if you had."

"I would have done it, too, I assure you." She frowned and clasped her hands. "I realize it wasn't very ladylike to threaten him and perhaps I should have restrained myself, but I've had to take care of myself for a long time, in some rather danger-ous situations, so I did what came naturally."

"I'm glad to hear it," he returned. "I was proud of you tonight and I'm even prouder to hear that you're willing and able to protect yourself."

Despite his welcome praise, a small wrinkle of puzzlement appeared between his dark eyebrows. "If it wasn't Leamington-Rudney or the duchess who upset you, did I do or say something to cause you distress tonight?"

"No, it wasn't anything you said or did." She de-cided to tell him what had happened in case there were repercussions she couldn't foresee. "Caro-line is quite upset with me. She seems to believe you were going to ask for her hand."

"No, never," he instantly replied, shaking his head. "Not even if I'd fallen into that little trap they set in the—"

He cleared his throat and said no more.

She wasn't about to let him stop there. "What sort of trap? And who set it?"

Dev ran his hand through his thick, waving hair, disheveling it completely, before he answered. "It was at their last ball. Caroline got me alone in the garden and tried to persuade me to kiss her. I refused and then her uncle appeared like a genie from a bottle. He might have been intending to declare I'd sullied her honor and so would have to marry her. If that was the plan, I could more easily believe her mother was behind it, not Caroline. She certainly seemed surprised by her uncle's arrival."

"She might be a better actress than you give her credit for, or more desperate," Thea said. Who knew better than she the lengths to which one might go for love?

"Whatever she thought was between us, she shouldn't have threatened you," he said. "I'll go over there in the morning and—"

"There's no need," Thea interrupted. "I understand that she's disappointed and the news of our wedding came as a shock. Surely in time Caroline will come to accept our marriage. After all, she's a lovely young woman and rich and titled, so she'll have her pick of other worthy young men."

Dev took a step closer and when he spoke, his voice was low and husky. "If I'd known Leamington-Rudney had dared to touch you, I would have challenged the blackguard to a duel on the spot."

She was very glad he hadn't. "He wouldn't be worth the effort."

Dev grinned, looking more like a youth than a mature young man. "Then I take it you would never have proposed marriage to the viscount?"

"Under no circumstances and no matter how desperate I was," she firmly agreed.

"I'm relieved to hear it. Otherwise I would be jealous of that toad.

"You look as if you don't believe me, but it's true," he went on, his deep voice soft and sincere. "You're a lovely woman, Thea — and it's not the fine new clothes or the way your hair is dressed, either, that makes me think so. It's the light in your eyes, your courage, your determination, that make you special, Thea."

As her heart raced and her body warmed, he gathered her in his arms and kissed her—not with fiery, primitive, demanding urgency, but tenderness. He caressed her not with lust, but with gentle desire.

And when he took her to bed, he made love to her that same way, although with no less passion.

Waking from a deep and restful sleep, Dev opened his eyes, then felt for Thea beside him.

She wasn't there.

He sat up abruptly and was relieved to see his wife standing by the window as the pale light of dawn touched the sky outside the tall window. Her hair was loose, and she wore only that silken nightgown.

He got out of bed and tugged on his trousers, then went to stand behind her. He wrapped his arms about her, enfolding her in the warmth of his embrace. "What are you thinking about so early in the morning?" he asked softly.

"Gladys."

That was unexpected. "Gladys?"

Still in his arms, she turned to face him. "I want her to be as happy as I am."

"Naturally, if she's your friend."

"She is, and I haven't had many friends." Thea laid her head on his naked chest, her breath warm on his skin. "Do you think the duke's son will come home this time?"

"Perhaps, but I wouldn't count on it. Trying to live up to his father's praise and expectations would be difficult for any man."

"If he does, will he really be so popular among the ladies?"

Dev put his hands on her shoulders and, confused, pulled back to look at her. "Paul's a nice fellow, but he's no Apollo or Adonis, either. He was the skinniest fellow at school and has a true Roman nose, a truly large Roman nose." He frowned. "What does it matter what Paul looks like or if he's popular?"

"I was wondering about Gladys's chances of securing his affection. I think she cares for him a great deal."

"You think Gladys...and Paul?" Dev returned, genuinely shocked.

"Why is it so strange to think they could fall in love?"

"For one thing, Paul doesn't like her. They're both nice people, but proud in their own way, especially Paul, and she's proven time and time again that she can run faster, ride better and shoot straighter than he can."

"That doesn't mean Gladys doesn't like him," Thea pointed out.

"You've never heard them quarrel. Normally she's the most genial and accommodating of women, but not with him. She contradicts everything he says until he loses his temper."

"That would be one way of getting his attention, at least."

He had never considered Gladys's actions in that light. And yet… "Even if they did fall in love, I doubt the duchess would allow their marriage."

"Why not? Gladys is an earl's daughter and the family is obviously wealthy."

"She may be an earl's daughter, but she's clumsy and not pretty or witty and she talks too much. Nor would Lady Byford be pleased."

"I think the countess would capitulate if the match made her daughter happy. As for the duchess, it would be Paul who would be marrying Gladys, not his mother. Do you think the duke would object?"

"He believes everything his son does is wonderful, and he'd be relieved Paul's choice is English."

"Then why shouldn't they marry, unless you think Paul won't stand up to his mother?"

"He would if he loved the girl enough. But this is Gladys we're talking about."

Thea raised her chin. "She's a fine woman and she'll make any man a fine wife, if he's wise enough to see it. And as for any previous enmity Paul may have because of her athletic prowess, he's been gone so long he must surely have had time to get over it."

"Perhaps," Dev answered warily. Thea had never seen his friend in a temper after losing another footrace to Gladys, or how that usually most amiable of girls could gloat.

"I think we should have a ball to welcome Paul home."

Dev suspected this was not a change of subject. "If you're thinking of having a ball with the intention of playing matchmaker for them, I'd reconsider. He may not come home for a long time yet, and even if he does, he's so quiet and shy—despite what his father believes—I doubt most people would even realize he's there."

She crossed her arms. "We should have a ball

anyway, whether or not it's to welcome your friend."

"So Gladys can meet other eligible young men?"

"Perhaps, although it's also important that we start to make a place for ourselves in society here, too."

A ball in his home meant noise and disruption. Nevertheless, she did have a point. "Very well. Choose a date and plan your ball. Mrs. Wessex will help you."

"I'm counting on that," Thea admitted. She put her arms around him and hugged him. "Thank you."

"As for Paul and Gladys, I wish you luck."

"Luck," she said with a sudden flash of temper. "How I hate that word! Luck and the wishing for it have been the bane of my existence for as long as I can remember."

In the next instant, the temper turned to sorrow.

"I'm sorry," she said softly. "I shouldn't be upset with you because my father lived to wager."

No, not for that, but if Sir John truly was her father and she ever learned the truth about that last game…

He moved away to hide the flush of shame stealing over him. "I'd best leave you to get dressed. I wouldn't want your maid to find me like this."

He bussed her lightly on the cheek and fled.

Two rainy days later, freshly shaven and dressed in his riding clothes, Dev trotted down the stairs heading for the dining room. It was a fine morning at last and he was looking forward to a good gallop, as well as the chance to decide what to do about Thea, or more precisely, his feelings about her.

Never had he felt for any woman the affection, respect and desire he felt for her. Never had he wanted to be with a woman as much as he wanted to be with her, both in bed and out.

Was that love?

And was it love that made him question whether or not he wanted the marriage ended even if Thea had lied about who she was?

He found Jackson at the bottom of the steps waiting to present him with a letter addressed in Roger's familiar hand.

He opened it and read the few lines his solicitor had written. Frowning, he glanced at his butler. "Please tell my wife I'll be gone for most of the day."

* * *

Sometime later, Dev scanned the dim confines of the tavern in a town a few miles from Dundrake. Ever since receiving the letter that morning, he'd feared Roger had brought him bad news. Otherwise he would surely have come to Dundrake Hall instead of asking to meet in this out-of-the-way place.

He spotted Roger leaning back against a none-too-clean wall. Drawing in a deep breath redolent of ale and sawdust and smoke, Dev threaded his way through the tables until he reached Roger and took a chair across from him. He'd no sooner sat than a serving woman in clothes that were also none too clean, her bodice loose and her breasts swaying, sauntered up to them.

"Ale, sir, or will it be wine…or maybe somethin' else, eh?" the woman asked, smiling and displaying a mouthful of teeth that made Dev suppress a shudder.

"Ale, if you please, and another for me friend," Roger replied, his accent slipping back to that of his poverty-stricken youth.

Dev waited until the serving wench had moved off, then inched his chair closer to the scarred wooden table. "Why are we meeting here instead of Dundrake Hall?"

"I thought it best not to meet there lest I encounter your wife."

Dev's heart sank. "You've discovered that Thea's not who she claims to be?" he asked, the extent of his pain beyond anything he'd thought he'd feel if that were so.

"She is indeed the daughter of Sir John Markham."

Dev felt as if he'd come back from the brink of a long and steep drop. "Thank God!"

Roger's eyes narrowed ever so slightly before he spoke again. "My man found the vicar in whose home she was burned. He also found the record of her baptism at St. Patrick's. Given everything he found in confirmation of the information provided, I think it most likely she is indeed Sir John's daughter."

Smiling with relief, Dev sat back in his chair as the serving wench arrived with the ale. One look at the beverage in the pewter mug and Dev decided not to drink it. Nevertheless, he paid for the drinks, then waited until the wench was out of earshot before he asked, "So why *are* we meeting here?"

"Even if your wife's identity is not in doubt, I've learned things about her father that are cause for concern. He gambled away the family fortune and he's been fleeing his creditors for years."

"Thea told me he'd lost all his money—that's why she proposed," he reminded his friend. "It makes sense that creditors would follow."

It also didn't take a great deal of imagination to envision Sir John letting his daughter cope with those creditors. That would explain her ability to appear calm and composed in almost any situation.

"There is something else," Roger said, dropping his voice lower, his expression as grim as Dev had ever seen—even worse than his father's at its worst. "My man was able to trace Sir John to Liverpool, but there is no evidence he actually boarded a ship there to Canada or anywhere else."

"What are you saying?"

"That Sir John may still be in England."

Dev frowned with both dismay and dread. "If he's not on a ship to Canada, where the devil is he?"

"My agents are trying to find out, so far without success."

"Could he have lost his passage money gambling?"

"It's possible. He did indulge in some wagers, but as far as my men have been able to ascertain, he won enough that he should have been able to pay for his passage. However, they may yet discover he had lost what he'd gained."

"Perhaps he chose another destination, or decided to sail from another port."

Roger's grim expression didn't change. "I've sent men to Glasgow, Wales, Dover, Plymouth, Cornwall and Lincolnshire. They have found no record of Sir John on any manifest of any vessel leaving England. Has your wife had any letters from him?"

"How could she? He's supposed to be in the middle of the Atlantic."

"Or so she told you."

A rock seemed to settle in Dev's stomach. "What are you implying?" he demanded, even though he knew full well what Roger suspected, as he immediately confirmed. "That she may be in contact with him and has kept that from you."

Another explanation occurred to Dev, one that offered little comfort. "Or Sir John could be dead."

Although he hoped for Thea's sake that he was wrong, her father could have bet against the wrong person and been murdered, his body hidden or tossed into the sea.

"Yes, he could be dead," Roger coolly agreed, "but my men have found no evidence of that, either."

That brought Dev a bit of relief, for Roger's men were very good at their jobs. But only a bit. In spite of whatever he'd done in the past, Thea loved her father and he would hate to have to tell her Sir John was dead.

"What if she *has* heard from him?" he asked. "If he stayed in England because he gambled away his passage money, she could be too ashamed and embarrassed to tell me."

"Or she might have known he never intended to leave the country and lied about that to gain your sympathy."

"She's never appealed to my sympathy. Ever."

"Experts in deceit excel at hiding their intentions. However, let us suppose she does believe he had sailed. He may have changed his mind for some unknown reason and chosen not to tell her. Perhaps he hasn't contacted her because he doesn't know where she is, or has yet to discover that she's married. If he does find out, though, and comes to you or your wife for money or to pay his debts—"

"I can afford it."

"No doubt, but that might only be the beginning of the demands he might make."

"He could demand all he liked. I need not agree."

"And your wife? What if she is not able to refuse his pleas?"

Dev thought of Thea's strength, her resolve, but also her apparent capacity to forgive her father almost anything. Against anyone else, including her husband, she might be strong, but her father? "She has her pin money and that's all. Even if Sir John asked, she would have to come to me for more money. She hasn't so far."

"You have a fair number of valuables in your house, Dev. Silver and jewelry, easily pawned."

That was also unfortunately true. "I haven't been told that anything is missing."

"I'm relieved to hear it."

Not nearly as much as he was to be able to truthfully say it.

The serving wench approached, until a look from Roger sent her scurrying back to the kitchen.

"I don't believe Thea is aware her father hasn't sailed—if he hasn't," Dev said in his wife's defense. "Mistakes have been made in ships' manifests before."

Roger's stern features softened a little. "I hate being the bearer of any news that causes you distress and I don't fault you for wanting to believe in your wife's honesty. I can see that in spite of your hasty nuptials, you care for her."

"You can, can you?"

Roger made a little smile and nodded. "You forget how well I know you. And it's possible that even if her father has contacted her, she wishes to distance herself from him and so has said nothing. But wherever he is and whatever your wife may or may not know, my first responsibility is your welfare and so I must voice my concerns."

"I appreciate that, Roger," Dev said. "Is there anything else you think I need to know?

"Only that there's no need for you to do anything immediately."

Dev did not agree. "I'm going to Liverpool myself," he said, rising.

Roger put out a detaining hand. "My agents—"

"Have no doubt checked all the well-known gambling hells," Dev interrupted. "But there are places in Liverpool that no agent of yours would ever be allowed to enter even if they knew they existed, places where men like Sir John and me are welcome."

Roger also got to his feet. "Then I should go with you. When are you planning to leave?"

"Now."

The solicitor's dark eyebrows rose. "Without returning to Dundrake Hall?"

"Yes."

"What about your wife? Won't she wonder where you are?"

"That's why you must go to Dundrake Hall and tell her I've gone to Liverpool on business. No need to say more."

Roger looked as if he'd rather walk over hot coals, which was probably true. Nevertheless, Dev had made his decision. "She'll believe my solicitor if he tells her there's no cause for alarm, because there isn't yet."

"And should she ask questions?"

Dev gave Roger the grimmest of grim smiles. "There is no one in the world better at discouraging queries than you."

Chapter Eleven

Finishing a late morning walk, Thea shivered and quickened her pace as she returned to Dundrake Hall. Soon it would be too cold to walk outside at all, so she had taken the opportunity to do so while she could. She had walked through a wood thick with pine, ash and oak and gone as far as the border of Dev's estate, where it abutted the Duke of Scane's vast acreage. The damp, misty air smelled of evergreen and rich earth made of leaves lost over the years. Startled squirrels scampered away through the undergrowth of bracken where the sun could reach the ground, and once a rabbit bounded away, its white tail like a sudden sighting of snow.

Just before turning back and beyond the boundary, she'd seen what appeared to be an abandoned cottage, perhaps used during the hunting season or by a charcoal burner. Despite its state of disrepair, it would have seemed palatial to many of the poor families she'd encountered in large cities, and it was a forceful reminder of her own days of poverty and fear.

Even so, she couldn't help feeling a sense of relief that she was free, if only for a little while, of the duties and responsibilities that came with being the mistress of a manor. It was more work than she'd anticipated, and now she'd added the planning of a ball—not that she was sorry for that. As she'd told Dev, it was important that they take their place in local society.

She glanced at the French doors leading to her husband's study, vividly remembering her trepidation the first time she'd approached Dundrake Hall through the garden. She'd had no idea what would happen. How glad she was that he'd agreed to marry her, especially after that frightening dream. All the terrors of the past, real or imagined, seemed to be behind her and a happier, secure life beginning.

Getting closer to the study, she caught sight of a familiar male figure standing near the fireplace with his back to the doors, looking up at the portrait of Sir Randolf.

That picture really ought to be taken down. Dev needed no reminders to be a good man. "Did you have a nice ride?" she asked after she opened the door and entered. "You were gone rather a long time."

The man who turned to face her was not her husband.

Instead it was as if the late baronet's portrait had come to life, except for the real man's vivid blue eyes.

"Who are you?" she demanded, instinctively backing toward the terrace.

"I'm sorry if I startled you, my lady. I'm Roger Bessborough, Sir Develin's solicitor," the man who shared Dev's broad shoulders and muscular build calmly replied. "I assume you're Lady Dundrake."

The shape of his face was different from Dev's—more square and angular. Nor did he sound like Dev. Mr. Bessborough's voice was rougher, and she had spent enough time with people trying to affect an upper-class accent to recognize the solicitor didn't come by his naturally.

"Yes, I am," she replied, wondering what he was doing there. "Won't you sit down? Unfortunately I don't think my husband is here at the moment. He may be out riding still. If he is, he should return shortly, should you care to wait."

Mr. Bessborough didn't accept her invitation. "I have not come here to see your husband. I came here to tell you that he's gone to Liverpool and isn't certain when he'll be returning."

"Why?" *And why has he sent his solicitor to tell me instead of telling me himself before he left this morning?*

"He has business, my lady, that he felt required his personal attention."

"What sort of business?"

"I regret I'm not at liberty to say."

Several business reasons came to mind, ones that her husband might prefer to keep confidential even from his wife or that he might not think a woman would either care about or understand.

Yet in spite of those possible explanations, there was something distinctly odd about her husband's unexpected departure. "He took no baggage with him."

The solicitor seemed unaffected by her concerned query. "I've spoken with the butler and he will see that the necessary articles are sent to Sir Develin's hotel in Liverpool."

"Which would be?"

"I have not yet been informed."

Thea's eyes narrowed. Dev's solicitor didn't know where he would be staying? Or perhaps he did but didn't want to tell her.

Another possible reason for Dev's abrupt departure and secrecy came to her, one that sent a spiral of dismay through her heart. She had given Dev leave to have lovers when she proposed they marry. Although it had seemed to her that all was well between them, perhaps he had a mistress in Liverpool. Nevertheless, that still didn't explain why he hadn't taken any baggage, unless the woman's summons had been urgent.

Perhaps Dev's mistress had used his solicitor to convey her appeal to Dev to come to her and that was really why Mr. Bessborough had come to Dundrake Hall. It might have been convenient for Dev to have Mr. Bessborough tell his wife where he'd gone, too. That would certainly save him having to make his excuses himself.

She raised her eyes and met the solicitor's steadfast gaze. "Will you stay for dinner, Mr. Bessborough?"

The solicitor flushed as if she'd asked him to strip naked before he shook his head. "No, thank you, my lady. I should start my journey back to London without delay. Please excuse me."

After giving her a slight bow, Mr. Bessborough strode from the room, leaving Thea to ponder her husband's unusual actions and what she should do if the reason for her dread proved to be true.

Two days later, Dev felt soiled just walking into the gambling hell. Unfortunately he had no choice except to search such places in Liverpool if he wanted to find Thea's father, who might or might not have sailed for Canada.

He'd already visited the shipping offices and, as Roger's agents had reported, hadn't found Sir John's name any ship's manifest sailing from Liverpool in the past few weeks. But neither had he found any evidence to suggest Sir John had stayed behind. Thea's father had stayed in no hotel, no inn, no tavern and none of the lodging houses Dev had visited thus far. There were a few more cheap ones to check. Not wanting to get bitten by fleas, however, he'd decided to try the gambling hells first. Perhaps after that, and even if he found out nothing about her father, he would write a letter to Thea. Every other time he'd started, he'd stopped, unsure what explanation he could give that wouldn't cause her any alarm.

"Sir Develin! What a pleasure! It's been too long!" the owner of the gambling hell called out when he spotted Dev at the entrance to the large, noisy room full of men wagering at games of chance. The smoke from cheroots swirled about like a fog in the candlelight, adding to the sense that Dev had entered some sort of underworld, one to which he no longer wanted to belong. Before he'd encountered Sir John, the lure of triumph, the need to prove he was better than other men at something, had made gambling seem like good sport. Since he'd learned the damage gambling could do, the hurt and harm it could cause to the innocent, he was sorry he hadn't found something else at which to excel.

"Hello, Bifkin," he said, nodding at the large, pale man with a long gray hair and thick gray beard who approached him.

Bifkin looked like Father Christmas down on

his luck—rather an appropriate notion. Dev also doubted the fellow ever saw the light of day.

"There's a spot for you at that table," Bifkin noted, pointing at a table where five men were engaged in a grimly silent, serious game of vingt-et-un.

Dev shook his head. "I haven't come to gamble. I've come for information."

Bifkin's bushy gray eyebrows lowered. "You know I don't 'peach," the man growled. "If you've got a debt to collect, that's naught my concern."

"It's a family matter," Dev said. "I'm looking for Sir John Markham. It's quite likely he'd have come here if he was in Liverpool."

"Never saw him. Never heard of him."

"There's a reward for any information concerning his whereabouts."

The bushy eyebrows drew together over Bifkin's red and bulbous nose. "How much?"

"Fifty pounds."

Bifkin let out a low whistle. "Blimey, wish I *had* met the man. That's a lot of brass."

"I just want to know where he can be found. You don't have to bring him to me. Send a message to the Regis Hotel here or if I've gone, to Dundrake

Hall. If your information proves useful, you'll be fifty pounds richer."

Bifkin scratched his beard and nodded. "I'll do my best, gov'nor. Sure you won't have a go?"

"Not tonight," Dev replied, turning to leave. *And not ever again, here or anywhere,* he vowed silently as he headed toward the door.

Where he nearly collided with Leamington-Rudney. The viscount stumbled over the threshold, obviously drunk and smelling as if he'd fallen into a cask of wine.

"Wha're you doing here?" the viscount demanded as he straightened, glaring at Dev as if his very presence was an insult.

"I'm searching for someone."

The florid color drained from Leamington-Rudney's face and he steadied himself with one hand on the nearest wall. "Wha' d'you care if she's run off? You don't give a brass farthing about her."

Dev stiffened, feeling as if an Arctic blast had hit him. *Surely he couldn't mean Thea. Please, God, don't let him be speaking of Thea!* "To whom are you referring?"

"Did her father send you? Not that he cares about her. The duchess's not much better." Leamington-Rudney sneered and Dev began to breathe again.

"Why shouldn't Caroline run off with me, eh?" the drunken viscount continued. "*I* like her—at least in bed."

Dev's relief was replaced by scornful disbelief. "Are you trying to tell me you and Caroline eloped?"

The viscount gave him a wicked grin. "*You* might get tricked into going to Gretna Green. *I'm* not so stupid."

Dev grabbed Leamington-Rudney by the collar and shoved him up against the wall. "You rotten cur!"

At the same time and despite his anger, he realized Caroline was still—and thankfully—free. Marriage to the viscount would be worse than hard labor.

"Gentlemen! None of that, if you please!" Bifkin declared, hurrying to separate them. "Take your quarrel outside!"

Dev ignored the owner of the gambling hell and held the squirming nobleman where he was. "Where is Caroline?"

"Still in bed," Leamington-Rudney gasped, his face growing redder.

"Where?" Dev snarled.

"The Ship's Inn."

It could be worse. That was a decent place, if not the finest.

Dev let go and Leamington-Rudney sank to his knees.

"If you're wise, my lord," Dev said to the coughing nobleman, "you'll get on the first ship out of port."

"She won't go with you!" the viscount shouted in the silence as Dev started for the door, for even the most hardened gamblers had stopped their games to stare. "Not now!"

Dev paused on the threshold and turned to regard the blackguard with all the disdain he felt. "Despite her unaccountable lapse of judgment running off with you, she's still my friend and worthy of my aid and protection, and she will have it."

"You can have her, then," the viscount retorted, rubbing his throat. "She'll be better in bed than that coldhearted wife of yours."

Dev took one step toward the viscount, who quickly moved behind Bifkin.

"Here, get away from me!" Bifkin cried, side-stepping away from Leamington-Rudney. The owner of the gambling hell scowled at Dev. "Do what you like to the bounder, but not here. I can't have no murder in my place."

"I have no intention of laying a hand on that poor excuse for a man," Dev replied before he turned on his heel and left them there.

After Dev had gone, Bifkin glared at the red-faced viscount. "You'd best leave, m'lord," he said, his hands on his broad hips.

"After I have a drink," Leamington-Rudney said hoarsely, "or I'll have this place shut down."

Bifkin nodded, albeit with obvious reluctance, then called for a servant to bring the man some wine.

Leamington-Rudney downed the wine in a gulp and wiped his thick lips with the back of his hand before heading for the door. "He's going to pay for this," he muttered.

Bifkin rolled his eyes and no one else paid the

least attention. They were all once again absorbed in their games of chance.

As soon as Dev left Bifkin's, he hailed a hackney coach and got to the Ship's Inn as quickly as he could. The tall, narrow building had once been home to a shipping merchant and bore the signs of excellent construction, from the oaken beams in the ceiling to the smooth, wide, pegged floorboards beneath his feet. Items decorating the main room, like the Turkey carpet and delicate lamps of Venetian glass, had come from all over the world.

Dev had no sooner entered than a young man with wispy brown hair and a weak chin appeared from a door beneath the wide stairway. "Good day, sir. We've a wonderful room vacant," he said eagerly.

"Thank you, but I don't require accommodation," Dev replied, doing his best to keep his voice calm and level so as not to alarm the fellow. "I'm looking for some acquaintances of mine, Lord Leamington-Rudney and a lady."

The young man frowned and rubbed his hands together nervously. "We have no one here by that name."

"The viscount may not wish his true name to be known, or the young lady's," Dev said. He decided on a lie of his own. "I'm the lady's solicitor and it's very important that I speak with her, Mr....?"

"Whitcombe."

Dev dropped his voice to a confidential whisper. "I fear there may have been some misinformation regarding the extent of the young man's fortune, Mr. Whitcome, that has only now come to light and may affect the marriage settlement."

The young man's pale blue eyes widened. "Oh dear! And her such a pretty—"

He flushed and fell silent, perhaps regretting that he'd betrayed Caroline's presence.

"Yes, she is," Dev agreed. "She's also a fine young woman deserving of a man's assistance, wouldn't you say?"

Whitcombe seemed to come to a decision and, to Dev's mind, the right one. "She's in the room at the far end of the hall on the second floor. The gentleman isn't with her at the moment."

"Thank you," Dev said sincerely, "and I'm sure she'll be most grateful, too."

He hurried up the stairs and along the corridor

to the room the young man had indicated. Once there, he knocked briskly.

"Go away!" a woman answered, a woman whose voice he recognized.

He stood close to the door and spoke just loud enough for her to hear. "Caroline, it's Dev. Please open the door."

He waited for what seemed an age, then called to her again. "Caroline, please open the door."

This time, he heard someone moving in the room before the door opened a crack, yet it was a gap wide enough to see a portion of Caroline's face. And a black eye.

"For the love of God, Caroline, please let me in!" he exclaimed, shoving his foot in the crack to prevent her from closing the door again.

To his relief, she moved back. She wore one of her day dresses, a pretty confection of silk and lace, but it had been torn at the sleeve, no doubt by Leamington-Rudney.

The room itself was a shambles, the bed in the corner unmade, dirty linen bunched up on the washstand, the water in the basin gray. Articles of clothing, male and female, were strewn about or half out of the two valises on the floor. Only ashes were in the hearth.

Caroline turned her back to him and gave him an order. "Go away, Develin."

"I'm not leaving without you," he said just as forcefully.

She whirled around and glared at him, revealing the black eye and another purple bruise on her cheek. "Go back to your home and your wife. You're married and happy."

He didn't care if Caroline hated him. There was no way in heaven he was going to leave her there. Fortunately he'd chosen not to stay in his usual hotel this trip. The staff at the Regis Hotel were much less likely to care if he asked for an additional room for a young lady and only for one night. "Pack your things. We're leaving."

Caroline's hands balled into fists at her sides. "I can't. I've got no home left except with Charles."

"He told me himself he doesn't intend to marry you."

"I know. He made that clear enough after he... we..." She shook her head. "It doesn't matter. I can't go back with you. Mama won't even let me through the door."

"Your father will," Dev said, certain the kind-hearted duke wouldn't deny food and shelter and comfort to his daughter.

"Mama rules there, not him."

"Then come back to Dundrake Hall and I'll speak to your father. I'm certain he'll help you."

"How? Send me off to Europe where nobody knows me or my shame? Maybe he would, but it wouldn't be the way he sent Paul, with all the spending money a person could want. He'll pay for some little hole for me to hide in and give me an allowance barely enough to survive on." She walked up to Dev and jabbed him in the chest with her finger. "What do *you* care what happens to me? You have your bride." She turned away. "Leave me to my misery."

"No. I won't leave you like this, with him." Dev walked around to face her and took her hands in his. "I care about you, Caroline."

"Only because I'm Paul's sister," she charged, choking back a sob and pulling her hands free.

"And because you deserve better than Leamington-Rudney." Dev could also easily imagine her fate when the viscount tired of her, as he surely would. "At least let me take you away from this place, to another inn or lodging house. Please, I beg of you."

"What's this? Sir Develin Dundrake is stooping to beg?"

"For your sake, I will."

Caroline raised her chin. "If I do go with you, your wife won't like it."

"Thea will understand."

"I doubt it. I wouldn't."

No, Caroline probably wouldn't, but she wasn't Thea.

Caroline straightened her shoulders and he could see how much she wanted to believe her next words. "Charles will come looking for me."

Dev shook his head. "No, Caroline, he won't," he said quietly.

She glared at him another moment, and then her face crumpled and she fell, sobbing, into his arms.

Sometime later that day, Leamington-Rudney thundered down the stairs of the Ship's Inn. "Where is she? The woman I was with?" he demanded of the young man watching him.

"She has left the inn, my lord," Whitcombe replied with the appearance of meek deference. In truth, he was rapidly contemplating summoning aid.

"What? When?"

"Some time ago," Whitcombe said, surreptitiously reaching for the cosh he kept in the left front pocket of his jacket.

"By herself?"

"No, sir. A gentleman was with her."

"What gentleman?"

"He said he was her solicitor."

"What did he look like?"

"Tall, dark hair, rather fierce."

"Dundrake's pet lawyer," Leamington-Rudney muttered angrily. He glared at the young man. "Where did they go?"

Whitcombe's hand closed around the handle of the cosh. "I really cannot say, my lord."

The viscount's eyes narrowed. He pulled out his wallet and tossed two pound notes on the counter. "Where are they?"

Whitcombe made no move to pick up the money. "I really cannot say, sir. It may have been to the magistrate, considering the lady's injuries."

Coloring, the viscount snatched up his money. "I'm leaving as soon as I've packed my things."

"Very good, sir," Whitcombe sincerely replied.

Chapter Twelve

Sir Develin's French chef regarded Thea with a baleful expression. "There is no need for such economy," he protested with the accent of a Parisian born and bred. "Sir Develin has never questioned the amount spent for food in all the years he's been in charge. He understands you cannot ask a builder to use inferior bricks and mortar."

Thea folded her hands in her lap and regarded Monsieur Bertrand with a look that had stood her in good stead with many an angry merchant or landlord. "Household matters are no longer my husband's concern," she pointed out to the peevish cook.

"You are an excellent chef," she went on, softening her tone as well as her expression, "and naturally when we have the ball in a few weeks' time, you will have no such restrictions. Indeed, I'm counting on you to suggest and prepare a menu that will make our first ball something to be remembered."

The chef brightened noticeably. "I promise you, my lady, I will make such food that you will be the envy of every hostess for miles around!"

"I'm quite sure of that, Monsieur," Thea replied. "However, in the meantime, we shall use more plain and inexpensive ingredients."

She caught sight of Mrs. Wessex hovering in the doorway and spoke before the chef could raise any more objections to her decision.

"That will be all for today, Monsieur," she said, beckoning for the housekeeper to enter.

The chef gave a baleful sigh, yet he realized he'd been dismissed. He walked past the housekeeper with a nod while Mrs. Wessex came farther into the morning room.

Thea hoped the housekeeper's arrival didn't mean a domestic crisis. She'd been mercifully free from any conflict in that regard so far.

"Still no word from Sir Develin?" Mrs. Wessex asked.

Thea kept any worry or dismay from her face as she answered with the same excuses she'd used to comfort herself as one day became two, then three, and still no word had arrived from her husband about when he might return. "Not yet. I suppose a bride must get used to her husband's ways, and he has yet to realize he has a wife who would like to know when he'll be coming home."

Mrs. Wessex gave her a reassuring smile. "Yes, that's it, I'm sure. He was always an impulsive boy, quick to laugh and get into mischief. Many's the time he'd come running to the kitchen and beg us to hide him from his fath—" The housekeeper swallowed the last of the word and smiled again. "As you say, he's new to being a husband."

"Is there something you require?" Thea asked, wondering if she'd forgotten to do something or issue an order. "Or do you have a question about the ball?"

Mrs. Wessex had been delighted to help with those arrangements, or so it had seemed. They also seemed never-ending, at least to Thea, and the ball was still over four weeks away.

"No, my lady," Mrs. Wessex said, a frown darkening her features. "It's Lady Gladys. She's arrived all in a flutter and wants to see you at once.

At least, I think that's what she said. She's in such a state, it was difficult to tell."

Thea rose at once. "Where is she? Why didn't you ask her to come here?"

"I put her in the drawing room. If she doesn't calm down, there's more space so less chance of...unfortunate accidents," Mrs. Wessex finished with a bit of a guilty look.

Something serious must have happened to upset Gladys so much. Perhaps Gladys's mother, or the earl had fallen ill...or maybe the duke's son had come home.

Whatever it was, Gladys was clearly in distress, so Thea hastened to the drawing room. She found Gladys, garbed in a wondrous creation of emerald-green velvet spencer jacket, long flowered gown and cunning tricorn hat with a drooping ostrich feather, striding about the room as if she must march or die.

"Gladys, what is it?" Thea cried as she hurried closer. "Not bad news, I hope?"

Gladys came to such an abrupt halt she nearly toppled onto the sofa. Facing Thea, she turned beet red when she saw Thea's concerned visage.

"Oh dear! I've given the wrong impression,"

she remorsefully exclaimed. "Nobody's died. At least nobody I know. I'm sure people I don't know have shuffled off this mortal coil recently, but then, that wouldn't trouble us, would it? People die all the time."

Thea took hold of Gladys's hands and pulled her down onto the sofa beside her. "Yet something *has* happened, I'm sure. Something important?"

Something about somebody named Paul, she wanted to add, but she held her tongue.

"Indeed yes, I'll say it has! The most astonishing thing! You'll never guess—" Gladys's hazel eyes narrowed. "I say, are you quite all right?"

"I'm fine, only a little tired."

"That's what you said the other day. You ought to try Mater's tonic. It does wonders for her."

Thea had no desire to sample the countess's tonic, and it wouldn't cure what ailed her anyway. "I'm quite all right, really. What is this astonishing thing?"

"You won't believe it! I didn't when I first heard, but I have it on good authority. I'm sure the vicar can be considered a good authority, don't you? I mean, if one can't trust a clergyman to be truthful, who can one trust? To be sure, some members of the clergy are terrible gossips, but not the rector here. The Reverend Mr. Furnival is a model of discretion, although he does tend to confide in Mater, especially in matters that concern the duchess. He practically had to beg the duchess for the living, you see, and she sends him notes on every sermon, like Sir Randolf used to do. Believe me, if there's anything that can anger a clergyman…"

Gladys finally stopped to draw a breath and Thea grabbed her chance. "What *is* this astonishing news?" she repeated, doubting now that it had anything to do with the duke's son.

"It's shocking! Truly. Well, perhaps not completely. I mean, I suppose one might have seen it coming, but I never thought…not Leamington-Rudney, at any rate!"

Thea would find it easy to believe any disreputable thing that fellow did. "What's he done?"

"He's run off with Caroline. Or Caroline's run off with him. Either way, they've run off together."

Thea stared at Gladys with dismay. Caroline and that odious viscount? Thea had seen no sign of any attachment whatsoever at the dinner party, and Caroline had been so upset about her marriage to Develin that eloping with Leamington-Rudney was the last thing Thea had expected of that young woman, or any woman of sense.

"Exactly!" Gladys exclaimed. "I was just as surprised. I spilled an entire cup of tea on myself when the Reverend Mr. Furnival told Mater and me. Ruined my dress completely. But it seems they ran off a few days ago, hopefully to Gretna Green, although nobody's sure yet."

About the time Dev had departed for Liverpool, Thea realized. An odd coincidence surely.

"They've managed to keep it secret for a time obviously, but it's no secret now. Apparently they found a note from Caroline after they discovered she was gone," Gladys continued. "Not even Caroline's maid knew about her plans. The poor creature was promptly sacked nonetheless. That was a mistake and not only because the maid had nothing to do with it. Gossip can be a disgruntled servant's revenge.

"The duchess is understandably beside herself, although it's not a bad match as things go, if one discounts Leamington-Rudney's propensity for drink. He's titled and rich and stands to inherit a good deal more. No, it's the scandal the duchess is upset about, especially when no one's sure they're actually married yet or ever will be."

"But to choose Leamington-Rudney of all men," Thea said with honest distress. "He's not fit to be any woman's husband."

Gladys sighed and when she spoke, she was calmer and her voice was full of pity. "You're right, of course. No amount of money can make up for a terrible husband, as I've told Mater a hundred times." Her gaze grew unexpectedly shrewd. "I suspect Caroline wanted to get away from her parents more than she wanted to marry. I fear the duchess has been impossible to live with ever since…"

Ever since Dev married another. Gladys didn't have to say what was passing through both their minds, and she didn't.

After looking around the room and although they were alone, Gladys lowered her voice to a confidential whisper. "I should warn you that the duchess is blaming you."

"Me?" Thea protested. "How am I responsible?"

"She says you and Develin gave Caroline the idea of eloping."

"We aren't the only couple who's ever gone to Gretna Green!"

"Of course not," Gladys agreed, "and nobody else would blame you. Still, you'd best warn Develin to stay away from the duke's seat for the next little while, even if Caroline and Leamington-Rudney marry."

Thea thought of another possible repercussion. "We were going to have a ball."

Gladys frowned as she pushed her spectacles back into place. "That could be difficult."

"I suppose we should postpone. Thankfully we haven't sent out the invitations yet. I'll tell Develin when he gets home."

"Home? Isn't he here?"

"He's gone to Liverpool for a few days, on business."

A look of consternation came to Gladys's face.

"What is it?" Thea asked. "What's wrong?"

Gladys tried to smile. "It's nothing, really. After all, not everyone who goes to Liverpool can expect to meet your husband there, even if they do always stay in the same hotel."

A horrible feeling of dread stole over Thea. "What do you mean?"

"It's just that Papa went to Liverpool directly after the duchess's dinner party and we had a letter from him yesterday. Usually when he and Develin are in Liverpool, they stay in the King's Arms, so they generally meet and have a dinner or drinks together. But he said he hasn't met a soul he knows this trip."

"Perhaps Dev decided to stay in a different hotel," Thea suggested, telling herself that was a likely explanation.

And hopefully not with another woman, she added in her thoughts.

"Yes, that's probably it," Gladys said with a relieved smile. "He might even have done so with the express intent of avoiding Papa. He's decided to follow Develin's example, you see, and build a charity school on the estate. I daresay he's been pestering Develin nearly to death about what to do, how large it should be and all that sort of thing.

"Yes, that *must* be it," Gladys carried on cheerfully. "And I wouldn't blame Develin a bit. Papa can be like a dog with a bone when he gets an idea in his head. I'm quite sure that if Develin told you he was going to Liverpool on business, he did."

"His solicitor told me." The moment those words left Thea's mouth, she wanted to call them back, especially when she saw the look on Gladys's face.

Fortunately it seemed Thea's friend's reaction was based not on the unusual method Dev had chosen to tell his wife he was going away, but on the solicitor himself. "You've met Mr. Bessborough?"

"Yes."

"Grim fellow, isn't he? But he's an excellent solicitor, I gather. Completely discreet and absolutely trustworthy."

"As a solicitor should be," Thea agreed.

"Especially when some young men need a solicitor to get them out of ticklish situations with women of a certain sort."

Gladys colored when she saw the dismay that Thea couldn't manage to hide. "Not Develin, I'm happy to say, although acquaintances of his have availed themselves of Mr. Bessborough's skill and a few more than once. Even if the women aren't completely honest, Mr. Bessborough always ensures that they're treated fairly." She dropped her voice to that confidential whisper again. "Papa said Mr. Bessborough nearly killed a client with his bare hands once when he found out the fellow had beaten his mistress to within an inch of her life. She recovered, fortunately, and the man fled to Australia. Good riddance, Papa said."

"And Mr. Bessborough? Was he arrested?"

"No, and even if he was, I'm sure Dev would have seen to it that he suffered no ill consequences for coming to the defense of a woman."

"Has Dev known Mr. Bessborough long?"

Gladys thoughtfully pursed her lips. "Oh, a number of years now. He hired Mr. Bessborough first for some mortgage matter or other, and steered some of his friends to him, and Papa, too—not that Papa's had any illicit doings with females, I assure you! Nothing would be further from his mind! But he does appreciate a good bit of legal work. He says Mr. Bessborough is the finest solicitor in London, and I believe it!"

"Is Mr. Bessborough related to my husband? They look a bit alike."

"Related? Oh, I don't think so!" Gladys said with a throaty laugh. "Roger Bessborough grew up in Cheapside!"

Thea refrained from pointing out that one's relatives could be born anywhere.

Gladys rose, smoothed down her dress and adjusted her hat. "Well, I must dash. Mater's expecting a bevy of visitors once word gets out about Caroline, and I'll have to help pour the tea. Give my best to Develin when he returns."

"I will," Thea said, walking Gladys to the door and incidentally shielding the smaller pieces of furniture.

The butler appeared as if by magic to escort Gladys to her waiting carriage, and with a wave, Gladys departed, tripping only once on her hem as she went out the front door.

After Gladys had gone and Jackson had closed the door behind her, Thea returned to the drawing room and stared, unseeing, at the barren garden.

Perhaps Caroline wasn't going to be the only young woman in the county with regrets.

And perhaps the time had come to get some answers about Dev's sudden and mysterious visit to Liverpool. Even if she learned he had a mistress there, it would be better than living in this perpetual state of anxiety and ignorance.

Her decision made, Thea went to her husband's study. Although she had the uneasy feeling that the man in the portrait was watching her, she searched the drawers until she found a letter bearing the address of Mr. Bessborough's chambers in London.

Opening another drawer, she took out a piece of foolscap, found a quill, sharpened the end with a few swift slices of a penknife, dipped it in the inkwell and began a letter to the solicitor. If he didn't respond within a week with information as to why her husband had gone to Liverpool and where he was staying, she wrote, she would go to Liverpool herself.

Regardless of her condition, too, although she did not include that.

If she was with child—and it was still too early to be completely certain—she could risk a journey. So far, other than the obvious lack of her monthly, the only other symptom was weariness. But those two signs could be signs of anxiety and sleeplessness, too.

She also did not inform the solicitor that she would begin by going to all the gaming hells that catered to aristocrats, including some that were very private indeed.

Or that it wouldn't be the first time she'd done

such a thing, although she hadn't been looking for her husband.

Her letter finished, she lit a candle, heated some sealing wax and sealed it.

As she started toward the door, she paused and looked up at the portrait over the fireplace. "What kind of father *were* you?" she asked aloud. "And what lessons did you teach your son?"

The next day Thea leaned her head against the back of the sofa in the large library of Dundrake Hall. It was quiet here, the books on the shelves helping to keep out any noise from the rest of the house. She wanted some peace and quiet, and time alone where none of the servants would ask her questions, or look at her askance because she didn't know when her husband would be coming back from Liverpool. No doubt they were all wondering why he'd gone, just as she was, but of course they wouldn't ask.

She still had had no word from him, and it was early yet to expect an answer from his solicitor.

She sighed heavily and closed her eyes. She was so tired, and yet she hadn't had a good night's sleep since her husband had gone. Instead she lay awake wondering and worrying, afraid he had secrets she hadn't yet uncovered, that for all her efforts to learn about the man she'd married, she was ignorant of serious sins or vices.

Sleep wouldn't come here, either. Sighing, she rose from the sofa and strolled along the shelves, running her fingers along the spines of the leather-covered books. Perhaps if she read something that she'd read before, she would relax and sleep would finally come.

At the far end of one of the shelves, she found an old volume of *Robinson Crusoe*, the spine cracked. She knew that story well, having read it many times while alone and waiting for her father to return, until he'd eventually pawned it.

She sat in the nearest chair, opened the book and paused when she saw something written in a childish hand on the flyleaf: *I'd like to be on an island by myself.*

Poor child, to want to be alone. She had hated spending time by herself, but if the writing belonged to her husband and being around people meant living with that hard-hearted Sir Randolf—

Jackson appeared at the door, looking rather put out. "If you please, my lady, Lord Leamington-Rudney has come and insists upon speaking with you. I've suggested to him in the strongest possible terms that you are not at home, for I must say, my lady, I believe he's in no fit state to speak to you or anybody. Unfortunately he refuses to believe me."

Thea rose and tucked the book back into its place on the shelf. "Is he drunk?"

"Possibly. Definitely highly agitated. I've summoned two of the footmen in case the viscount requires assistance to leave."

Even before Jackson had finished speaking, Leamington-Rudney shoved his way past the butler into the room. The viscount's face was unshaven, his hair was unkempt and his clothes rumpled and travel-stained. She could smell the ale and cheroot smoke from where she stood.

"My lady, I *must* speak with you!" he exclaimed.

Although he looked and smelled as many men did after a long night of drinking and gambling, something she was unfortunately familiar with, Thea realized he probably wasn't drunk. Exhausted and clearly upset, but not drunk.

"You look ill, my lord," she said, staying where she was, glad Jackson was there, and even more glad when two tall, broad-chested footmen appeared behind the butler.

"My lord, might I suggest you return another

time when you are in a more fit state to converse with Lady Dundrake?" Jackson said.

"She won't want me to go, not until I tell her what I've discovered about her husband and Lady Caroline," Leamington-Rudney declared while the footmen sidled forward until they stood beside the butler.

An icy pall of dread settled over Thea. "Jackson, please leave us, and take the footmen with you."

"But, my lady—" the butler began.

"Please," she insisted.

"We shall be outside the library door should you require us, my lady."

"Thank you, Jackson."

When the servants had gone, Thea addressed the viscount. "Now, my lord, what have you to tell me that is so important?"

Leamington-Rudney came closer. "Lady Caroline and your husband are lovers."

Thea struggled to remain calm and remember who was speaking. "It was my understanding that she had eloped with *you*."

"That's the story he's spreading, is it?"

"I was told—and not by my husband—that you

and Lady Caroline had eloped and presumably gone to Gretna Green. Sir Develin's in Liverpool."

"So is she, and while she might have left with me, it was your husband she was going to. After we got to Liverpool, he came there and took her."

In spite of the fear arising within her, Thea managed to sound composed as she raised an interrogative eyebrow and said, "Took her?"

"He came to the inn where we were staying and they left together, that whore and your husband," Leamington-Rudney angrily replied. "I should have guessed she was only using me to escape from her parents and get to him, or she wouldn't have come to my bed so easily." The viscount frowned mournfully. "And here I was, all ready to offer to marry her, too."

Thea was sure that was a lie. It was easier to believe the viscount had seduced Caroline into running off with him, expecting her to have faith in his promise of lawful marriage. But like a bad gambler, he was poor at bluffing. That maudlin look on his face was as good as an admission that he wasn't telling the truth.

And if he was lying about that, was anything he said true?

Emboldened and relieved by that realization, she straightened her shoulders. "If what you say is true, my lord—and I don't believe for a moment that it is—what do you expect me to do about it?"

The viscount's watery eyes widened. "I...I..." he stammered.

Thea gracefully swept aside her skirts and sat down. "There's little a wife can do against a philandering husband unless she wishes to cause an even greater scandal by seeking a divorce. If I did that, what would happen next? How will I live? I have no means of support other than my husband's, and he would not be likely to offer me anything if I dragged his name through the mud."

Leamington-Rudney studied her a moment, then sidled closer, like a snake. "If your husband is fool enough to chase after other women, as I assure you he does, you need not suffer from a lack of attention, my pretty lady. What's sauce for the goose, after all..." he murmured, reaching out for her.

Thea glared at him with disdain. "However my husband or other men may behave, my lord, *I* will not dishonor myself or my marriage vows with you or anyone else. Now, unless you have more to say to me, please go," she commanded, raising her arm and pointing at the door.

Leamington-Rudney scowled. "You're well matched for arrogance, that's for certain. Very well, I'll leave you. But you've married a heartless blackguard, my lady, and if you ever decide to pay him back in kind, I'll be waiting."

"If you think I'm such a woman, you'll be waiting a very long time."

With another scowl, the viscount turned on his heel and strode out of the room.

After he was gone, Thea went to the bell pull and was about to give it a firm tug to summon the butler and order the carriage to take her to Liverpool at once, until she remembered the bargain she had made with Sir Develin Dundrake.

Even if the viscount hadn't lied, even if Dev and Caroline were lovers, or he had some other paramour in Liverpool, she had given him leave to do so. She could not go back on her word now. She couldn't chase after him and demand that he be faithful to her.

Just as her pride demanded that she not beg for his affection.

Even if her heart was broken.

Chapter Thirteen

Dev trotted up the steps to the back entrance of Dundrake Hall. Although it was still the afternoon, he was bone-tired and not only because of the journey back from Liverpool. It had been wearying keeping Caroline's spirits up on the way home and even more tiring dealing with the duke, who at least had agreed to see him. The duchess had refused to come downstairs at all. The duke, poor man, had aged a year since the last time Dev had seen him. Fortunately, despite what had happened and as Dev had expected, the duke needed little persuasion to speak with his daughter. When Caroline met her father in the library, she'd tried not to cry, and so had he. That reticence hadn't lasted long, though, and soon enough they were embracing. Then the duke himself had suggested that he provide Carolyn with a living somewhere in Europe—"Wherever you like, my dear!" In the meantime, while they decided upon the city and subsequent arrangements were made, she could stay in a little cottage on the edge of his estate. "Out of the way of prying eyes and nosy gossips," her father had added.

He didn't say "and your mother, too," but Dev was sure all three were thinking it, and that was for the best as well.

Now that Caroline's future was settled, he could hardly wait to see Thea. Because he had no more knowledge of her father's whereabouts than when he'd left, he would say nothing to her of his real reason for going to Liverpool; "business" would have to do. As for whether he would go back to Liverpool or leave the search for information about Sir John to Roger and his men, he had yet to decide.

He opened the door and nearly collided with Jackson. "Sir Develin!" the butler cried with surprise. "We didn't realize you were expected."

Dev handed Jackson his hat and gloves and shrugged off his greatcoat. "I wasn't. Where is Lady Dundrake?"

"Her morning room, sir."

"We aren't to be disturbed," Dev called over his shoulder as he headed that way.

He found Thea standing by the French doors and looking out at the garden until he called her name. She whirled around, her expression one of surprise and joy—until her smile faded and something like suspicion came to her bright eyes.

But that was not what disturbed him most. He was taken aback by the paleness of her complexion. "Are you ill?"

"No," she replied calmly as she sat on the nearest chair and folded her hands in her lap. "I trust you had a safe journey home. How is Lady Caroline?"

How the devil did she know he'd been with Caroline? he wondered, taking a seat opposite her. "So you've heard what's happened?"

"I was told Caroline ran off with Lord Leamington-Rudney and not, apparently, to Gretna Green. They went to Liverpool instead." Her expression changed ever so slightly. "I've also been informed that although she ran off with Lord Leamington-Rudney, he was but the means for her to get to Liverpool to be with you."

"What?" Dev cried, staring at her with disbelief

that quickly turned to annoyance. "That's outrageous!"

"You *were* with her in Liverpool, were you not?" his wife inquired as if it were nothing to her whether he'd been with Caroline in Liverpool or anywhere else.

"Yes, for a bit, but we didn't plan to meet."

Thea's expression remained just as placid. "If you do have a liaison with Caroline, that is within the bounds of our agreement. All I ask is that you be discreet."

She sounded as if it were perfectly fine with her if he committed adultery.

To be sure, there had been that provision in their agreement before they wed, but he'd come to believe, to hope, that her feelings for him had changed. Deepened, perhaps even to love.

Yet if she was so quick to think the worst of him, if she could believe so readily that he had a lover, he had to be wrong.

And if that was so, perhaps he was merely the means to a comfortable, secure life after all.

Determined not to show how much her words had hurt him, he managed to reply in that same calm, composed way, "Whether you believe me or not—and I must admit I'm rather surprised to discover you would put so much credence in gossip—I found out Caroline was in Liverpool only by chance. Once I had, however, and learned how she had come to be there and with whom, I resolved to help her if she was willing to accept my aid. For that I will make no apologies and I'm glad she did. Leamington-Rudney hadn't just seduced and deceived her. He'd beaten her."

Thea winced. "Then I'm happy she had a champion in you."

Champion? What did *that* mean? Whatever Thea meant, he wasn't about to demean himself by asking, or do anything that sounded like pleading for forgiveness or affection. He wouldn't display such weakness to his father, and he wouldn't do it with her. "I was able to convince her to return home with me."

Thea's gray eyes widened and her lips turned down in a frown. "You've brought her *here*?"

It was an emotional reaction, at least, if not one that he was pleased to see. "No. She's staying in a cottage on her father's estate. The duke is going to send her to live in Europe."

Once more that look of steely determination

came to his wife's visage. Surely she wouldn't be sorry that the duke was willing to help his daughter.

"Does she *want* to go?" Thea demanded. "Or is she being sent into exile even though she's the one more sinned against than sinning?"

While he was glad Thea's anger wasn't aimed at Caroline, clearly Thea had no real understanding of what Caroline would face if she remained in England. "Yes, she agreed."

"Naturally she would if she had no other choices offered to her."

"What other choice does she have? She's the disgraced daughter of a duke. She shared a man's bed without benefit of marriage. If she stays in England she'll be snubbed, ignored and subjected to the most lewd sort of speculation. She'll be considered a whore, available to any man of rank who cares to have her. For her own safety and peace of mind, she should leave the country."

Thea didn't look the least bit convinced. "I know what it's like to be punished and live in disgrace," she said, "and I wouldn't wish that upon her, or anyone."

Dev's patience frayed. "What do you suggest? That she propose marriage to Leamington-Rudney?"

His wife's cheeks reddened, but her expression remained resolute. "Never. Never would I counsel any woman to give herself to such a man. And as I said, it should be the viscount who suffers, not her."

Tired and frustrated, Dev had no wish to continue this pointless conversation. Caroline would find sanctuary in Europe and that would be the end of it. "A life far from here, where no one knows her or the scandal, is Caroline's best hope for a happy future. Now, my lady, I'm tired and I'm going to change my clothes."

"A moment if you please, Sir Develin," his wife said, moving to block his progress toward the door. "If you didn't go to Liverpool to be with Caroline, why did you go?"

"I had business there."

"If that business was nothing sordid or shameful, why send your solicitor to tell me where you had gone and then never write to tell me when you would come home?"

"I had neither the time nor the inclination,"

Dev replied before he marched from the room and slammed the door behind him.

After Dev had gone, Thea sat and put her hands to her temples, trying to rub away the ache that had started with her husband's unexpected return.

If only she'd had some warning he was back, she would have been prepared. Instead she'd felt like a rabbit that sensed danger, freezing and walling off her feelings. She should never have revealed what Lord Leamington-Rudney had said, especially when she couldn't believe a word out of the viscount's mouth. Dev was right to be angry about that—but was she not also justified in demanding an explanation for his absence?

Under the terms of their agreement, financial security was to be her reward for marrying him. If that was in jeopardy, if that was why he'd gone to Liverpool, she should know.

It would almost have been better to find out he and Caroline were lovers. At least then she would have an answer.

As for poor Caroline, she'd met other women who had been cast out of their families and forced to fend for themselves after similar mistakes. Too many wound up selling themselves and dulling their pain with cheap gin.

But not Geraldine, the baker's daughter in London. She'd been jilted the day before her wedding by the butcher's brother. Instead of slinking about like a wounded dog, she had sued her fiancé for breach of promise and won, getting back every ha'penny she'd spent on the wedding. More than that, people who heard of her success regarded her with respectful awe.

There was an important difference, of course. Geraldine hadn't spent the night with the butcher's brother.

But neither was she a duke's daughter who could afford the best solicitor in London.

Thea might never learn what had sent her husband to Liverpool, but at least she could offer Caroline an alternative to exile.

It wasn't easy slipping out of Dundrake Hall the next morning without any of the servants noticing. Thea had to wait until her maid had finished helping her dress and Thea had dismissed her. Only then could she get her new warm and fur-trimmed pelisse from the wardrobe and new bonnet. After making sure none of the maids were in the hall, she'd hurried to the stairs, checked them for the presence of any servants and tiptoed quickly down. A furtive glance into the main hall showed that the footmen, hall boy and Jackson were either finishing their own breakfast or otherwise occupied. Running lightly to the door, she opened it only as wide as necessary and squeezed out into the fresh, damp morning air.

She hesitated a moment there, listening for any sounds that might indicate that Dev hadn't already gone on his morning ride. He hadn't told her he was going to do so; she assumed he was, based on her experience. Last night he'd barely said three words at dinner, as silent and grim as the first days of their marriage. He hadn't come to her bedroom last night, either, but then, she hadn't expected him. Not last night.

All was silent, so she gathered up her skirts and made a swift rush around the house and along the hedge at the side of the garden to the wood, heading to that little cottage she'd noticed the other day. Hopefully that would be the one Develin had spoken of in the morning room, where Caroline would be.

The autumn air was thick with the scent of wet foliage, but only from the dew, although that was heavier than she'd expected. Walking quickly, she kept her gaze on the path. Even so, there were a few places she nearly stumbled over a root in her haste. Fortunately it didn't take her long to reach the cottage, and her brisk pace ensured that she was quite warm.

As Thea drew near, the door of the cottage opened and Caroline, plainly attired in a simple gown, her hair untidily knotted at her neck, appeared, although she was half-hidden by the door. "What do *you* want?" she demanded.

"To offer you my friendship," Thea replied, continuing toward her.

The door opened a little wider, revealing more of Caroline's suspicious expression, as well as a purple bruise and blackened eye marring her pretty face. "Why?"

Thea came to halt a few feet from the cottage. Caroline looked tired and thinner, too, and Thea's sympathy grew. However, she kept any pity, likely to be unwelcome, from her voice. "Because I wish to."

"You want to be my friend, do you?" Caroline

retorted. "Or have you come here to gloat over my misfortune? Isn't it enough that you got Develin and I got ruined?"

Caroline might look weary and worn, but there was still a spark of proud defiance in her voice and visage that Thea was glad to see. "No, that isn't why I've come," she replied, "or to say sympathetic nothings that will not do you any good. May I come in?"

She thought Caroline was going to refuse, but after a moment, the young woman shrugged and said, "Very well," before moving back inside the cottage.

Following her, Thea found herself in a small but clean stone building with a dirt floor and a brick hearth. A fire warmed the cottage furnished with what were clearly castoffs from the duke's manor.

Feeling somewhat tired after her walk, she gestured at one of the chairs near the hearth. "May I?" she asked.

"If you wish," Caroline sullenly replied.

"My husband told me it was purely by chance that he discovered you were in Liverpool," Thea began without preamble. "He never said how."

"I didn't write to him and beg for his aid, if

that's what you think," Caroline said. "He told me he met that lout Leamington-Rudney and discovered I had run off with him. Charles was vain enough to brag that he wasn't going to marry me, so Dev took it upon himself to help me."

"You don't sound very grateful," Thea noted.

Caroline sat, twisting her hands in her lap as she continued to meet Thea's steadfast gaze. "Of course I am." Her gaze faltered and her cheeks flushed. "And I'm ashamed to the core of my soul, if that's what you want to hear."

"I take no pleasure in what's happened to you," Thea said. "In fact, I hope to offer you a way to restore your wounded pride."

"Why would *you* want to help *me*?" Caroline demanded. "Unless you want to spite my mother, I suppose."

"My offer has nothing to do with her and everything to do with a woman who was lied to and is made to suffer while the man who deceived her gets away virtually unscathed."

Thea reached out and took Caroline's cold hands in hers. "Before I met Develin, my family had fallen on hard times. That dress I was wearing when we first met was one of only three I owned.

So you can believe me when I say I understand how it feels to be scorned and belittled, to be treated as unworthy, and how hard it can be to retain your self-respect.

"I can also understand why you would run off with a man who made you feel attractive and desirable and who offered to marry you. I can even understand if part of you wanted to make my husband jealous."

Caroline's eyes narrowed, but Thea continued undaunted. "Then instead of marrying you, the viscount went back on his promise and left you with a ruined reputation."

Caroline looked away, staring out the small window to the trees beyond. "I was in love with Develin, or thought I was. I was sure he'd offer to marry me and instead he came home with *you*."

Today Thea could ignore her scorn. Caroline was in pain, suffering from wounded pride and a broken heart. "I'm sorry," she said softly, meaning it.

Caroline turned back to her, her expression hard, her eyes hot with unshed tears. "So am I."

"Dev told me he never gave you cause to believe he wanted to marry you."

Caroline jumped to her feet and walked to the far wall of the small cottage before facing her again. For a moment, she looked at Thea defiantly, but only for a moment before her shoulders slumped as if in defeat. "No, he didn't," she admitted. "I wanted him, but he never wanted me."

She came back and sat again, now regarding Thea with a more humble mien. "And you're right. I needed to hear I was beautiful and wanted, that a man loved me, even if it was Leamington-Rudney. He wrote me adoring letters and said if I would honor him with my hand in marriage, we'd go to Gretna Green just like you and Develin and be wed." She took a deep breath and the fire of scorn returned to her eyes, but this time the disdain was for herself. "Like a fool, I believed him, just as I foolishly told myself Develin's attention meant he cared for me." Her hands balled into fists in her lap. "No man's ever going to make a fool of me again!"

"I believe you," Thea said firmly. "What if there's a way to show Lord Leamington-Rudney that you won't be treated like discarded baggage?"

"How?" Caroline demanded before she gave

Thea a bitter little smile. "I can't challenge him to a duel."

"You can sue him for breach of promise."

Caroline's eyes widened with stunned surprise. "Sue him?"

"Yes, especially if you still have the letters he wrote offering to marry you."

"What? And become even more infamous?" Caroline exclaimed.

"There's going to be a scandal regardless, and if you sue, all will see that you were betrayed by a cad. You'll also be warning other young women about him. I know of another jilted bride who did just that," Thea explained, and she briefly described Geraldine's legal triumph.

"I do have his letters," Caroline said, getting to her feet and hurrying to a small valise near the window. She opened it and drew out a packet of letters tied with a green ribbon. "I thought of burning them but was afraid some portion would escape and a servant would find it. I was going to throw them overboard on my way to the Continent."

Regarding Thea warily, she held them close to her chest. "Do you want to read them?"

"No," Thea replied, shaking her head. "As long as you have them as proof for your lawyer should you decide to sue."

Her eyebrows knit, Caroline sank onto a nearby wooden chair. "Take the cad to court," she murmured before she looked up at Thea and smiled, beautiful despite the black eye and the bruise. "It would serve him right."

Dev walked toward the duke's cottage through the early-morning mist. He'd had a tense dinner with Thea the night before, during which each had said only what was necessary. He'd spent the rest of that night pacing in his bedroom.

His father had often condemned him for a lustful, weak-willed, impetuous fool. He would have been surprised by the resolve his son had displayed last night, staying away from the woman who stirred so much desire in him and whose presence he'd come to enjoy.

Until yesterday.

He'd been so taken aback by Thea's manner and her calm acceptance of the suggestion of adultery on his part that he was beginning to doubt her sincerity about anything, including her passionate responses. And if he was wrong about that, what else was he wrong about? How much could he trust her about anything?

He reached the cottage and knocked on the door. At least for now, he had something practical with which to occupy his mind and his time, and that was getting Caroline safely to Europe.

"Who is it?" Caroline called out.

After he answered, she opened the door and gestured for him to enter.

Wearing a rather plain, dark gown and with her hair tightly and simply dressed, the duke's daughter looked like some sort of nun or Quaker.

He hoped this was a temporary reaction to her distressing situation. Caroline had always been a cheerful person, and he would be sorry to find out that her nature had been permanently altered.

He spotted a horsehair trunk near the small window. "I trust you'll be ready to leave with me early tomorrow morning. I'll take you to London to meet with my solicitor, and then escort you to Dover. One of Mr. Bessborough's agents will meet you in France."

Caroline lifted her chin and straightened her shoulders—rather like his wife about to voice a strong opinion. "I appreciate all you've done for me, Develin, and all the plans you've made, and for helping me to reconcile with my father. But I'm not going."

Poor girl. She must be more afraid of such a major change to her circumstances than he had realized. "You'll have letters of introduction and a considerable allowance, as well as the assistance of Mr. Bessborough's contacts and your father's, too," he assured her. "You should be safe and comfortable."

"I'm not going to Europe," Caroline repeated, a stubborn glint to her eyes that also—and unfortunately—reminded him of Thea.

"Your father and I both agree that's for the best," he said, this time somewhat warily.

"I don't," Caroline replied, "and neither does your wife."

His wife? What did Thea have to do—

"She thinks I should sue the viscount for breach of promise."

"What?" Of all the foolish, ridiculous—"What the devil are you talking about?"

"Thea came to see me yesterday. She told me about another young woman who'd been jilted and what she'd done, and it did not entail fleeing the country like a whipped dog."

He still couldn't quite fathom what Caroline was saying. "*My wife* came to see you?"

"Yes, and I was as surprised as you are that she did. She's truly a kind and sympathetic woman, and clever, too. She said that if I had proof that Charles offered to marry me—and I do—I should sue him for breach of promise. That's what I intend to do."

Dev stared with dumbfounded disbelief at the regal young woman whose cheeks were flushed and whose green eyes sparkled as she continued. "Everyone is going to learn what happened to me anyway, so why not make that cad's betrayal public knowledge, too?"

Dev tried to overlook Thea's unexpected involvement and concentrate on Caroline. "But you went away with Leamington-Rudney. You stayed with him without being married. There's no denying that."

Caroline blushed and looked down at her toes. "No, there isn't, to my eternal regret."

"Then taking the viscount to court will only create more gossip and make your life more difficult."

"I realize you think you know best, but you're

not a woman scorned, Develin," Caroline said, her tone slightly softer, the look in her eyes pleading. "I have to do what *I* think is best for me, and I agree with Thea. By suing, I will show the world the kind of blackguard the viscount is, and even if I must suffer more because of gossip, he should also endure some social repercussions." Her tone gentled even more and she took his hands in hers. "If you ever cared for me, you'll help me by going with me to London and introducing me to your solicitor. It's well known Mr. Bessborough is the best in the city." She let go and stepped back, her voice and visage hardening again. "If you won't, I'll go to London anyway and find another solicitor to represent me."

"And if Mr. Bessborough counsels you not to sue?" he asked.

"I will listen to what he has to say, just as I did to your wife, and then make my own decision."

"Is there nothing I can say that will make you change your mind?"

"No, and there's nothing my father can say, either." Her eyes grew moist, but her voice was firm when she said, "Please, Dev, help me do this. If I don't, the viscount has made me look nothing more than a weak-willed, gullible fool. The suit will also serve as a warning to other young women that he's a cad and a scoundrel. That will give me some comfort, some hope that something good has come from my shame."

Dev sighed and ran a hand through his hair. Caroline seemed so sure of her decision he doubted there were any more objections he could make that would convince her to change her mind.

Perhaps Roger would have more luck in that regard. "We'll leave for London tomorrow as we planned and see what my solicitor thinks about a lawsuit."

Caroline nodded and, after Dev said his farewell, watched him stride away through the trees. Then she closed the door, leaned her cheek against it and started to cry.

A short while later, Dev marched into the morning room where his wife was deep in conversation with the housekeeper.

"If you'll please excuse us, Mrs. Wessex," he said with stern intensity. "I need to speak to my wife. Alone."

Chapter Fourteen

Thea's jaw clenched. She'd been expecting this confrontation since she'd gone to see Caroline that morning. Because Dev was a male aristocrat, it was no wonder he didn't understand her reasoning.

Mrs. Wessex, though, was obviously shocked by Dev's manner, and no wonder. He looked and sounded furiously angry.

"If you please, Mrs. Wessex," he repeated.

The housekeeper regarded Thea worriedly.

Not wanting to alarm the housekeeper any more than she already was, Thea marshaled her ability to appear more in control than she felt and gave Mrs. Wessex an encouraging smile. "It's quite all right, Mrs. Wessex," she said. "I'm sure whatever has upset Sir Develin, we'll be able to discuss it in a calm and rational manner."

Her words had the desired effect on both Dev and the housekeeper. Mrs. Wessex left the room and her husband appeared slightly more composed before he sat on the edge of the chair opposite her, meeting her steady gaze with a searching one of his own.

"What were you thinking, telling Caroline she should sue for breach of promise?" he asked at once. "Do you truly believe dragging the whole affair through the courts will make things easier for her? How can it, when their affair will be public knowledge, discussed at every ball, fete and dinner party for months?"

"If Caroline were a weak and feeble woman, I wouldn't have gone to her this morning and suggested it. Fortunately she has letters the viscount wrote that prove he lied to her about his intentions, and by exposing Leamington-Rudney for the cad he is, Caroline will not only regain a measure of self-respect and assuage her wounded pride, but she'll help prevent other young women from being seduced by that disgraceful scoundrel."

"Her story *might* save other young women from a similar fate," Dev countered, "but it might not. And Caroline will certainly suffer more." He ran his hand through his hair with frustration. "Obviously you are too naive to appreciate the damage scandal can do a duke's daughter."

"Naive?" Thea retorted, his words and his disdain tearing open barely healed wounds. "You call *me* naive when I've seen the scorn from former friends as my father lost his wealth and position? When I've had to search for my father in gambling hells and taverns from the time I was thirteen? How do you think men treated a girl in such circumstances? The things they said, the ways they tried to touch me? How can I be *naive* when I watched my mother die of poverty and despair while my father continued to gamble, and nothing I said or did could convince him to stop? You have *no* idea what I had to learn if we were to survive.

"But for all the pain and shame, I grew stronger, as Caroline will. As I did, she's learning that in this world, a woman must stand up for herself if she's to have any self-respect, no matter how difficult or what people might say. *That's* why I believe Caroline should stay and fight, as I stayed rather than leave England with—"

She nearly said too much before she caught herself and turned away.

Too late.

Dev marched around to face her. "What were you going to say, Thea? Weren't you abandoned by your father? Didn't he abscond and sail without you?"

"I *was* abandoned by my father—many times!" she retorted. "He would leave me for hours and even days. I was determined not to live that way any longer." She took a deep breath and told the truth because there was no point to hide it from Dev anymore. "So yes, when he wanted me to sail with him, I said no and came to you instead."

"*If* he sailed," her husband said coldly. "There's no evidence he ever boarded a ship for Halifax."

Thea's stunned disbelief quickly turned to dread. "What are you saying?"

"He wasn't listed on the manifest of any ship leaving Liverpool in the past few weeks."

Dread and disbelief became increasing fear. "That has to be a mistake! He *must* have sailed!"

"You haven't had any communication with him?"

"No, of course not!" she cried. "I was sure he

was at sea. He must be at sea! Where else could he be?"

"That's what my solicitor and I have been trying to find out. That's why I went to Liverpool."

Anger and dismay joined with her fear. "Why didn't you tell me my father was missing?"

"I thought to spare you from worry." Dev leaned close, studying her features as if she were a coded message he was trying to decipher. "Do you truly have no idea where your father is?"

"No, I do not, and I don't appreciate being interrogated this way!"

She started to go past him, forcing him to move out of the way as she strode to the windows. By the time she turned back to face her husband, the resolve and defiant pride that had come to her aid so often had returned. "Wherever my father is, whatever he's done, you can't play the virtuous martyr with me. When you gambled with my father, the cards were marked—and not by him."

As her husband's face turned pale, she came closer, glaring at him with recrimination. "You can't deny it, not to me. My father pocketed the deck after the last game you played, the one that left him penniless. He'd done that before, pawning the used decks for a few pennies. When he told me what had happened, I checked the cards carefully before he could sell them. I've been around enough gamblers and card sharps to recognize the marks. No wonder you won everything."

Her husband's expression darkened. "I won't deny it. I wanted a swift end to the game and I thought he'd quit when he began to lose so much, but he kept playing."

"Because he didn't realize he was playing with a *cheat*," she charged. "No one knows, because I've told no one. *I* saved your reputation."

Instead of being grateful or remorseful, he lowered his eyebrows and he regarded her with cold suspicion. "And if I hadn't agreed to marry you, what then, my lady?"

He had guessed her plan, the one she had been so happy not to need, but she wouldn't tell him that. Not now. "Fortunately you did marry me and your reputation remains unsullied."

"While you got a rich and titled husband."

"You took advantage of my father's vice."

"*I* took advantage? What did you do, coming here like some poor abandoned orphan?"

"I didn't plead or beg. I simply put a proposition to you that you were quite free to reject. You did not."

"No doubt you wish I had. Then you could simply have tried to blackmail me. You wouldn't have had to be intimate with me." He walked closer, his dark eyes full of angry accusation. "Who is the cheat now, my lady? And what other secrets are you keeping?"

"As many as you, I daresay.'

His nostrils flared and his eyes widened for the briefest of moments, telling her he did have other secrets. That shouldn't have been so surprising or disappointing, but it was.

"So our marriage is a bargain between rogues," he said grimly, "one who cheated to get out of a game of cards and the other a liar willing to trade on a man's guilt to get what she wanted. And now you have my name and all the comforts being my wife affords you."

Although she backed away from him, she felt righteous indignation, not fear. *"Comforts?"* she repeated scornfully. "Do you think it's a comfort to know you could be with other women and I gave you leave to do so? That I dare not ask where you go or why or when you will return no matter how much it hurts or humiliates me? Have you any notion at all how it feels to see the questioning looks from the servants that I'm apparently ignorant of such things?"

"You set the terms of our agreement, not I. If you'd rather break our bargain—"

"Not in this life!" she declared, wondering if he'd planned to make her so angry she would leave him.

He turned on his heel and marched to the door, then hesitated on the threshold before glancing back at her over his shoulder, his gaze cold and hard as marble. "Tomorrow I'm going to London with Caroline, where hopefully my solicitor will talk her out of this foolish notion of suing the viscount. Now you need not feel humiliated should anyone ask where I am. As for when I'll return, I don't even know myself and that will have to do."

After Dev had left her, Thea sank onto the nearest chair. She hadn't meant to tell him she knew the cards had been marked unless and until he'd refused to marry her. Only then would she have threatened him with exposure as a cheat, to get enough money to live on for a year or two until she found another means to survive. That would have been a last, desperate resort. Marriage had been a desperate hope. When that had come to pass and especially when they had shared such passionate desire, she'd begun to believe her one and only gamble had paid off.

Now...now she felt lower than the worst scoundrel in the world.

And a pregnant one at that.

She sighed and looked around the lovely room. This estate had seemed like heaven on earth the first time she saw it, when she believed her father was on his way to a distant shore to begin his life anew, or so she'd hoped, and although she'd feared deep in her heart that he could never change. But now she was forced to realize she really didn't know what her father had done after she left him. Or what might have happened to him.

For the first time in her life she prayed he had gambled away all his money in a card game and that was why he hadn't taken ship. That he was still somewhere in Liverpool, doing his best to regain what he had lost. As long as he was living!

She must try to find him. She *would* try to find him, and now that whatever affection or desire her husband had felt for her had likely been destroyed, she would do so by herself, as she'd had to do so many other things.

Two days later, Dev paced in the drawing room of his Mayfair town house. It was smaller than the drawing room at Dundrake Hall, but even more expensively decorated, with plasterwork and expensive paintings of English landscapes and thick damask upholstery and draperies. He'd decided it would be better for Caroline and Roger to meet at his home than Roger's chambers. They were grim rooms, darkly paneled.

Now, though, he wasn't so sure meeting here was the best idea. If they'd gone to Roger's chambers, he wouldn't be stuck here waiting. And thinking. And wondering what he was going to do about his marriage.

Before he made any decisions about that, they must first try to talk Caroline out of this ludicrous notion of suing Leamington-Rudney for breach of promise. Whatever Thea thought about the restoration of Caroline's self-respect, and although the idea of protecting unsuspecting females was worthy, the gossip would surely make things much worse for Caroline and take longer to die down.

When he heard someone arrive at the front door, he hurried to the hall, where he saw one of the footmen admit Roger. He returned to the drawing room and went to the bell pull. When a maid immediately appeared at the other door, he sent her to fetch Lady Caroline, then stayed by the hearth.

Roger entered the drawing room, took a quick survey of Dev and closed the door behind him.

"What's happened?" he asked, his dark eyebrows lowered as he joined Dev by the fire. "By the tone of your letter, I assume it's important. Is it something to do with your wife or her father?"

"Have your men found out anything more about Sir John?"

"Not yet. Has he contacted your wife?"

"Not that I know of, and she said that as far as she was aware, he sailed for Canada. But we can discuss that later. I asked you here today for a different reason. You've heard me speak of my friend Paul, the Duke of Scane's son?"

Roger nodded. "The young Apollo?"

"I'm sure I've also mentioned his sister, Caroline."

"Yes," Roger answered with a hint of wariness. "I believe you said she's very pretty."

"Quite," Dev agreed. "She's gotten herself in trouble."

"With you?"

"God, no! With Lord Leamington-Rudney. She ran off with the lout after he promised to marry her, but they never went to Gretna Green. He took her to Liverpool instead. I found them there and persuaded her to come home with me. Her father was going to send her to Europe and provide her with an allowance—the wisest course, no doubt—until my wife suggested that Caroline sue the viscount for breach of promise. I want you to convince Caroline that would be a disaster."

Roger's expression altered, again only slightly, to what Dev called his "legal face."

"Is Lady Caroline with child?"

That thought hadn't occurred to Dev. "I don't know," he grimly replied. "I don't think so. I hope not."

"If she is, would she consider marrying the viscount for the child's sake?"

"That would be worse than any scandal," Dev said with firm conviction.

"Having heard of some of his more unsavory activities, I concur."

"So even if there is a child, surely you agree that she should take her father's offer and live abroad, where no one knows what she's done."

Roger didn't answer right away, and when he did, he was guarded. "I agree that a lawsuit can be difficult for a young lady to endure. However—"

He fell silent when Caroline herself entered from the dining room.

She was very pale, and although the bruises on her face had faded, there were still signs of a black eye and a nasty mark. Her hair was simply dressed and the only jewelry she wore was a little gold chain around her neck that Paul had given her on her twelfth birthday. Her attire was youthful and charming, a pretty cream day gown embroidered with little pink roses that suited her better than anything her mother would have chosen for her. She held a packet of letters, probably from the viscount and the evidence Thea had mentioned.

"Lady Caroline," Dev said, moving toward her, "this is Roger Bessborough, my solicitor."

He turned toward his friend, to find Roger regarding Carolyn with something like…surprise?

Astonishment? No, it was more akin to reverence, like a man beholding a miracle.

Caroline, meanwhile, blushed and stared at the hem of her gown, more bashful than he'd ever seen her, no doubt because of the reason she was there.

"Thank you for the introduction, Sir Develin," Roger said, his tone and expression once again that of an attorney at work. "As the discussion will be of a legal nature, the lady and I should be alone."

Having faith that Roger would put the ramifications of any lawsuit to Caroline in such a way that she would surely change her mind, Dev nodded.

"Ring for the footman when you're finished," he said, starting for the door.

Neither Caroline nor Roger moved, or said a single word.

After more than an hour of anxious pacing and more indecisive thinking about Thea and his marriage, Dev was summoned to the drawing room. Roger was there; Caroline was not.

"I suggested Lady Caroline rest before dinner," Roger explained. Then he looked intently at Dev and said, "We are suing the viscount for breach of promise."

Dev's jaw dropped. "You don't mean to say she talked you into agreeing with that ridiculous notion?"

Roger didn't bat an eyelash. "I believe her case has merit, yes. She has letters that are evidence of a promise to marry, one that the viscount did not fulfill."

"What can be gained by a lawsuit?" Dev demanded. "She doesn't want him to marry her, does she?"

"No, nor is she with child. She's suing because she wants to show the ton that the viscount is a scoundrel. I also believe your wife was right to suggest that by taking the viscount to court, Lady Caroline will regain some measure of her pride and self-respect."

"The scandal will destroy what pride and self-respect she has left," Dev protested.

"I think not. Lady Caroline strikes me as a woman strong enough to endure the gossip as long as she can prove she was deceived by a heartless cad."

Dev sat heavily, then quickly marshaled another

argument. "Not only will gossip run wild, but it might cause a break between Caroline and the rest of her family. She might not care about her mother, but her father and brother—"

"She told me she's never been close to them. To be sure, she has some regret about the possibility of losing her father and brother's goodwill, but I agree her own self-respect is more important."

Dev let his breath out slowly. "You really think she ought to sue."

"I really think she has a right to make her own decision in this matter, and based on the evidence I've seen, she has a good case against the scoundrel."

"I feel like a man on a sinking raft."

Roger's expression changed from coldly rational attorney to concerned friend. "I appreciate that you care for her because she's Paul's sister, but I have to ask. Is there anything more to your feelings for her?"

Dev shook his head and answered honestly, "No, never. If Caroline thought otherwise, she was mistaken."

Feeling the need for a drink, he went to the tray holding a decanter of brandy and glasses and poured a considerable amount into two of the glasses. He held one out to Roger, who shook his head. "Drinking will not make it easier for you to accept Lady Caroline's decision."

"Or anything else," Dev said before he took a quick gulp. "I recall the last days of my mother's unfortunate life."

"As difficult as it may be for you to accept," Roger said with quiet compassion, "we must allow Lady Caroline to make her own decision in this matter—or to change her mind should she do so. She's suffered a great deal."

"I realize that."

"I wonder if you, or I, or any man, can truly understand how used and humiliated a woman in such circumstances can feel."

"I suppose not," Dev answered with a sigh.

A long moment of silence stretched between them, each thinking of his own mother and how she'd been deceived by a man. The same man.

"It's time I got back to my chambers," Roger said.

Dev nodded and walked with him to the door.

After Roger had gone, Dev absently picked up the letters that had arrived that day. Most were invitations he could easily refuse and he set them aside.

One was addressed in Mrs. Wessex's familiar spidery hand, except it looked even more poorly written than usual, as if with great agitation.

He immediately tore that one open. It was dated the day before and said,

Sir Develin: I hardly know what to write. Your wife has left the house without a word to anyone. When her absence was discovered, Jackson immediately dispatched some of the footmen to search for her in case she'd been out walking and was injured. When she wasn't found on the estate, Jackson and I took the liberty of going to the village, where Jackson learned—discreetly!—that she boarded the coach for Liverpool. We don't know more than that. This may not be surprising to you. Nevertheless, I felt it my duty to tell you in case it is, and that we are all worried and pray for the safe return of both you and your wife. Sincerely, Violet Wessex

The rest of the correspondence dropped from Dev's hand as he read the letter again. Thea had gone to Liverpool? Alone and without telling anyone?

Perhaps she'd gone to meet her father, or—

He spotted another letter in the pile that had fallen and scattered on the floor, one addressed in his wife's hand. He snatched it up and ripped it open.

Develin—I've gone to Liverpool to look for my father. I shan't be gone long. I'm familiar with the city and its dangers and I won't take any unnecessary risks, but I cannot rest until I've done my best to find him. Thea

Chapter Fifteen

Shivering in her old pelisse and bonnet, Thea rapped on the cracked wooden door in the ancient brick building down a filthy lane by the wharfs of Liverpool. She had been in the city for three days and had yet to find out whether her father had boarded a ship bound for Halifax or not. As Dev had said, Sir John Markham wasn't listed on any ship's manifest, but neither had he been seen at the lodgings they'd stayed in before. Nor had she found anyone who'd gambled or shared a meal with him since she left him there.

This was the last place she knew to inquire, the worst of all the gambling hells her father had frequented. As she'd made her way here, more than one seaman, more than one drunk, more than one prostitute looking for customers, had watched her walking down the cobbled street smelling of tar and salt water and fish. One or two of the men had called out to her, asking how much, but she ignored them and kept going until she reached the unfortunately familiar lane, then the door leading to the sort of gambling hell a man like Dev would never hear about. This was a place for poor, desperate men playing for shillings and pennies, not noblemen wagering small fortunes.

A narrow slot in the door shot open and a quarter of a face, including a rheumy brown eye, appeared. "Wha'd'ya want?" a deep voice growled.

"I'm lookin' for me father," she replied, exchanging her upper-class accent for a lowborn Irish one, her tone pleading as she let the tears come to her eyes. Tears had often proved effective with even the most hardened of doorkeepers. "His name's Mayhew, John Mayhew."

Her father had long ago assumed an alias and learned to speak like a less aristocratic, educated man when he was driven to play in such places, as she had when she came to fetch him. If she didn't seek him out, he would often play day and night, without food or rest, until he collapsed.

There had been no John Mayhew on any ship's manifest, either.

The man shifted, trying to get a better look at her. "What's it worth t'ya?"

Pleading and tears were not going to work with this one and she clutched the neck of her pelisse more tightly. "I have a little money."

"Maybe it ain't money I want."

"Money is all I've got t' offer."

"No, it ain't." Again the man moved, this time to open the door a bit wider, so she could see more of his unshaven, pockmarked face. His clothes were dirty, and he smelled of beer and sweat.

He ran his tongue over his thick lips. "I can think of a few ways *you* can pay."

This was not the first time such a proposition had been put to her, so while his suggestion was repellant, she wasn't shocked. "Either you tell me or I'm going t' the Big Man. He likes me and he'll make you sorry if you don't tell me."

The nickname of the ruffian who ran the docks had the effect she hoped. The man at the door scowled, then said, "Mayhew ain't here. Ain't been here for weeks."

She nodded and turned to go, only to find the end of the lane blocked by a huge, burly fellow leading a group of equally tough-looking men.

The Big Man and his gang.

The door to the gaming room closed with a dull thud behind her.

"Well, now, who've we got here, eh?" the Big Man asked as he came toward her. He was not just tall, but bulky, his upper body evincing powerful muscles probably developed unloading ships. His thighs were wide as tree trunks.

Thea began to back away until her nose told her someone was behind her and she stopped before she collided with one of his men.

"Ain't you a dainty little thing?" the Big Man said, strolling closer. "New to the docks, are ya?"

"And who might you be, big fella?" she answered coyly and as if she had no idea.

The man drew himself to his full height—almost six and a half feet. "Able Fields. They call me the Big Man because I'm big everywhere."

"A seaman, are ya? And this lot would be your shipmates?"

"I run the docks," Fields replied as the rest of his gang chuckled. "Anything happens here, I know about it," he boasted. "Any buying, selling or trading takes place, I get a cut. Anybody don't want to pay winds up in the harbor."

"A man o' power, then," Thea said as if she was impressed. "Well, well, I've been wastin' me time elsewhere. How'd you like to buy a girl a drink, Mr. Fields?"

"How about I buy the girl?" he replied with a leer.

"Mebbe," she returned, although she'd sooner dive into the harbor and try to swim to Ireland. "Drink first, and if ye can tell me if ye've heard anything of me da, maybe it'll be free."

"Who's he?"

"John Mayhew."

The Big Man mused a moment, then turned to a weasel-like, much smaller man on his right. "Ain't that the name o' the fella nearly fell off the gang-plank on that ship goin' to Canada?"

"It was John Mayhew, all right," Weasel-face confirmed.

"So he got on the ship, then?" she asked, trying not to betray her relief.

Fields reached out and dragged her close. He smelled worse than the man at the door of the gambling hell. "So now you're all alone in Liverpool and needin' the protection of a strong man like me, eh?"

"Needin' a drink, that's certain," she replied, hoping he'd let her go.

He did, but only for an instant before he grabbed her hand and knocked loudly on the door to the gaming hell. "Open up, ya bastard!" he shouted.

The door opened and Fields pulled Thea inside.

Dev slowed his exhausted horse to a trot and rode through the gates of an inn near the outskirts of Liverpool. He had changed mounts twice already; mercifully this would be the last time before he reached the city.

A groom ran out and took hold of the horse's bridle.

"Does the coach to Liverpool stop here?" Dev asked, dismounting.

"Aye, sir."

"Was there a young woman traveling alone to Liverpool recently?"

The groom eyed him warily. "I just looks after the horses, sir."

Dev reached into his pocket and took out a silver coin. He did not hand it over at once. "You would have noticed her. She's very pretty."

The groom shifted as the horse refooted. "Well, now, sir, seems to me there mighta bin."

Dev still did not give up the coin. Instead he rolled it between his fingers so that the silver glinted in the weak autumn sunlight. "Might have been, or was?"

"Was, sir, wearing a drab pelisse and a straw bonnet that's seen better days. Brown hair she had, and very pretty, like you said."

Thea, without a doubt, and he was grateful she'd worn that memorably ugly pelisse.

"I want a fresh horse at once," he ordered. "I'll be leaving as soon as I've had a drink and something to eat."

He tossed the coin to the groom. He caught it, then tugged his forelock. "Aye, sir."

Dev nodded and strode into the modest inn. He'd made only brief stops on his way to Liverpool and didn't intend to linger long here, either. He had to get to Liverpool and find Thea. If she was looking for her father among the gambling hells there, he had no time to waste.

Fortunately for Thea, Able Fields was more interested in drinking and playing cards than toying with her, at least for the time being.

So she fetched his drinks in the dirty, dingy hell while trying to conquer the queasiness caused by the stench of stale sweat, sawdust and ale. Most of the time she was able to keep some distance between herself and the large man, but not always. A few times Fields hauled her down onto his lap, only to shove her off when a new hand was dealt or he wanted another drink. Nevertheless, she knew that as soon as the game palled or the drink took stronger hold, she would be in danger of molestation or worse, and she searched for ways to escape without detection.

Finally there came a particularly close game. As the Big Man's attention was focused on the hand he was about to play—a good one, as she well knew, just as she knew he was dealing from the bottom of the deck—she inched her way to the rickety stairs leading back down to the alley.

She was nearly there when Field's voice boomed across the room. "You dirty, lying cheat!"

At the same time, a knife flew past Thea's head and stuck, quivering, in the frame of the door.

Gasping, she turned to see Fields lunge across the table at the filthy, greasy-haired man sitting opposite him. That man's chair tumbled backward, taking them both with it and breaking beneath their weight. Undeterred, the men rolled on the floor, each bashing the other with his fists while coarsely cursing. Field's gang moved out of the way, leaving the two men to battle it out. Some even started to laugh and shout encouragement.

This was Thea's chance and she took it, flying down the stairs and out into the street. She ran as fast and as far as she could, ignoring anyone who called out to her, until she came to a street of finer shops. Only then did she stop, drawing in great, deep breaths of fresh air, paying no heed to the crowd of curious onlookers who began to surround her.

Dev was getting more and more desperate and afraid. Each gambling hell or tavern he visited seeking Thea was worse than the last—dirtier and darker, filled with worse kinds of men. He had hoped he would find her quickly, or at least obtain some information that would help him to find her. Instead it was as if she, like her father, had disappeared from the face of the earth.

Perhaps she'd been lying to him all along and knew exactly where Sir John was and had gone to meet him. But Dev didn't want to believe that, or that she was capable of deceiving him so thor-

oughly. After all, she had certainly seemed genuinely shocked when he told her Sir John apparently
wasn't on any ship to Canada.

Nevertheless, if she had been lying and had deceived him, he had to find out, no matter how it
hurt him.

Even if it broke his heart.

He spotted a commotion farther down the street,
then gasped at the sight of a familiar straw bonnet—an ugly straw bonnet, the sort a poor farmer's wife would wear.

He sprinted toward the little knot of men and
women surrounding a woman gasping for breath
who said, in a determined voice he knew so well,
"Thank you, but I'm really quite all right!"

"Thea!" he cried, shoving his way toward her.

"Dev!" she exclaimed.

And then she was in his arms, holding him
tightly while he clasped her to him as if he never
wanted to let her go. No matter what she'd done,
he didn't want to let her go.

"Oh, Dev," she whispered as if just as glad and
relieved to see him. "Let's get away from here,
please."

"Are you hurt?" he asked, drawing back to search her lovely, exhausted face.

"No, I'm fine. Only tired."

He took her hand just as an older, well-dressed gentleman in the fashion of a decade ago and wearing a Welsh wig moved to intercept them. "Are you sure you want to go with this fellow?" he asked Thea, his tone kind, but the look he gave Dev wary and suspicious.

"He's my husband."

The man didn't immediately move.

"You heard her. I'm her husband," Dev said, his concern for Thea and his desire to get her safely away to his hotel making him brusque.

The man and a few others around them ran a measuring gaze over Thea and then Dev. "This young woman is your wife?" the first man asked, raising an eyebrow with a look that said, "You are finely dressed yet this woman you claim is your wife is dressed like that?"

"I assure you, she is," Dev swiftly replied, his patience fraying.

"Thank you for your concern," Thea said more diplomatically, "but he truly is my husband. You mustn't blame him for my attire. These clothes were my choice, and I got lost and panicked." She clutched Dev's arm. "I can't tell you how glad I am he found me."

There could be no doubting her sincerity, not on Dev's part or any of the onlookers, either.

"As long as you're not in danger," the older man said, moving out of their way at last.

Dev put his arm around his wife and together they hurried down the street.

"Where are we going?" Thea asked as they continued toward the more fashionable part of the city.

"My hotel, the King's Arms. You're sure you're not hurt?"

"Yes." She wanted to ask what he was doing here, why he'd come back to Liverpool and how he'd found her, but was too tired and afraid of what he might answer to say anything more, until he spoke first. "Did you find out anything about your father?"

She hadn't expected that, or the gentle kindness in his voice. But before she could answer, a large man stepped out of an alley. A large, familiar man.

"What d'ya think ye're doing, ya swab?" Fields demanded, eying Dev angrily, his beefy hands on his hips and his gang behind him.

Her husband regarded the Big Man with cool aplomb. "I'm walking with my wife, not that it's any business of yours."

"Wife?" Fields returned with a disdainful sniff, as skeptical as the helpful older man had been, but for a very different reason. "That's rich! Since when's a British toff married t' an Irish whore?"

Dev shot a puzzled glance at Thea.

"Never mind what he says. We should get away from these men," she urgently whispered.

Instead of following her heartfelt suggestion, Dev let go of her hand and planted his feet. "How dare you insult my wife?"

"Think you're brave, do ya?" Fields returned, pulling a knife from his thick leather belt—a large knife that he held with the practiced ease of someone who was used to using it.

Neither he nor Thea had counted on Dev reaching behind his back and bringing forth a pistol, which he pointed at the ruffian's head. "If I were you, I would leave us alone," he said calmly, "before I put a lead ball in your brain."

The ruffian's gang began backing away while the Big Man's eyes narrowed to mere beady slits. "What game's this, eh?"

"We could call it Go Away or I'll Shoot," Dev replied, his pistol still aimed at the man's head, his arm steady as a rock.

Fields looked past Dev to Thea, who held her breath, then back to Dev. "She's the sort likes to play games, eh? And you come to her rescue, do ya? Gives ya both a thrill, does it?"

Despite his disdainful words—and to Thea's vast relief—Fields started to back away.

"I wouldn't come round again, either one o' ya," he charged, "or you're liable to wind up playin' *my* little game. Floatin' in the Harbor, I calls it." He turned on his heel and made a swift gesture to his gang. "Come on, lads, let's get out o' here. We got things to do."

Dev did not lower his pistol until the brute and his gang disappeared around a corner. When they were finally gone, Thea relaxed and put her hand gently on his arm. "Please, Dev, let's go."

He needed no further urging. He tucked his pistol back into his waistband, then hailed a nearby hackney coach. "To the King's Arms and as quick as you can," he ordered as he helped Thea inside.

Once in the coach, Thea leaned back against the worn squabs and closed her eyes, desperately trying to control her dizziness and nausea and calm her racing heart. Unfortunately the rocking of the cab only made her feel worse.

"Are you ill?"

She opened her eyes to see Dev regarding her with a wrinkle of concern between his dark brows. She was too tired to tell him about the child she was carrying and too weary to deal with his reaction should he be less than pleased, so she shook her head.

"How the devil did you get mixed up with a lout like that?" he asked. "And why does he think you're an Irish whore?"

She sighed and answered truthfully, "There are places in Liverpool the gentry don't know and wouldn't get in if they did. I pretended to be a poor Irish woman to gain admittance, and as for the epithet, I suspect Fields calls most women whores.

"But whatever danger I was in," she continued,

her vitality returning with the excitement of what she'd learned, "it was worth it. My father *did* get on board a ship sailing for Halifax. One of those awful men saw him. He remembers because my father nearly fell off the gangplank."

"And you believed the fellow?"

In the face of Dev's skepticism, her delight and relief diminished slightly. "He had no reason to lie."

"Such men have no reason to be truthful, either."

"What purpose would it serve for him to lie to me about a man getting on board a ship?" she demanded.

Dev's countenance softened. "I want to believe your father got on the ship, too." He moved to sit beside her, and there was tenderness in his dark eyes. "We'll say no more about it for now. Rest your head on my shoulder, Thea. You're safe now, and I'll keep you safe. I am your husband, after all."

Dev said no more to Thea about her journey to Liverpool or the reason for it that night or the next day as they journeyed back to Dundrake Hall. He was too concerned about Thea's state of health to question her. She ate very little at dinner and while she fell asleep as soon as they returned to their room, she seemed less rested than he that morning even though he'd spent the night in a chair.

She continued to deny that she was ill when he asked her at breakfast, but she did not look well and by the time they finally got to Dundrake Hall, it was all he could do not to pick her up and carry her up the stairs to her bedroom. He didn't because he was afraid she would rebuff his efforts in front of the servants, and they already had enough reason to believe things were troubled between their master and mistress without adding to their concern.

Nevertheless, after Thea had gone upstairs with her maid, he immediately asked Mrs. Wessex to join him in the study.

"We're glad to have you back, Sir Develin," the housekeeper said with a wide smile. "And Lady Dundrake, too, of course."

"As am I after our silly misunderstanding." That was all the explanation he was going to give for

Thea's departure and his subsequent journey to Liverpool. "Has my wife been ill?"

"Nooo, not exactly," the housekeeper replied cautiously.

Her tentative manner did nothing to assuage Dev's fear. "Has she seen a physician?"

"Not yet. Nor has your wife said anything to me about doing so, but then it's early days yet," Mrs. Wessex said, her gravity giving way to another smile.

"I fail to see anything amusing about an illness," Dev said, taken aback by the housekeeper's apparent lack of concern.

"I didn't say I thought she was sick," Mrs. Wessex said quickly, serious once again. "I think she's expecting."

"What is she expecting?" he demanded. Her father's return? That he might send her away?

Mrs. Wessex positivity beamed. "Lord love you, Sir Develin, a *baby*. I think she's expecting a baby."

Stunned, Dev stared at the housekeeper for a full minute before speaking, and even then, all he could say was, "Baby?"

"It's not a surprise to you, surely?" the housekeeper said with a knowing look that made him blush.

"She hasn't said a word to me about it," he replied in his defense.

She hadn't said a word to him about it.

Maybe she feared he wouldn't be pleased or that he'd be like his own father, cold and stern and distant.

Mrs. Wessex reached out and patted his hand, the gesture a bit familiar for a servant, even one of long standing, but welcome, too. "She might not be sure yet."

That explanation eased the worst of his dismay and he put his hand on the older woman's shoulder. "Thank you."

A sympathetic look came to Mrs. Wessex's features. "Being with child makes a woman's feelings as rough as the sea in a storm, so be gentle with her, Sir Develin. She's a sweet thing, and a good mistress, and she cares for you a great deal. You mustn't think that because she doesn't say so she doesn't feel it. She's the same as you that way, I expect."

Dev felt the heat of a blush. No, he had never

told Thea how he felt. How could he, when he hadn't been sure himself until she went away?

What if she didn't feel the same way about him? Suppose she still considered their marriage a bargain of mutual convenience? Would it be wise to let her know how his feelings had changed and how easily she could break his heart?

Or should he keep that to himself, as he had so many other things?

Chapter Sixteen

Regardless of what Mrs. Wessex thought about the need to send for a physician, Dev took matters into his own hands and sent one of the footman to the village to ask Dr. Havish to come as soon as possible.

The doctor immediately obliged and it was clear he'd been given to understand he was urgently required.

"My wife hasn't fallen seriously ill," Dev hastened to explain to the middle-aged physician as the doctor handed his greatcoat to the butler, "or at least, I hope not. I've just found out she's with child and—"

"Like most first-time fathers, you're worried," the doctor said with a sympathetic smile, picking up his medical bag.

"Yes. I'm sorry if I've unnecessarily called you away from a more serious case."

"It's quite all right, Sir Develin," Dr. Havish said, his shrewd eyes gleaming. "In fact, you've saved me from having to listen to Lady Byford extol the virtues of the latest elixir some charlatan has sold her. Fortunately the ingredients are harmless. Now, if you'll be so good as to direct me to your wife…?"

Dev started for the stairs. "We've been out of town," he said, trying not to look as ashamed as he felt. He should have paid more attention to Thea's physical state before he went to London. "I fear she may have overtaxed her strength."

"I wouldn't worry, Sir Develin. Weariness is to be expected in her condition."

When they reached Thea's bedroom, the doctor spoke before Dev opened the door. "I find it best to examine the ladies alone, Sir Develin. They tend to be more forthcoming that way. I'll speak to you when I've finished."

"I'll just let her know you're here."

Dr. Havish frowned. "She isn't expecting me?"

"I thought it best not to tell her. She insists she's well, but I want to be sure there's nothing amiss."

The doctor shrugged his rounded shoulders and Dev knocked on the door. It was quickly opened by Alice Cartwright, who couldn't look more surprised if the prince regent had come to call.

"Is my wife awake?" Dev asked.

"Yes, sir."

"Good," he said, walking past the maid into the bedroom.

Thea sat near the hearth, dressed in one of her pretty new dresses, with her hair loose about her shoulders. She looked lovely and rather fragile, and he desperately hoped everyone who told him not to worry was right.

"I've sent for the doctor to make sure you're quite well," he said without preamble and regardless of the presence of her maid. "He's waiting outside."

He expected her to say that she was quite all right, that she didn't need a doctor and he should send the man away.

Instead she nodded. "Very well."

She wasn't going to argue or refuse? Did that mean she *wasn't* feeling well? That something really was wrong?

He hurried out of the bedroom and bade the doctor enter.

* * *

It felt like a hundred years had passed before the door to Thea's bedroom opened and her maid appeared. "Dr. Havish says you may come in now, Sir Develin."

He immediately strode into the room. Momentarily ignoring the doctor and the maid, he focused his attention on Thea now lying under the bedcovers, her expression serene—which was not, in itself, reassuring. He could well believe she could look calm and composed even if she was sitting on a bed of nails.

"There's nothing to be alarmed about, Sir Develin," the doctor said before Dev could speak. "Your wife's a little worn out, as you said, but all should be well provided she rests and is kept free from worry. And she should have some strong broth every afternoon."

Dev let out his breath. He had never felt so relieved in his life. "Of course, Doctor."

"Good." The older man smiled and picked up his medical bag. "You heard me, I trust, my lady," he said to Thea. "Rest and no worry."

"Yes, Doctor," she replied with a meekness that shocked Dev. If Dr. Havish hadn't said she was all right, he would have suspected her response was a sign of serious illness.

"Good day, Sir Develin, my lady," the doctor said, nodding at them both. "Don't hesitate to summon me again should you have any concerns."

"I will, Dr. Havish," Thea said, still serene. She then addressed her maid. "Please show the doctor out."

The young woman did as she was asked, leaving Dev and Thea alone.

Dev spoke at once. "I'm sorry if you're upset that I sent for Dr. Havish," he said sincerely. "I wanted to make sure you aren't ill."

She smiled then, a sight that was almost as much of a relief as the doctor's assurance. "I'm glad you sent for the doctor. I thought everything was all right, but it's a relief to know for certain."

Dev approached the bed. "If I'd known you were with child earlier, I wouldn't have gone to London."

"I thought it was too early to be certain," she explained.

She toyed with the edge of the silk coverlet and regarded him with a remorseful look that went straight to his heart. "I wish you'd told me about my father."

"I had no certain information and wanted to ascertain his whereabouts before I suggested he wasn't on the ship," he replied. "I truly wanted to spare you any unnecessary concern."

She sighed heavily. "It seems as if I've been worrying about my father most of my life."

He sat on the bed and gently took her hand in his. "I'll make sure that Roger's men continue to try to locate your father. In the meantime, you must rest and try not to worry."

"That won't be easy, I'm afraid," Thea noted with another sigh, "but I'll try."

"Dear me, I hope I'm not intruding!"

Regardless of her declaration, Lady Gladys came hurtling into the bedroom. As always, she was dressed in a fashionable outfit, this one an emerald-green velvet riding habit with a wide skirt looped up to enable her to walk without tripping. Almost. She caught her foot on the edge of the carpet, then righted herself with practiced ease. At nearly the same time, she swept the long veil of her hat away from her face with the back of her gloved hand.

"I came for a visit and met Dr. Havish leaving," she continued. "He tells me you're not sick, which I assure you was a vast relief after the fright seeing him gave me. And then he said you'd been away. Another shock, I must say. I had no idea you'd gone anywhere, and in your condition, too!"

Dev frowned and got to his feet. "Did *everybody* know except me?"

"Of course not!" Gladys hurriedly replied. "We were only guessing until Dr. Havish confirmed it just now. I asked him, of course, and practically had to pry it out of him. Fortunately the good man realizes Mater would worry him to death unless he told me why you'd summoned him, so he revealed all—in strictest confidence, naturally. We're not even to tell Papa, although Mater already told him what we suspected. Still, I'll do my best."

"I think my wife should rest now, Gladys, if you don't mind," Dev said kindly, but firmly, too.

"Quite right and you must forgive me for barging in here like a battering ram and although your maid—who can be quite fierce, I must say!—did her best, and Mrs. Wessex, too, I simply had to see for myself that Thea was well or Mater wouldn't have believed me and she likely would have come roaring over here like Boudica with potions and lotions and who knows what. Leeches wouldn't surprise." Gladys's eyes sparkled behind her spectacles and she triumphantly concluded, "So I've really done you a service!"

"For which we are eternally grateful," Dev said, guiding her to the door as if he was a sheep dog and she an errant lamb. "Give your parents our best."

"I'll come for a visit soon!" Thea called after them.

"I'm seriously considering putting a large lock on that door," Dev muttered as he came back into the room after Gladys had gone and closed the door.

"She means well," Thea said, getting out of the bed and drawing on the bedrobe that had been laid across the bottom of it.

"You shouldn't be up!"

"I'm not an invalid," she replied with the resolve that was so much a part of her nature. "As long as I rest, I'll be fine and the baby, too, and I have a host of servants to help me."

He supposed it would be useless to argue with her any further, but there was something else he *was* prepared to take a stand on. "We cannot have the ball."

She stared at him as if he'd suggested cutting off a limb. "We must!"

"No. It'll be too much for you."

"I think *I* should be the judge of that. Mrs. Wessex and I have already made most of the arrangements."

"But there's always a lot to consider as the day draws near—how many will really attend, will the food and drink be adequate, will it rain?" His mouth a hard line of determination, he shook his head. "No, Thea, there will be no ball at Dundrake Hall while you're with child."

Thea's expression was no less determined. "Planning a ball with the help of an army of servants is a lot less trouble than wondering where your next meal is coming from or how you're going to pay the rent. And we *must* have the ball. I've told you why it's important, and it still is. I can rest in the afternoons every day."

"I don't give a damn about a ball! I care about *you.*"

Thea's expression gentled, reminding him of the first night they'd been married, when she seemed so innocent and vulnerable. "I care about you, too, and that's the main reason to have this ball, so you don't lose your place in society because you married me."

Thrilled to hear she cared and, somewhat mollified, he said, "We can have a ball after the baby's born."

She gave him a wry smile. "When you think I'll have less to do? Or more vitality?"

She did have a point, although… "But the doctor—"

"I'll take care, Dev," she assured him. "After all, I *want* to have your baby. I want that very much."

"You do? You aren't worried…?" He paused, then voiced the concern he'd been harboring since he learned she was pregnant. "You aren't worried I'll be like my father?"

Looking up into her husband's dark brown eyes, Thea put her hands lightly on his shoulders and said, "Not for a moment."

It was as if something leaden had fallen from

his chest for the first time since he learned about the baby.

As if he were completely free.

Because of her.

"I love you, Thea," he said softly and with all the sincerity of complete truth, "more than I've ever loved anyone or thought I would or could. I love you with all my heart, poor gift that it is. Call me what you will—a liar, a cheat, a scoundrel, a dishonorable rogue—and you'd be right. But one thing prevents me from being completely sorry for all that I've done. It brought you to me, Thea. You're like a clean page in a book yet to be written. You've given me hope that I can be a better man and that I can have the one thing I've never had before—a loving family, provided you can forgive your stubborn, arrogant oaf of a husband, and give me another chance."

Thea studied the handsome face of the man before her. How many times had she heard her father say he only needed one more chance to make good? To return their family to its former glory, or at least provide a decent meal?

But always she had seen the greedy gleam lurking in his eyes that told her the urge to gamble still held sway over him. Today, here, when she looked into her husband's eyes, she saw only his longing and his love, and knew that all her hopeful wishes had come true. "I love you, Dev, with all *my* heart. Nor am I an angel who has done no wrong. I, too, lied like any dishonest rogue, but I saw no other way to get close to you." She laid her head on his shoulder. "I've wanted to be your wife since I saw you leaving a gambling hell with some of your friends six months ago."

"Six *months* ago?"

She nodded. "There was a poor flower seller nearby and you bought a nosegay from her, paying more than she asked. One of your friends sneered at you for a fool and another said you should save your money for brandy or cheroots, but you merely smiled. I fell in love with you that night, I think, and I've been in love with you ever since. So you see, it wasn't only out of necessity that I came to you."

"I'm so very glad you did," he whispered before he pulled her close and kissed her. Tenderly. Ardently.

She responded in kind, then with increasing passion, until he broke the kiss.

"You've been standing long enough," he said, sitting on a chair near the hearth and drawing her down upon his lap. Toying with a lock of her thick hair, he stared at the fire in the hearth and spoke without looking at her, his voice soft and low. "I want to tell you why I tried to ignore my feelings for you for so long, even when they would have brought me joy."

He glanced at her and, when she nodded, continued. "One day when I was very young, I heard my parents arguing. It was a terrible quarrel, with bitter accusations on my mother's part and cold, stern disapproval on his. I learned then that my father had never loved my mother and never would, and more besides that made me despise him. That was the beginning of the end for my mother, too, I think. She began to drink more and more wine every day until it killed her. That quarrel didn't just destroy her and any affection I had for my father. It made something else die in me, too—the notion that there was such a thing as true and lasting love."

He looked at Thea with sorrow in his dark eyes. "I've felt lust plenty of times and I've made friends, but love?" He shook his head. "I decided that was a lie concocted by romantic fools and believed it until the day you came here. That was the beginning of a new lesson for me—that there is such a thing as sincere, lasting love and that I could share it.

"But oh, Thea," he went on with a ragged sigh, "you brought shame with you, too. You were like my sin made flesh, come to chastise me as I deserved to be chastised because I cheated when I played that game with your father. Not to win all his money to break him or because I was greedy, but because I was so proud and arrogant and—of all the poor excuses!—I had friends waiting for me elsewhere. But when I suggested ending the game, he derided me for a coward and poor loser. Even before I knew what losing had meant to you and your father, I decided to end it another way and took the opportunity during a break in the game to mark a deck. It was stupid and reckless, especially when he didn't stop, not even when he had to borrow more to play. Eventually I realized to my shame that the vice had a stronger hold on him than I suspected and I finally walked away. But by then, the damage had been done. I'm truly sorry, Thea, that I didn't stop playing sooner and that I acted with dishonor. No guilt, no remorse, can erase what I did. Can you ever forgive me?"

How could she not? And not only because he asked her. She was hardly blameless herself. "Of course I do, and I hope you'll forgive me for the lies I told and the way I deceived you."

"Gladly, Thea, gladly!"

With love in his eyes, Dev smiled and held her close. "However it happened, we're together now, and I promise to love you and be faithful to you for the rest of my life."

"As I pledge the same to you," she vowed.

They kissed again, their desire blossoming, their need growing as they held each other.

After another few moments, Dev carried his wife to bed, where neither of them rested, or at least not for a while.

Sometime later, as Thea and Dev lay in each other's arms, naked and blissfully satisfied, Thea nestled against her husband and studied his handsome profile. She thought of his father, and how that man's harsh features had been softened somewhat in his son. She was sure Dev's nature was kinder and gentler, too, and she'd meant what she'd said about Dev being a good father.

But Dev was not the only man who looked like the late, stern baronet, and thoughts of children brought that other man to mind. "Dev," she ventured, running her fingertip around his ear, "I want to ask you something."

Smiling, he turned his head to look at her and raised a dark, inquisitive eyebrow.

"Is Mr. Bessborough any relation to you?"

He made no effort to hide his surprise. "What makes you ask that?"

"You look rather alike. He even sounds like you sometimes, although the way he speaks makes me believe he's not of the same rank. I could believe he was your father's by-blow, though."

"He is," her husband admitted. "Roger Bessborough is my illegitimate half brother. But you're the only one other than Roger who knows that."

"Other people haven't seen you together and wondered?"

He shook his head. "We aren't usually seen together. More important, though, it's Roger's wish that the true nature of our relationship be kept confidential. He fears he'll lose clients if they dis-cover the circumstances of his birth."

"Perhaps. On the other hand, being the son of a baronet, even an illegitimate one, could be seen as impressive and therefore beneficial. He may find he has more clients among the merchants and businessmen of the city who are not mem-bers of the ton."

"He also keeps the secret for his mother's sake. The end of her life was neither an easy nor a vir-tuous one."

That was an explanation Thea could better un-derstand, and her sympathy for the stern solici-tor increased. "How long have you known about him?"

"Since I was five years old and heard my mother cast it up to my father. He didn't even try to deny it. Indeed he used it as a weapon against her, say-ing it proved that the lack of children after me had to be her fault, not his."

How difficult that must have been for a boy to hear! "I'm so sorry, Develin!"

"Roger's the only bastard I'm aware of. I think if there'd been others, I would have heard that, too."

"At least your father looked out for him and found him a profession."

Develin gave a scornful laugh. "That wasn't my father's doing. He abandoned Roger and his mother when Roger was a baby. She'd been a servant, so she had no education, and she had no family or friends to help her, either. I suppose I don't have to tell you what that means, or that she died young because of it."

Thea had encountered many women in similar circumstances and knew that often even the pretty ones raised in prosperous homes eventually wound up walking the streets and drowning their shame and sorrow in gin shops, or the nearest river. "No, you don't have to tell me."

"When I was sixteen," Dev continued, "I searched for Roger and found him working in a smithy. He didn't want to listen to me at first, until I pointed out I had no reason to lie about who I was or why I wanted to help him. I offered to pay for his education, such as I could afford, and later found a solicitor for him to clerk under after Roger said he'd like to study the law. I never told my father what I was doing with my money.

As far as he was concerned, I was wasting all my pocket money on wine, women and song."

"And your relationship with your father suffered accordingly."

"By that time I had no relationship with my father, other than to consider him a sort of bank from which to withdraw funds."

At a rate of interest she could well imagine.

Touched by his past, relieved that he trusted her enough to tell her about Roger, and most of all yearning to ease the pain he still obviously felt, she put her arms around him. "You're a good man, Dev. You haven't just helped your half brother. The charity schools you fund will help many more young women like his mother. I'm so proud to be your wife!"

He smiled then with true joy and happiness. "As I'm proud to be your husband. And I think it's past time I sent a wedding announcement to the *Times.*"

Thea started to laugh. "I imagined that, too, when I was dreaming of becoming your wife."

"It seems I have a wife who's imaginative as well as determined."

"As I have a very imaginative husband. Or do all husbands do...what you just did?"

"I suspect not, although more fools them."

"Do you like doing that?"

"I like that it gives you pleasure."

A soft knocking at the door interrupted them, followed by the subdued voice of Thea's maid. "If you please, my lady, it's time to dress for dinner if you're going to come down."

"Just a moment," Thea called out, starting to get out of bed.

Dev held her back. "Let's stay here. You need to rest, and I think I do, too."

"The doctor also said I should eat," she replied with a twinkle in her eye, "and what will the servants think if we linger here?"

"That we want to be alone," he said, "but heaven forbid we outrage the servants with our impropriety!"

"We can be as improper as we like later," she said, her voice low and sultry as she watched him get out of bed.

Dev's eyebrows rose and then he slowly smiled.

A few days later, Mrs. Wessex sat beside Thea in the morning room discussing the arrangements for the upcoming ball. Dev had raised no more objections and had even added a few more names to the guest list.

"We shall have to decide on the flowers," the housekeeper said. "They will, of course, have to match your gown."

"Naturally," Thea said, although she was still not used to having unlimited funds or new ball gowns, either.

Mrs. Lemmuel had finished the last of her new clothes and the sapphire-blue ball gown trimmed with Brussels lace, the skirt tucked and shirred, the bodice as low as could be considered proper, was a marvel. Wanting it to be a surprise, she hadn't let Dev see it yet, although he did know it was blue.

"I beg your pardon, my lady," Jackson intoned from the doorway. "Lady Gladys is—"

"Here, and I hope you don't mind me barging in like this," the young woman said, rushing into the room, this time deftly sidestepping a small table. She wore a bright yellow pelisse and a small navy blue tricorn hat trimmed with the same yellow. Her dress was likewise navy blue, falling in folds from the empire waist. Her boots were soft brown leather and her lace gloves as white as a summer's cloud.

"I've been *dying* to come for a visit," she went on, "only Papa fell off his horse and sprained his ankle. You might not think that's much of an excuse, but the poor dear is the most impatient patient and I'm the only one who doesn't get annoyed with him. I understand him, you see. He hates enforced idleness. Wants to be up and about despite the good doctor's orders."

Thea could appreciate that. It took a good deal of persuasion to get Dev to agree that she didn't need to stay in bed all day. Not that she minded the persuading or didn't guess what he really meant. And she'd been wondering why her friend hadn't been to call. "Will you please bring us some tea, Mrs. Wessex?"

The housekeeper, who hadn't been quite able to hide her pique that their conference had been interrupted, rose and swept out of the room.

"Oh dear, I didn't mean to offend Mrs. Wessex!" Gladys cried with real dismay as she sat, her spectacles glittering in the morning light.

"It's all right. We can finish that discussion another time," Thea replied. "I'm sorry to hear about your father's injury."

"He'll be fine in another few days, Dr. Havish says. Not like the duchess, I'm sorry to say."

"What's happened to the duchess? Is she ill?" Thea asked with sincere concern. She didn't like the woman, but she didn't wish her any harm, either, and she could well imagine the toll her daughter's scandalous behavior had taken on the older woman.

"Not sick exactly, but Mater says you'd hardly know her. She's like a shadow. Of course the moment Mater heard she wasn't doing well, she went to see her right away with her favorite tonic. I can tell you're surprised. I wasn't. Mater's a kindhearted person, and for all her differences with the duchess, well, they're of an age, so I think Mater felt for her. Not that *I'd* ever entertain the notion of running off with a man even if I was desperately in love, which is about as likely as a trip to the moon.

"And while Mater can be quite blunt, she can also be soft-spoken if the situation warrants, as this one does. She's been to see the duchess every day—a kindness for the duchess and it gets Mater out of the house as well, so all parties benefit."

"Perhaps I should visit the duchess, too, if company helps," Thea suggested.

Gladys flushed and shook her head. "I applaud the urge, but it would be better if you didn't. Just the mention of your name or Dev's sets her to ranting. She still blames you, you see, for her daughter's behavior. Easier to blame you than her own child, I suppose."

Thea sighed and nodded her agreement. "How is the duke?"

"Not nearly as downcast as his wife, that's for certain. But then, he's got something else to rally his spirits," Gladys said, her cheeks turning a brighter shade of pink.

Although Thea had an inkling of what had brought the blush to Gladys's face, she couldn't resist feigning ignorance. "And what might that be?"

"The poor man is still under the impression his son will be returning soon. He seems to forget the marquess is nothing if not inconsistent." Gladys spoke with uncharacteristic pertness and Thea wondered if Dev was right about Gladys's feelings for Paul after all.

"You're looking well, I must say!" Gladys declared, clearly keen to change the subject. "My word, such a fright you gave me! And how is your husband? Delighted about the little stranger?"

"Yes, he's very happy about the baby," Thea was pleased to reply.

Mrs. Wessex entered the room, bearing a tea tray that she set down before Thea and Gladys. "Thank you," Thea said, deciding it might be better to wait for the housekeeper to leave the room before speaking again.

The notion of reticence didn't seem to enter Gladys's head, however. "Are you still having the ball?" she asked as Thea handed her a cup of tea.

"Yes."

"Excellent!" Gladys exclaimed. "Mater thought maybe not, but I couldn't see a little thing like being with child, especially when it's early days, stopping you. And a wise thing it is, too. Plenty of people are simply dying to meet you."

That was not as thrilling to Thea as Gladys seemed to expect. "I hope I'm not a disappointment."

Gladys gave her a warm, reassuring smile. "You can't be." She set down her tea, jostling the cup so much, it nearly tipped, before she leaned forward and spoke with grave intensity. "There is something I simply *must* discuss with you. Do you think my new ball gown should be lavender, pink or Nile green?"

Chapter Seventeen

"It's true," Dev said softly, appearing behind Thea as she stood in front of the looking glass in her bedroom. The night of the ball had finally arrived and it was almost time to go downstairs to greet their guests. "I have the loveliest wife in England and the cleverest and bravest, too. Indeed I can think of only one thing she lacks."

Frowning, but with smiling eyes, Thea turned to face him. "And what would that be, sir? It cannot be a handsome, kind, loving husband, for that I surely have. I also have a fine roof over my head, plenty of food to eat and nice clothes to wear, a child on the way and..." She twirled, letting the silk skirt of her empire-waist blue ball gown trimmed with lace three inches wide flare. "A very pretty ball gown."

Something of her delight diminished. "That I

hope plenty of people will see." She clasped her hands. "Oh, Dev, what if nobody comes?"

He gave her a reassuring smile that made him look even more dashing in his evening clothes. His cravat and collar framed his strong jaw, and his black tailcoat emphasized his broad shoulders, as his breeches and stockings revealed his leanly muscular legs. "Dr. Havish told you not to worry, and really, there's no need. I'm sure everyone we've invited will come. Perhaps not the duke and duchess, but otherwise, nobody's sent their regrets, have they? And the roads are dry." His smile grew a little sly. "I suspect there are plenty of people curious to see my bride."

"That's not completely reassuring," Thea replied, bending over her dressing table and adjusting one of the little curls her maid had spent several minutes arranging. "They'll surely think you married beneath you," she added, straightening.

"If they think that, they're fools." He came closer and reached into a pocket, withdrawing a long velvet box. "Much as I'm appreciating the space between your neck and the edge of your bodice, it looks a little barren. This should help."

"Oh, Dev!" she gasped as he opened the box to reveal a silver and sapphire necklace, the filament thin, the jewels large. "It's beautiful!"

He put the box on her dressing table and took out the necklace. "Let me put it on," he said, and she dutifully turned her back to him. "This was my mother's, and it was her mother's before her. It was the one thing of hers my father never sold."

"I'll love it for her sake, too, then," Thea said quietly, fingering the necklace after he closed the clasp. She turned to him again and saw the love shining in his eyes. "I wish I could have known her."

"She would have liked you, although she might have found you a bit intimidating," he admitted.

"As I'm sure my father would like you once he got over losing to you," she said, suppressing a sigh. "I wish we knew where he was!"

He embraced her gently. "If he sailed to Canada, it would take at least this long to get a letter from him, and Roger's men have found no evidence that he's met with foul play."

She returned his hug. "You're right, of course. Now we'd best go down and prepare to meet our guests," she said, placing her hand on his arm.

They had no sooner reached the entrance to the ballroom than they heard a commotion in the hall.

"Who can that be? It's a little early for any of the guests to be arriving," Thea said, glancing warily at her husband.

"We'd best go see," he replied, and she could tell by his expression that he was equally puzzled and concerned.

Until they saw Roger, dressed in pristine, fine-fitting evening clothes and a red-faced Caroline in a cream-colored ball gown, her thick blond hair plainly styled but needing no embellishment to be beautiful, standing in the foyer.

Thea had sent them invitations but hadn't expected them to attend. A swift glance at Dev, following close behind, proved he was equally surprised.

Anyone seeing the solicitor in evening dress would find it easy to believe he was the son of a nobleman, while Caroline looked grimly determined or as if she'd rather be anywhere else.

In spite of Caroline's expression, Thea hurried forward to welcome them. "Good evening, Lady Caroline, Mr. Bessborough."

"We're delighted you could come," Dev added as he came to stand beside her.

Caroline slid a rather displeased glance at Roger. "My legal counsel said it would help the suit if I acted as if all was well."

"*And* since she is clearly unable to play the weeping victim," Roger said, likewise obviously displeased. "In such a situation, it's best not to try to act it."

"Well, in any case, here you are!" Dev said while Jackson took away Roger's hat and great-coat and Thea's maid appeared to escort Caroline to one of the bedrooms that was to be used as a lady's dressing room. The disgraced noblewoman went off with her head high and a scathing backward glance at the attorney.

"Trouble with Lady Caroline?" Dev asked as they made their way to the ballroom brightened by nearly five hundred candles, the light reflected and magnified by the mirrored walls. Large bouquets of hothouse roses, white like the lace of Thea's gown, stood on tables, their scent perfuming the room. The raised platform at the far end of the room where the musicians would play was already prepared with stands for their music.

"She is a very stubborn, opinionated woman," Roger replied.

"Rather like my wife," Dev noted.

"In other words," Thea said with a toss of her head, "she speaks her own mind and doesn't easily go along with your suggestions."

"My legal advice," Roger corrected.

"Whatever you wish to call it. But she did come with you. Has she been to see her parents?"

"Her mother refused to see her, and her father wasn't there."

That was unfortunate, if not surprising. "Where are you staying?"

"I've taken rooms for Lady Caroline and myself at the inn in Dundrake."

"We'll be happy to have you both stay here," Thea offered.

"Perhaps Lady Caroline will avail herself of your kindness. I must return to London first thing in the morning."

"Very well, I'll ask her," Thea said.

With a nod, Roger moved away toward the anteroom where the refreshments would be served. Meanwhile, Jackson appeared at the main entrance to the ballroom. He had barely taken up the position he would have as the rest of the guests arrived when he immediately announced, "The Earl and Countess of Byford, Lady Gladys Fitzwalter!"

The earl and his wife and daughter came forward, smiling and looking about with admiration and approval, at least on the countess's part. Thea rather suspected the earl didn't notice a room's décor any more than he paid heed to the latest fashion in men's clothing.

His wife no doubt did, though, and Thea was glad to see her satisfied appraisal.

"Good evening, my lord, my lady, Lady Gladys," Dev said.

"Good evening to you and your charming wife," the earl declared, giving Thea a nod before addressing Dev again. "Have you heard about my new hunter? Lovely animal and a bargain, too!"

"You can tell him all about the beast later," Lady Byford said. Like her daughter, she wore a gown that might have come from Paris, or perhaps ancient Greece, judging by the flowing folds of lavender satin. It was beautiful without being overpowering, and trimmed by a thin band of gold, understated and well suited to the older woman's maturity.

Momentarily ignoring Dev, the countess fixed her gaze on Thea. "How are you, my dear?"

"Quite well, thank you."

"So Gladys informs me, but *I* think you're a little too pale. I'll send you some of Dr. Delamonte's tonic. It will revive you, I'm sure!"

Thea merely smiled in response to the countess's offer before the older woman moved farther into the room. "You look lovely tonight," she said to Gladys.

The Nile green of Gladys's gown brought out the color of her eyes and suited her complexion perfectly. Like her mother's, her gown was inspired by classic Greek statues, and its low-cut bodice emphasized her stately figure, long neck and excellent posture. Her brown hair had been dressed in braids coiled around her head, with little curls on her forehead, making her look both pretty and mature in the best way. To be sure, the spectacles took something away, but her radiant smile and excited visage easily overcame any detriment they posed. "Do you really think so? I'm still not sure the green was the best choice."

"It's perfect. You look like a wood nymph."

"As long as I don't look like an old tree," Gladys replied with a rueful grin. "Truly Mrs. Lemmuel is outdoing herself these days. Your gown is delightful. I especially like the little cap sleeves and the lace around the bodice. Next time I shall ask for lace, too." She looked around the ballroom. "I see we're the first to arrive."

"Mr. Bessborough and Lady Caroline are here. Didn't you see her in the dressing room?"

"Didn't go. Just handed my cloak to one of the footmen," Gladys admitted. Like Thea, she surveyed the ballroom again and neither she nor Thea saw the solicitor.

"That's odd. He *was* here," Thea said. She tapped her husband on the shoulder. "Where's Mr. Bessborough?"

"On the terrace indulging in a cheroot, I expect," Dev replied.

"Filthy, disgusting habit!" the countess declared, having moved closer while her husband headed for the warmth of the fireplace. "Come along, Gladys. I don't want to stand in a draft all night."

Gladys gave Thea and Dev another rueful smile before she followed her mother into the brightly lit ballroom. The members of the small orchestra hired for the evening began to take their places, preparing to play a selection of chamber music as the rest of the guests arrived.

It was soon apparent that Thea had been worried about the number of guests for nothing. Everyone they had invited came, with one exception: the Duke and Duchess of Scane.

Then Caroline came into the ballroom from the door leading to the anteroom. Heads turned, and a few of the more waspish women whispered behind their fans.

Without a word between them, Dev and Thea immediately moved toward her and greeted her warmly.

Thea went on to add, and loudly enough for any curious onlookers to overhear, "I hope you'll consider staying here with us for a few days. We'd be happy to have you."

Caroline stiffened ever so slightly. "Thank you, but I think it's best I don't. I should go back to London tomorrow. Mr. Bessborough has been kind enough to pay my coach fare and lodgings there, and I wouldn't want to waste his hard-earned money."

"If it's a question of funds—" Dev began.

"The Duke and Duchess of Scane!" Jackson announced. "The Marquess of Haltonbrook!"

"Good God! Paul!" Dev gasped, turning around as swiftly as Thea.

Everyone else stared, too. The duke stood in the doorway grinning from ear to ear. His dour wife, dressed in black from head to toe as if she was in mourning, looked like a shadow of her former self. Behind them, half-hidden by the butler, was a tall young man who had to be the Marquess of Haltonbrook or, as his father called him, *the young Apollo!*

"Sorry to be so late," the duke said loudly enough for all to hear before striding forward through the assembly toward Dev and Thea like a hot knife through butter. *"The young Apollo!* didn't arrive until late his afternoon and without a word of warning, too. Could have knocked me down with a quill!" He half turned and called out, "Come along, Apollo! You have to meet Sir Develin's wife!"

From what Dev had told her, Thea expected to meet a very thin, not very attractive young man with a long nose. Instead she found herself staring at a young man who could have posed for a statue of Apollo.

It was true the duke's son had an aquiline nose, but it was more than balanced by his broad forehead and strong jaw, the sharp planes of his cheeks and well-cut lips. Dark hair, expertly trimmed, waved upon his head. His evening clothes emphasized his broad shoulders, trim waist and lean, muscular legs.

All in all, he was nearly as handsome as her husband and a very far cry from the gangly, homely fellow she'd envisioned.

"Oh my word!" she heard Gladys breathe behind her.

A swift glance proved that Dev was equally shocked.

His surprise quickly gave way to true delight, however. He grabbed his friend's hand and shook it with enthusiasm while Paul looked just as pleased.

The duke beamed like a man seeing a vision of heaven as he addressed Thea. "My lady, may I present my son, the Marquess of Haltonbrook?"

The young Apollo turned toward her with another smile and reached out to kiss her hand. "I'm delighted, my lady. Truly," he said, his voice deep and his accent bearing the cosmopolitan traces of years on the Continent.

"I'm so pleased to meet my husband's good friend," she said sincerely.

"Not as pleased as Dev was to meet you, my lady, I have no doubt," Paul returned graciously. "I've never seen him looking so well and happy."

Thea blushed and smiled, but at the same time, she realized the duchess had been all but forgotten. New lines of strain had come to the woman's features, and she looked pale and drained.

Thea moved past Paul and took his mother by the arm, intending to lead her to a nearby chair on the edge of the room.

"Young woman, I don't require your aid in any way, shape or form," the duchess hissed in a low whisper, proving she was not completely unaffected by recent events.

Thea let go of the woman's arm, but only for a moment, until she realized the duchess wasn't steady on her feet.

"Get me out of this crowd!" the duchess muttered, her breathing rapid. "I won't be stared at like something on display at a fair!"

Thea did as she was asked, leading the older woman to the anteroom where she could sit in a shadowed corner and get something to eat and drink, too.

Only to discover Caroline was there, standing in the shadows near the servants' entrance, a door disguised as one of the wall panels.

"Good evening, Mama," Caroline said, coming forward, her expression tense but unflinching.

"Caroline!" Her mother's exclamation seemed both a plea and an accusation.

Caroline halted and her expression changed from determined defiance to worried dread. "Mama! You're ill!"

The duchess pulled away from Thea and took a step toward Caroline, but only one. "If I were, I wouldn't be in this...I wouldn't be here," she replied, her haughty pride once more evident, if slightly weakened. "Why are *you* here?"

"My solicitor thought it best that I appear among society. Mr. Bessborough is here, too, if you or Papa wish to speak to him."

"No, I do not."

"Mama," Caroline said firmly, but with dismay in her eyes, "I'm well aware I've disgraced the

Margaret Moore

family. I'm trying to remedy that the best I can. It would be easier if I had your help."

"And what of your brother?" the duchess demanded. "What of Paul's future?"

"I have no fear of gossip and scandal," a male voice said nearby.

Thea and the duchess turned to find the young Apollo approaching, an affectionate smile on his handsome face before he hugged his sister.

"We shall brazen it out, all of us," he said resolutely, letting go of his sister and facing his mother. "Together, our family can face anything. Did our family not arrive with William the Conqueror himself and survive the War of the Roses? The plague? And Cromwell? Yet the house of the Duke of Scane still stands and proudly, too. Are you going to let that little cad Leamington-Rudney destroy what centuries of warfare and upheaval could not?"

Her mother straightened as if shot by an arrow. "My son, you are right! Our family is more ancient than anyone else's here, and our forebears were royalty." She slipped her arm through her daughter's and then her son's and said, "Come along, my dears. Let us show those gossiping old biddies what we're made of!"

Without so much as a backward glance at Thea, the mother and her children marched back to the ballroom, leaving Thea surprised and surprisingly relieved to see the duchess so quickly return to form.

"Oh my dear! This has been the most marvelous night of my life!" Gladys enthused as she joined Thea at the punch bowl in the anteroom a few hours later. "To think I actually danced the first dance! No doubt Mr. Bessborough asked me as a kindness, but still! I've never been asked by anybody for the first dance. Usually it takes a few before some of the gentlemen recall I'll have a considerable dowry and even then, I can tell they aren't happy to be saddled with me."

"You dance very well," Thea said, trying not to yawn.

The ball was proving to be as successful as she'd wished, albeit with an undercurrent of scandalized whispers even after Caroline, her parents and her brother had departed early in the evening. Paul had shown that not only had his appearance altered for the better as he matured, but so had his manners, for he was certainly not shy. He moved about the ballroom engaging in pleasant conversation with all the guests and, judging by the response of the ladies, making a very favorable impression. Thea suspected he would find himself in the same social position Dev had once occupied: that of the greatest catch of the marriage market.

During one of the breaks in the dancing, Paul had pleaded fatigue from the journey home in his deep, smooth voice and promised to come for a longer visit the next day, while Caroline had seemed more full of energy than ever, perhaps because no one had dared to snub her. Moreover, the duchess had demonstrated her forgiveness by allowing her daughter to stay at the ducal residence that night. Mr. Bessborough had likewise taken his leave early, reminding them he needed to get back to London as soon as possible.

"I've had a cartful of dancing lessons," Gladys went on, "but nothing can be done about my height. No man likes to look diminished by a woman. Fortunately your Mr. Bessborough is sufficiently tall. Indeed I quite felt like a sylph beside him. What a pity he's a solicitor!"

Thea looked at her friend with surprise and some dismay. "He's a very good solicitor and a most excellent man."

"Oh, I know all that. I meant it's a pity he's not a barrister. I can just see him in wig and robes demolishing a villain on the stand, can't you? I'm sure he'd make a murderer squirm!"

"Yes, I can see that." Thea assumed a look of innocent speculation. "I'm surprised he's not married."

Whatever she had thought about a possible attachment between Gladys and Paul, at least on Gladys's part, this evening had dispelled the notion. After the surprise of Paul's arrival, Gladys had spent most of the evening at her mother's side, not so much as glancing at the male belle of the ball, not even when he was speaking to the countess. Nor had Paul made any effort to speak to Gladys beyond a very brief and formal greeting.

Gladys smiled and waggled a finger at her. "None of that sort of thing, if you please. He's not my sort of young man at all. Too stern by half. Can you see him putting up with my chatter? I can't. Not in several millennia. No, he needs a woman more like you. Or Caroline, if it comes to that.

"But it won't. Even after what's happened, Caroline would never marry a mere solicitor. That would be the final straw for her Mama, and I daresay her allowance would be completely cut off. Caroline could never be poor, or even what we would consider poor. She hasn't that kind of cleverness."

"But for the right man, perhaps...?"

Gladys shook her head emphatically. "Caroline would make a poor man miserable."

Gladys had known the duke's daughter longer, so Thea bowed to her opinion and said no more about that. "Lord Haltonbrook was not what I expected. I really didn't think any man could live up to the duke's praises."

"Yes, he's turned out to be quite handsome, like the ugly duckling in the fairy tale," Gladys carelessly replied, confirming Thea's notion that she'd been mistaken about Gladys's feelings for the marquess and that Dev had been right.

"Oh dear!" Gladys cried, looking across the room toward the men gathered around the window and as alarmed as if the tablecloth had caught fire. "Your poor husband's been cornered by Papa. No doubt Papa's talking his ear off about the new school. I'd best go rescue him."

Gladys immediately set off toward the earl and his companions.

Thea made no effort to follow. Dev was more than capable of extricating himself from a boring conversation if he wanted to, so she took the opportunity to sit down and rest her tired feet.

She'd no sooner done so than there was a slight commotion outside the room. Wondering what was wrong, hoping it was nothing serious, she rose again just as Jackson came to the door. His face was red, his manner agitated.

Out of the corner of her eye, she saw Dev, looking equally worried, start forward.

"Sir John Markham!" Jackson announced.

Thea came to a dead halt and stared with amazement as her father, alive and well, stepped out from behind the butler.

"Father!" she gasped before rushing headlong into his open arms.

Chapter Eighteen

Dev's first instinct was to hurry after his wife until Roger appeared at his elbow and put a detaining hand on his arm. His half brother didn't say anything; his expression alone was enough to remind Dev of his suspicions about Sir John's possible attempt to wring money from his daughter's husband.

Dev nodded in acknowledgment of that silent caution and, aware that there were several other people staring at the tableau in the doorway, continued toward his wife and her father.

"As delighted as I am by your return, Sir John," he said, "perhaps we should adjourn to somewhere more private."

The older gentleman whose face Dev well remembered nodded and gently removed his daughter's clinging arms from around his neck. "Yes,

yes, of course. I didn't mean to interrupt your ball, but I didn't know you were having one."

Sir John's voice was just as Dev remembered, too, although it lacked the accusatory or wheedling tone of that memorable night.

Thea held on to her father's arm, then reached for Dev's hand, smiling at him through her tears.

He wished he could feel such joy at the prodigal's return, but he couldn't, not until he knew where the man had been, why he'd kept his whereabouts secret and if he wanted anything from them now that he had reappeared.

Dev took a candelabra from a table in the hall and led them to his study, where his father's wrathful visage seemed to regard Sir John with the same suspicions as Roger.

"Where have you been, Father?" Thea asked, her relief tinged with concern. "We thought you were on your way to Canada."

Her father didn't answer right away. Instead he took hold of Thea's hands and spread them wide, surveying her. "Let me look at you! You're as beautiful as your sainted mother."

A more discernible expression of dismay came to Thea's face, and she pulled her hands away while also surveying her father from head to toe. "Why didn't you get on the ship like you told me you were going to? And where did you get those clothes?"

Only then did Dev realize how finely dressed Sir John was.

"I'll tell you everything in a moment," he replied, looking from Thea to Dev and back again. "First I want to hear about you and this marriage. You could have bowled me over with a pebble when I saw the announcement in the *Times*." He fixed a gaze as steadfast as his daughter's on Dev. "You went to look for her after what you'd done, didn't you? I thought you might. You seemed the kindhearted sort. And once you met her, you fell in love with her, eh?"

Although part of that was true, Dev was not impressed by the man's assumptions. They seemed to absolve him of any need to be concerned about his daughter's welfare.

"I had no idea you had a daughter," he informed the older man.

Thea lightly touched Dev's arm, then addressed her father. "*I* sought *him* out, Father. It was my suggestion that we marry." Her cheeks reddened, but she went boldly on. "I told him that since he had won my dowry, he should have the bride."

Obviously astonished, Sir John felt for the sofa nearby and sat down. "I've always known you were a brave, bold girl, but I never imagined...I thought you'd find yourself a place as a teacher or governess, or some lady's companion, or maybe a husband, but I never thought you'd..." He wiped his forehead with his hand before he looked up at Dev. "And you said yes?"

"She had a point."

He would say nothing about the sort of freedom she'd offered in return because that was utterly unimportant now.

Thea started to speak, and fearing she was going to reveal that part of their bargain, he interrupted. "Fortunately it's turned out for the best. We're very happy together."

"Is that true, Thea?" her father asked, apparently finally aware of the hardships and dangers his daughter might have faced alone.

"Yes," she replied, sitting beside him and taking his hand in hers. "And we're going to have a baby."

Sir John's eyes widened with surprise and delight. "A grandchild!" he cried, hugging his daughter. "A grandchild!"

"Yes, we're both delighted about that," Dev said, and, sweeping his coattails aside, he sat in a chair opposite them. "Why don't you tell us where you've been all this time?"

"Well, now, I will," Sir John replied, moving a little away from Thea but continuing to hold her hand. "I was going to get on that ship, I truly was, until I met an old friend of mine and decided to have a game of cards. Just one, mind. No more, I told myself."

He sighed and, not looking at Thea, said, "I kept playing. By the time he'd had enough and I'd had a bite to eat and something to drink and a bit of a rest, the ship had sailed. I was beside myself, thinking how upset my darling girl would be if she found out and that ashamed of myself, too." He glanced at Thea, his expression remorseful. "I said to myself, I can't let her find out. I had a bit of money left, so I took a stage north to Glasgow and got another ship, to Dublin."

"Dublin!" Thea exclaimed. "You've been in Dublin all this time?"

"Dublin first, then Belfast, and a few days in

Limerick. 'twas in Limerick where I was at my worst. I'd lost everything by then, all that I'd won and then some. I had nothing to eat, nothing to sell except the clothes on my back. And most of all, I'd lost you, too, Thea. You were right to leave me. If you'd stayed and looked after me as you'd done for so long, I might never have realized the mess I'd made of my life, and yours.

"I was so full of regret and shame I came near to doing myself in, until I thought of all the times I'd been like that before and you'd always managed to make me feel better. You always said there were better days ahead and I'd always believed you. So I decided to do what you would do if you were in my place—although," he admitted with the hint of a smile, "I never thought of marriage."

Not many would, Dev silently concurred.

"I got a job as a clerk in a warehouse," Sir John continued. "I found out one of the other clerks was embezzling funds to pay for his gambling—I knew all the signs, you see—and the owner gave me a reward. I was going to save up a bit more and then go back to London to look for you, but then I saw your wedding announcement in the *Times.*"

He gave her a wistful smile. "I wasn't going

to come after that. I thought, 'She thinks I'm far away and she's better off without me.' Then one night I was in the pub having my dinner when I heard this drunken fellow grumbling about Sir Develin Drake and his busybody of a wife nobody seemed to know anything about and something about another woman.

"Well, you can bet..." He cleared his throat. "You can be sure I wanted to find out more, so I offered to buy the fellow another drink or five. Turns out he's a viscount—"

"Leamington-Rudney!" Thea cried with sudden comprehension.

"Exactly, in the flesh," her father answered with a nod, "although pretty pickled flesh it was. I gather you've been a thorn in his side, the pair of you."

"You could say that," Dev agreed. "I didn't realize he was in Ireland."

"I take it he hopes nobody does. You might want to send somebody after him before he sails for South America or some such place once he sobers up. *If* he sobers up. And if the drink or a fall or a fight doesn't kill him first.

"Still, the man did me a favor. He made it pretty

clear you're happily married. 'Like something out of a stinking ballad,' was his kind way of putting it, so I thought since things seemed to have come right for all of us, I'd risk a visit. I got him to tell me where you were, and here I am!"

"Things *have* come right, Father," Thea assured him. She smiled at Dev. "They couldn't have come out any better."

"Thanks to your bold daughter," Dev added.

She reached out and clasped Develin's hand. "I took the chance to have something I always wanted. You could even say I gambled, and won."

Her father rapidly shook his head. "No more talk of gambling or games of chance, if you please."

Laughing, Thea hugged her father again. Dev wasn't quite so ready to believe the man could give up the vice that had ruled him for so long, but this wasn't the time to voice those doubts.

"I think we could all use something to drink," he said, heading for the brandy.

"I won't deny it's not easy keeping away from the cards," Sir John admitted after they'd all had a sip of brandy. "But I've managed so far."

"And if you live with us, we'll help you keep that vow," Thea said.

Perhaps it was time to voice those doubts, Dev thought, until Sir John shook his head and said, "Oh no, no! That would be too much. I couldn't impose on you like that. Besides, I've got my job in Ireland to go back to. I can't let O'Muckle down, not after he took a chance hiring me." The older man got to his feet and pulled his daughter to hers. "Come on, my lovely girl. Let's get back to the ball. I feel like dancing a jig! We'll have to be careful, though. We've got my grandchild to think of!"

The next morning Jackson informed Dev that Mr. Bessborough wished to speak with him in the study. Wondering what had happened to delay Roger's return to London, Dev found his half brother pacing beneath the portrait of the man he so resembled in feature, if not at all in nature.

"Good morning," Dev said, stifling a yawn. It had been a long night and he hadn't fallen asleep until the wee hours. "As pleased as I am to see you, I thought you had to return to London right away."

"That was before your father-in-law made his sudden and unexpected appearance," the solicitor replied, looking even grimmer than the late Sir Randolf's portrait.

Dev held up his hand. "Before you say another word, I have no doubts that he's Thea father and I believe his explanation for his apparent disappearance." He told Roger where Thea's father had been and what he'd been doing, finishing with the news that Leamington-Rudney had fled to Ireland.

"I had heard the viscount had left London and was likely trying to get outside the reach of British law. I'll send my men to Limerick at once to try to prevent that and bring him back to London," Roger said.

"And if you've missed him? Will that be the end of the suit?"

Roger's jaw clenched. "Unfortunately I fear not even the lack of a defendant will entice Lady Caroline to drop the suit."

"If Caroline's so much trouble, you could always suggest she find another solicitor," Dev said, watching his half brother carefully.

He was rewarded by the slight flush that colored Roger's cheeks. "I may have to do that," he said. "However, I didn't come here to discuss Lady Caroline. I'm concerned about the unexpected return of your father-in-law. Do you think he intends to ask you for money?"

"Actually no, I don't. And he seems quite determined to go back to Ireland."

"For your sake, I hope he does," Roger said. "Now, since I really do have business I must attend to, I should be on my way. Don't hesitate to contact me if Sir John tries to wheedle money out of you."

"I will," Dev assured him.

Some months later, after Leamington-Rudney had been found and rather forcefully persuaded to return to London, Sir Develin Dundrake and his wife stood in the village church preparing for the baptism of their son, a squirming bundle of joy to be named Paul Roger John. Although little Paul was undoubtedly the most wonderful child the world had ever seen, Thea was nevertheless concerned that he would cry. Develin was too happy with his son to be worried about such a minor catastrophe. Little Paul could raise the roof with his howls and that would be all right with Dev.

Lady Gladys was there, too, for she was to be little Paul's godmother, a request that had left her silent before she burst into tears and nodded her agreement. At the church, she hovered over the infant like an overly enthusiastic angel, paying little heed to any of the other guests, including the Marquess of Haltonbrook.

The young Apollo had taken the request to be godfather with a little more aplomb, but no less delight, and seemed as determined to maintain an air of dignity as Gladys was to forget it.

The Duke of Scane thought it only natural that his son would be asked and beamed upon the congregation like a benevolent overlord. The duchess sniffed when she heard of the request but stayed blessedly silent, while Caroline conducted herself as if she'd never done anything wrong in her life.

Roger Bessborough was there, too, although he had refused the request to be a godparent. He was far too busy with his practice to be concerned with the upbringing of anyone's son, he'd explained, and Lady Caroline's suit was proving particularly complicated, rather like the lady herself. Anyone watching them would have assumed they could barely stand to be in the same building. Dev, however, knew better, at least where his half brother was concerned. He well remembered what it was like to try not to fall in love with seemingly every breath.

Even more excited and delighted than little Paul's parents was Sir John Markham. In the years to come, as Thea and Develin's family grew in love and happiness—perhaps aided by the supernatural powers of a piece of stale, sawdustlike fruitcake brought out on the baptismal day but never tasted—Sir John became both a friend and confidant to their children, a playmate and adviser of the best kind. He also kept his word and never played cards again.

Of all the people in the church that day, though, none was happier than Thea. She had been determined to have a better future and had succeeded against all odds. She had a home and a husband who loved her as much as she loved him, and now a child, too.

And none felt more blessed than Sir Develin Drake. He had cheated and acted with dishonor, yet he had been redeemed by the love of the most clever, passionate, desirable and determined woman he had ever met. No prayer he offered up could ever convey his gratitude, just as no words, no kiss, no caress could ever properly convey the depth of his love for her.

But he tried. For the rest of his life, as long as he lived, he did his best to show her—and succeeded admirably.

* * * * *

If you enjoyed this story,
you won't want to miss these
other great reads from Margaret Moore

HIGHLAND ROGUE, LONDON MISS
HIGHLAND HEIRESS
CASTLE OF THE WOLF
BRIDE FOR A KNIGHT
SCOUNDREL OF DUNBOROUGH